SWEETER THAN WINE . . .

John moved his fingertips from her neck up to Crystal's face, then with the slightest amount of pressure, he pulled her face toward his.

"No," Crystal murmured quietly. "No."

But though she resisted him with her words, she let her lips be drawn to his, and when their mouths came together, she knew it was all so right.

John's lips were like fire and ice. Never had anything tasted sweeter, and yet, been so fraught with danger. Never had anything frightened her so, and yet drawn her so powerfully to it.

John's fingers left her face and moved down to the tiny buttons of her nightgown. A second later, she felt the cool night air on her naked, burning flesh. His hand cupped her breast and her nipple strained upward.

The top buttons of her gown were open so that both breasts were exposed, and aching in sweet agony from the supplications of his lips.

"I love you, Crystal," John whispered in her ear. "I love you, and I want you. I want you . . . now."

River of Passion

Paula Fairman

PINNACLE BOOKS   NEW YORK

RIVER OF PASSION

Copyright © 1983 by Script Representatives, Inc.

An original Pinnacle Books edition, published for the first time anywhere.

First printing, November 1983

ISBN: 0-523-41995-3

Can. ISBN: 0-523-43047-7

Cover illustration by John Solie

Printed in the United States of America

PINNACLE BOOKS, INC.
1430 Broadway
New York, New York 10018

9 8 7 6 5 4 3 2 1

RIVER
OF PASSION

Chapter One

Crystal Lee was a voluptuous young woman of eighteen, with hair the color of polished copper and eyes as green as emerald flame. She was tall and willowy thin, with full breasts and a well-rounded derriere. Because she lived and worked in a man's world, she attracted not only covetous stares, but sometimes a pinch or a lingering touch as she moved through the crowds of men who worked the docks and boats of the Mississippi River.

Despite the occasional indignities visited upon her as she moved among this breed of men, Crystal greatly relished her work, for every moment was teeming with a zest for life. There was an urgency and excitement to this world which could be found in no other.

1

Crystal was the daughter of a Missouri riverboat captain, and she had been raised to this life. She was not merely a casual bystander either, for she had shown an eagerness to learn which her father appreciated. Now, despite the fact that she was a woman, there was very little around the boat she couldn't do. She could supervise the loading of cargo in order to provide the correct ballast and balance for the boat, or she could keep books on the income from passengers and freight. She could perform expert mechanical work on the boilers and engines, and, most importantly, she could pilot the boat through the most difficult channels and passages of the river.

In the spring of 1879, her father's boat, which was named *The Missouri Mist*, sailed down the Missouri River to St. Louis. Once it arrived in the gateway city, it began taking on a load of cargo and passengers for the return trip up the Missouri to Fort Benton, Montana. This was the first trip of the new season, and Crystal was, as always, excited by it.

But there was another type of excitement which heated Crystal's blood as well. There were certain, awakening sensations in her body which sometimes caused her to be aware of an unexplained pleasure, and yet, leave her with a gnawing desire for some mysterious fulfillment. Crystal asked herself questions about these feelings, but they were questions which she could not answer.

Crystal particularly liked to stand at the stern of the boat when it was underway. She liked to feel her own body throb in rhythmic response to the engine's powerful beat. She would watch in fascination as the pumping piston rod would turn the huge paddle wheel. The spinning paddle wheel took 240 dips of water every single minute, thus pushing the boat through the water with its powerful thrusts.

Sometimes Crystal would feel drawn toward it as a woman is drawn to her lover, and she would stand there watching and feeling her body pulse with excitement. At such times she was deliciously aware of these new and strange urgings, yet vaguely hungry for a mysterious something more. It was a bittersweet feeling and Crystal allowed it to wash through her body as she floated with its pleasurable sensations, even though a small, unheeded voice cautioned her against it.

Crystal was still a virgin. There were times, however, when the excitement of being underway, coupled with the awakening feelings of her own body stirred her so that, unbidden, erotic thoughts would be born. During such times she allowed fantasies without form, and desires without definition, to play upon her mind. She realized, therefore, that she was a woman with a passionate nature, though in truth she had never had that nature tested, nor did she want to. She was afraid, without admitting it to herself, that she would fail any such test should it occur.

Often when she realized she was allowing such thoughts to have their way with her, she would walk to the bow of the boat and stand there and let the cool river water splash on her until her mind and her body were purged of such lascivious ideas. She was therefore, relieved when the *Missouri Mist* arrived in St. Louis. Perhaps a period of time in the city, with the desirable influences of its libraries, concerts, and lectures would free her mind of these unwholesome meanderings.

It was a busy time while the *Missouri Mist* was tied up in St. Louis, but because her father encouraged Crystal to further her education, she found frequent opportunity to visit all the city of St. Louis had to offer in the pursuit of culture.

For one week the crew of the *Missouri Mist* labored long, hard days to prepare for the return journey. Crystal was relieved of all that, however. With her father's blessing, Crystal took in all the sights, sounds and sensations a young girl would never experience under normal conditions. She attended concerts and art showings, lectures and museum exhibits.

It was at a museum exhibit that she first saw him, the most handsome man she had ever laid eyes upon.

He was standing near an exhibit on ancient Egypt. His arms were folded across his body, though one hand was raised to his chin. His head was cocked slightly, almost with an air of arrogance, and he was studying the exhibit very carefully. He was dressed in an expensive looking, fawn-colored, three-piece suit. He had dark hair, and dark eyes, a narrow nose, and lips, which, though Crystal couldn't think of the word, could only be described as sensuous. His handsome features looked as though they belonged in such a costume, but his shoulders and arms tended to belie that, for they appeared much larger and more powerful than the shoulders and arms of most men who were so elegantly dressed. Crystal stared, and for just a moment she experienced a strange difficulty in breathing, and a quickening of her pulse as she looked at him. Her reaction to him surprised and frightened her somewhat, and she forced herself to walk away quickly, before the man realized that she was staring at him.

Crystal was angry with herself for reacting so to a stranger, so she pursued the rest of her sightseeing with renewed vigor. Finally, on the last day before departure, Crystal returned to the boat. She was as excited as ever about the journey on the next day, but she was fortified with the stabilizing influence of her visit to the educational and cultural aspects of the city.

From the boat, she was able to enjoy the city in panorama. It could have been a Currier and Ives print come to life. In the distance one could see the trees and fields of Illinois, then the broad, silver sweep of the Mississippi River, and finally the majesty of St. Louis itself. The city sprawled north and south along the west side of the river for nearly three miles. It had been recently rebuilt to glistening splendor, after the devastating riverside fire that had taken out fifteen blocks a few years earlier.

At LaClede's Landing, there were more than two score boats, bow-in to the riverbank, pulling with the current against the thick hawsers which held them fast. About half the boats were for the Mississippi River trade, and they were the side-wheelers; large, stately wedding-cake-like boats with gilt, glitter and glamor. Their staterooms were carpeted with the finest Oriental rugs and inlayed with the most exquisite woods and tiles. Ornate chandeliers hung in magnificent opulence in the dining rooms and salons, as each boat competed with the other for the passenger with the taste for luxury.

The other half of the boats at the landing were designed for the Missouri River trade. They were much smaller, sturdier, stern-wheelers, with a shallow draught and a powerful engine The engine had a steam-pressure escape valve which made a cannonlike roar that could be heard for miles when the boats worked their way up the river. The passenger accommodations on these boats were smaller and much more spartan.

The Mississippi River boats had a relatively easy run of no more than eleven hundred miles down a river which grew wider and deeper with each mile, until it reached New Orleans. The Missouri boats on the other hand, had a torturous, narrow, twisting, obstacle course of a river, which ran more than three thousand miles via a circuitous route from St. Louis to Fort Benton, Montana. The Missouri boats fought snags, and bars, rocks, sudden shifting of channels, weather, miles of complete isolation, occasional river pirates, and, often, hostile Indians. It took a special breed of man to work the Missouri River boats, and Missouri boatmen looked with disdain upon those who made their living on the Mississippi River. They called them Drawing Room Dandies, and they claimed they could outdrink, outcuss and outfight, or outanything, any Mississippi River boatman could do.

It was just that sort of attitude which caused many a boatman to wind up in a St. Louis city jail, arrested for public drunkenness, disturbing the peace, fighting, damaging private property, and sometimes, even inciting a riot.

On the last night before the *Missouri Mist* was scheduled to depart, just such a fight erupted in Clancey's Bar, a favorite hang-out for the rivermen. As a result of the fight, twenty-three boatmen from both rivers were thrown into jail to await payment of fines and damages by their captains.

Three of these men were from the *Missouri Mist*. Captain Marsh Lee had just received word of this, when Crystal returned to the boat.

"Well, daughter," Marsh Lee said, smiling at Crystal. "Did you have a good time?"

"Yes," Crystal said. "I went to the museum today and saw several fascinating things."

Crystal suddenly recalled the handsome young man she had seen there. Indeed, he had been the more fascinating than any of the exhibits, and as she thought of him, she felt her face flame. She was blushing! She stammered, praying that her father wouldn't notice. "Oh, and, uh, I heard a very good lecture about the South Sea Islands," she went on, quickly.

"I'm glad you had a good time, darlin'," Marsh said. He sighed, and looked at the message he was holding. "Some of the others from the boat have had a good time as well, only I'm afraid their good time wasn't quite as innocent as yours."

"Oh, no, Dad, don't tell me! Someone is in jail?"

"Willie, Hank and Pete," Marsh said.

"Oh, dear me. It seems they will never learn."

"Darlin', I hate to ask you, but I simply can't go down there. I have too many things to attend to here. Would you go bail them out for me?"

"Of course I will," Crystal said.

A short while later, Crystal stepped down from a buckboard in front of the First Precinct Police

Station. For a moment she was standing under the gas lantern which lit the front steps, and her red hair and green eyes sparkled so prettily that she might well have been one of the many young debutantes who were preparing for the Veiled Prophet's Ball, rather than an eighteen-year-old girl arriving at a police station to bail out a crew of rowdy boatmen.

"Miss, are you sure you don't want me to come in with you?" the buckboard driver asked. "This here is a police station."

"No," Crystal answered. "I'll be all right. I've done this before. But I would like you to wait for me, please."

"Yes'm," the driver said. "I'll wait." He tied the reins to a ring on the footboard, then leaned back, tipped his hat forward across his eyes, folded his arms across his chest, and closed his eyes.

Crystal walked up the concrete steps to the front door, pushed it open and stepped inside. A tall police officer with a high dome hat and a long, blue coat, was standing by the wall.

"You comin' for the night court?" he asked.

"No," Crystal said. "I wish to speak with the fines-clerk."

"The fines-clerk? He's got a desk back there with the desk sergeant. It's the second door on your right."

"Thank you," Crystal said.

Crystal walked on down the hall. She passed a

large, double-door which was open, and she looked through it. She could see night court in session. The judge was leaning back in his chair, his eyelids drooping heavily under bushy, white eyebrows. The prosecutor was making a point, and he was emphasizing his statements by pounding his hand into his fist. The accused was at his table, looking properly contrite.

Crystal went into the room the police officer had indicated. It was a large, stark-looking room, with bare, wooden benches and stained walls. On one wall was a large calendar with the year "1879," in bold, blacktype, just below the picture. The picture was an idealistic full-color drawing of a farm, with fields of corn, pumpkins, squash, melons and tomatoes, all portrayed at the simultaneous and unrealistic peak of ripeness. On the sheet below the day was the month, May, with every day until today's date, the 9th, dutifully crossed out. Beside the calendar was a large, bold-faced clock. The time was 8:45.

The desk sergeant was writing in a ledger and when Crystal stepped up to his desk he didn't acknowledge her until she cleared her throat.

"I'll be with you in a moment," he said, still not looking up.

Crystal waited for another, long moment, until finally the desk sergeant did look up. When he saw that the person before him was not the type who normally appeared here, but instead was a beautiful young girl, he smiled broadly and put the pen down.

"Excuse me, miss," he said, touching the brim of his hat. It, like the hat on the policeman by the door, was high-domed, with a shining brass shield on the front. "What can I do for you?"

"I believe you are holding three men in your jail," Crystal said.

The desk sergeant laughed. "Miss, we're holding a mite more'n that, I'd say."

"These are boatmen."

"Most of our prisoners are," the sergeant said again. "Which three men are you concerned with?"

"Willie Parsons, Hank Guthrie and Pete Stanley," Crystal said. "They are crewmen from my father's boat, the *Missouri Mist*. I'd like to pay their fines and any damages they may have caused, if that is possible."

"Well, now," the sergeant said. "I suppose it would be, but the judge hasn't put a fine on 'em yet. They're up at nine o'clock, in night court," he said. "If you'd care to go in there, the judge will hear the case, then affix the fine and damages. If you pay the bailiff, the judge'll let 'em go free."

"Thank you," Crystal said.

"Officer Morris, take this young lady to night court, if you would, please," the desk sergeant said to a nearby officer. The desk sergeant twirled the ends of his mustache, and preened somewhat importantly for Crystal.

"Thank you, again," Crystal said.

"My pleasure, ma'am," the desk sergeant said. His eyes reflected the fact that not all of his pleasure was in doing the favor for the young girl. Some of his pleasure, quite obviously, came from looking at her.

The police officer appointed by the desk sergeant to escort Crystal, took her into the courtroom, then found a place for her near the very front. He touched his hat in a half-salute, then left, while Crystal settled down, feeling the stares of the others who had watched with interest as she entered.

A railing separated the gallery of the courtroom from the counsel tables and the judge's bench. Behind the bench, the judge sat in somber robes, listening to the argument of one of the lawyers.

"Counselor, it is obvious to me that this case is going to go far beyond it's allotted time," the judge said. "Therefore, I suggest we move it from this docket to the day court."

"Defense has no objections."

"So moved," the judge said, hitting the bench with his gavel. "Bailiff, call the next case, please."

"The court calls: Willie Parsons, Hank Guthrie and Pete Stanley," the bailiff said. "Your Honor, the defendants are charged with starting a fight, inciting a riot, and extensive damage to private property."

"Boatmen?" the judge asked in a long-suffering sigh.

12

"Yes, Your Honor. Missouri River Boatmen."

"That hardly comes as a surprise," the judge said. "Bring the defendants in."

"Your Honor, I object!" Crystal suddenly shouted, standing up from her seat.

There was a gasp of surprise from everyone in the courtroom, then a tittering of laughter. The judge banged his gavel a few times until order was restored, then he looked at Crystal with an expression which was more of shock, than of anger.

"Young lady, did I hear you properly?" the judge asked. "Did you say the words, 'I object'?"

"Yes, Your Honor, I did say it, and I do object," Crystal said.

"I see." The judge stroked his chin and looked at Crystal, studying her for a moment. "Tell me, Miss, are you licensed by the bar of Missouri?"

"I beg your pardon?"

"Are you a lawyer?"

"No, sir. Of course I'm not a lawyer. Why would you ask that?"

"Why indeed?" the judge replied. He sighed. "If you are not a lawyer, madam, then by what right do you object to anything said in my court, let alone, anything the bench may have to say?"

"Your Honor, you said you were not surprised that the three men in question were Missouri River boatmen. That makes it sound as if all Missouri River boatmen are troublemakers."

"Unfortunately, madam, it has been my sad experience that, if not all, then certainly a large majority of the Missouri River boatmen are troublemakers. However, in deference to your expressed exception to this matter, I shall withdraw my statement, contingent upon exacting a promise from you that you will not interrupt these proceedings again."

"I . . . I promise, Your Honor," Crystal said.

Crystal had spoken on impulse, and now she was the center of attention. She regretted the impulse which had made her speak, and she wished she could find a hole to sink into.

"Very well, madam, you have my apology for the inference my statement may have made. I withdraw my remark, and instruct the bailiff to bring the three defendants before the bench."

There was a smattering of laughter, and Crystal sat back down with her cheeks flaming. The judge rapped the gavel a few more times, and the laughter, mercifully subsided.

A moment later, Willie Parsons, Hank Guthrie, and Pete Stanley, stood before the bench, each man in handcuffs, and each man with his eyes downcast in contrition. Despite the inglorious condition of their present situation, Crystal couldn't help but feel a swell of pride in these men. They were not only the finest boatmen she had ever known, they were the finest of men. They were all honorary uncles to her, and they had been a part of her life for as long as she could remember. She loved them as dearly as any young girl could ever love her own flesh and blood uncles.

"Will one of you gentlemen speak for the lot, or do each of you wish to make a statement?" the judge asked.

"I'll speak for all of us, Your Worship," Willie said in the faint English accent he had never lost, despite more than thirty years in America.

"And you are?"

"My name is Willie Parsons, Your Grace," Willie said. "I am an educated man," he added proudly.

"Very well, Mr. Parsons," the judge said. "You may proceed."

"Well, you see, Your Lordship, it was like this," Willie started.

"Wait a minute, hold on here," the judge interrupted. "Now I have sat quietly while you called me a 'Worship' and a 'Grace.' But I remind you, Mr. Parsons, that in this country, there are no Lords. You may properly address me as 'Your Honor'."

"Very well, Mr. Parsons," the judge said. "You sayin', it was like this. Hank, Pete and I are members of the crew of the *Missouri Mist*, sir, and we are proud of it. We've been workin' hard these last few days, gettin' ready for a trip up the Missouri to Fort Benton, Montana ... as trying a journey as any man has ever made since Moses led his people out into the wilderness, Your Honor. Our good captain is a noble man by the name of

Marsh Lee, and no more noble nor fine a man has ever drawn a breath than that prince of a fellow, I can tell you. Earlier today, Captain Lee generously allowed that by our toils, we of the loyal crew had earned the right to a small 'bon-voyage' —respite as it were—at the drinking establishment of our choice. Our choice being Clancey's, we proceeded forthwith, whereupon we began to attend to the avowed purpose of our visit to said establishment, that being to imbibe in the spirits which flow so freely therein."

"Mr. Parsons, please?" The judge said. "Would you get on with it? For God's sake, man, you sound like a solicitor in a Dickens novel."

Willie smiled broadly. "Why, I do thank you, sir, that is most kind of you," he said. "But, as you request, I shall continue. My friends, Hank Guthrie and Pete Stanley, and may I add here, sir, that no man could ever want for two finer or more noble friends?"

"By all means, add that," the judge said. The gallery laughed.

"Thank you, Your Honor," Willie said. "Anyway, there we were, standin' at the bar, just peacefully imbibing, when in came five ne'er-do-wells, who, from the look of their pasty complexions and narrow, cruel eyes, could only have been Mississippi River scum."

"Mississippi River scum," the judge repeated.

"Yes, Your Grace ... er, Your Honor," Willie said. He cleared his throat and went on.

"At any rate I said to my companions, 'Gentlemen,' I said. 'Gentlemen,' says I. 'I beg of you to pay no heed to the likes of those who have just entered, for it is not our wish to be the instigators of trouble.' Didn't I say that, lads?"

"Aye, Your Honor," Hank said. "That's just what ole' Willie said, all right."

"Yes, sir, 'n he said it in them very words, too," Pete put in.

"It is gratifying, Mr. Parsons, to see that your friends can talk," the judge said.

"Oh, they can talk, Your Honor. It's just that I talk better," Willie said, before going on. "At any rate, we turned away from those river scum, and continued to converse among ourselves, when one of them chanced to pass a remark which was most inflamatory in nature. He said, and I quote, Your Honor, 'you three men must be off that pissant that's tied up alongside the *Virginia Dare*.' I replied as politely as I could, Your Honor. 'Sir,' says I. 'That is no pissant. That is the gallant Missouri River vessel, the *Missouri Mist*.' Well, one would have thought that such a forceful affirmation of our pride in our vessel would preclude any further derisive comments, but if one were to think that, one would be mistaken. For indeed, no sooner were the words out of my mouth, than one of the other gentlemen passed another inflammatory

17

remark, this one of so foul a nature that I shan't repeat it here, in the presence of your august ears. Upon hearing that unkind remark, I then made an inquiry as to whether or not the marriage arrangements of the parents, not only of that particular soul, but indeed of all the gentlemen in his company, had been completed prior to their birth. From that simple inquiry, the Mississippi River boatmen became unreasonably angry, and they commenced to throw punches. As I am sure you can understand, my colleagues and I had no recourse but to defend ourselves. The resultant fight did cause rather extensive damage, as several others then saw fit to join in. But, as you can see, Your Honor, we are clearly not to blame," Willie concluded.

"You have convinced me, Mr. Parsons," the judge said. "Neither you, nor your friends, will be held as solely responsible for the fight, or the resultant damages."

Willie smiled and he and the others shook hands as best they could, with handcuffs still in place.

"However," the judge continued, "you must share responsibility with everyone else, and you must pay your share of the damages and the fines. I fine each of you twenty-five dollars, and assess damages at twenty-five dollars apiece."

"Fifty dol——" Your Honor, that's one hundred and fifty dollars for the three of us!" Willie said.

"Yes," the judge replied. "Yes, it is. It is not lost

upon me that that is a great deal of money for men of your means, and in your situation. It is my hope, however, that such a penalty will aid you in your endeavor to be even more careful in the future."

"But your Honor, how are we to come by such money?" Willie asked.

"Perhaps your captain could be persuaded to pay the amount for you," the judge suggested.

"No, sir," Willie said. "I'll sit and rot in your jail, Your Honor, before I make such an imposition upon that noble man."

"You don't have to sit in jail, Willie, I'm here to pay for all of you," Crystal said, standing again.

"You?" the judge said. He looked at Willie and the other two men, then he looked back at Crystal. "Well, I will say that I'm not surprised, and this time I won't apologize. Bailiff, take these three men to the fine's clerk. When their fines have been paid, release them to this young woman."

"Yes, Your Honor," the bailiff said. "Right this way, men."

The bailiff took the three men through a door at the back of the courtroom, while Crystal had to leave via the front door. She had farther to go, so by the time she arrived the three men were already standing in front of the fine's clerk's desk. The bailiff was opening their handcuffs. "Here's the money," Crystal said, taking the money from her bag.

"And here is your receipt," the fine's clerk said. "These three men belong to you now, Miss, though why in heaven's name anyone would want them is beyond me."

"Thank you," Crystal said. "Come along, boys, I have a buckboard out front."

"Miss Crystal, darlin'," Willie said, as they walked down the concrete steps in front of the building. "I can never find the words to express my thanks for your intervention, nor my shame that it had to come to this."

Crystal chuckled. "Willie, I can't believe that the time will ever come when you can't find the words for anything."

The driver, hearing Crystal's voice, pushed his hat back, then sat up. He looked at the three men accompanying her with some misgiving, but as she seemed to have them under control, he made no comment.

"Take us down to the river," Crystal said. "Take us to the *Missouri Mist*."

"The *Missouri Mist*?" the carriage driver said. "What is that, a steamboat or a barge?"

"I'll thank you to keep a civil tongue in your head, sir, when you speak of the *Missouri Mist*," Willie said.

"Willie, I'm sure the gentleman meant no disrespect," Crystal said quickly, lest she have another fight on her hands.

"Then, in order to inform the . . . gentleman . . ."

Willie said, and he set the word, gentleman, apart from the rest of the sentence, "I'll inform him that the *Missouri Mist* is a steamboat. She is the finest steamboat on the Missouri river, or any other river for that matter. Why, she's that good that she'll make five knots across grass if there's a good, heavy dew."

Crystal smiled, but she said nothing. She had enough faith in the boat to think that it might do just that.

Chapter Two

John Riley leaned back in his chair and examined the hand of cards that he was holding. Had someone scrutinized John Riley with the same intensity as John was scrutinizing his cards, they would have seen a tall, dark man with deep brown eyes, and a pleasing arrangement of features. They would also have noticed that his collar appeared to choke him somewhat, and his fine-cut jacket seemed somewhat restrictive. Or, perhaps that was just an illusion, brought on by the way John felt in his clothes, because he was a mountain man who was much more comfortable in skins and denim, than he was in silks and brocades.

John was in silks and brocades for a purpose, however; he had only recently returned from a mission to Washington, D.C. where he had pleaded the case of the Mandan Indians. John was not a lawyer, nor was he an Indian agent. In fact, his only connection with the Indians was a long-term friendship which had developed out of mutual respect. It was that friendship and respect which led Crazy Wolf to ask John to represent them in a complaint against the United States government.

John had undertaken the task out of a sense of responsibility to his friends, certainly not out of any desire to walk through the halls of power.

John had taken advantage of his trip back east to see and do things he had never done. He watched the United States Congress in action, and left wondering how anything was ever done. He saw a telephone, and marveled at the genius which would allow a man's voice to be carried over a wire. He saw magic lantern shows, and concerts and fine art exhibits. But he had seen nothing as interesting as the beautiful red-headed girl he saw in the St. Louis Museum this very afternoon.

The girl was breath-takingly pretty, and John had to fight against the desire to walk over to her and ask her her name. He let the opportunity slip by him, however, and she left before he ever said a word to her. He would probably never see her again, but that didn't lessen his appreciation of her beauty. He vowed that he would think of her often, and remember her, the way he remembered particularly beautiful sunsets.

Tomorrow, John would be taking a riverboat

back up the Missouri, where he would carry his report to the Mandan Indians, then get on with his life as a trapper. This was his last day in the city, so he decided that he would spend it playing cards. Now he was faced with a decision as to what he should do in the game.

"Why don't you just fold?" the man across the table asked.

Whereas John Riley was over thirty, the one who spoke was in his early twenties. It wasn't only an age difference which set the men apart, however. John was dark and muscular; his gambling adversary was fair-haired, with watery blue eyes and a pale skin which looked as if it never saw sun light. And he lacked John's muscular structure, as he was much more trim in appearance. There was about him, though, a certain sense of danger, and somehow it seemed accented by the way he stroked a small diamond-shaped mark on his cheek. He was a professional gambler, and everything about him looked the part.

"Why should I fold, sir?" John asked. "I believe I am holding the winning hand."

The gambling man smiled and he moved his forefinger from the mark on his cheek to tap the back of his cards, which were lying face-down on the table.

"That's what makes this game so interesting, isn't it?" the professional gambler said. "I think my hand is better than yours, and you believe

24

your hand to be better than mine. However, I have advanced a wager of fifty dollars to back up my statement. Now you must either call or fold. That is how the game is played."

John looked at his hand again. He held three tens and two fives. He had discarded the Ace of Spades to draw the third ten, and he was reasonably certain that the risk of calling was worth taking. He had to be sure though, because he had no more money to lose. Should he lose this bet he would have to find some means of raising more money before he returned home. The sensible thing to do, he realized, would be to fold. But he couldn't fold. Pots had been won all night on hands of lesser value. He reached into his inside jacket pocket and pulled out his billfold. He extracted the last fifty dollars and lay it on the pile of money which was stacked in the center of the table. If he won the pot, he would not only have enough money to complete his journey, he would also have enough for a grub-stake for the winter's trapping. John sighed made his decision.

"I call," he said.

The gambler smiled.

"Well now, isn't that nice?" he said. "Here, I thought you were going to fold and I would have to be satisfied just with what was on the table. Instead, you added fifty dollars. Thank you, that makes it much sweeter." He dropped his hand in front of him. "Full house, Kings over Aces," he said.

"I'm afraid that beats me," John said, laying his own hand down.

"Yes, it does, doesn't it?" the gambler said, with a small laugh. He started to rake the money toward himself. "Have you any more money, mountain man? I hear you went to Washington for the Indians. Maybe you've got some of their money. I'd be happy to relieve you of the burden of carrying it," he added with an evil chuckle.

"No, thanks," John said. "I suppose I've had enough gambling for one night. Gentlemen," he said to the others around the table, all of whom had folded in his hand before he had. "If you will excuse me, I'll. . . ." suddenly John stopped in midsentence, and he stared at the winning hand the gambler had so proudly displayed. When the gambler saw John looking, he reached down quickly and flipped his cards over, then pulled them back into the rest of the deck.

"Just a minute," John said. "I'd like to see that hand again."

"What for?" the gambler asked. "You paid to look at it, you didn't buy it. You've seen it. It was the winning hand."

"King's over Aces, yes, I know," John said. "But one of the Aces was the Ace of Spades, wasn't it?"

"It was the Ace of Clubs," the gambler said. He started to shuffle the cards, even as he spoke.

"No, it was the Ace of Spades," one of the other men said. "I saw it."

"Ace of Clubs, Ace of Spades, what difference does it make?" the gambler asked. By now the entire deck had been thoroughly shuffled.

"It makes a lot of difference," John said. "You see, my discard was an Ace of Spades."

"Well, then that proves it," the gambler said. "If you discarded the Ace of Spades, my card had to be an Ace of Clubs."

"Your card was an Ace of Spades," John said coolly.

The gambler looked at John and his watery blue eyes narrowed, and flashed a dangerous kind of light.

"Mister, what is it you are trying to say?"

"I'm saying you are a liar and a card cheat," John said easily. "You either had another Ace of Spades palmed, or you, somehow, got into the discard pile."

"Mister, I don't know what kind of a life you've been living up in the mountains with the Indians, but here, in the city, cheating is frowned upon. An accusation like the one you just made can get you killed. I'm going to let it go by this time, because I have an idea you don't really understand what you're doing."

The man reached for the money in the center of the table.

"No," John Riley said, and his voice rang loud

and clear throughout the entire lobby of the hotel where the game was being played. "You're not going to take that money by deceit. Leave it on the table. The rest of us will take out what we put in."

Suddenly the gambler had a small pistol in his hand. It appeared so quickly that most of the people, including John Riley, were totally surprised by his action. The gambler took off his hat and started putting the money into it, while holding the others at bay with his pistol.

"Gents, my apologies about this," he said. "But I'll not stand by and be robbed of my winnings."

"Winnings? You mean loot, don't you. You didn't win that money, you're stealing it," John said.

"Well, now, I'm afraid there is only my word against yours about that, isn't there?" the gambler asked. "And, I've got witnesses." He held up a small pistol, a pepper-box, with six barrels. "In fact, I have six witnesses, right here in this pepper box. Now, as this establishment is no longer to my liking, I shall seek more favorable climes elsewhere. If you would excuse me?"

The gambler backed slowly out of the room, holding John Riley and the others at bay with his pistol. So cool was he, that many others in the lobby were not even aware of the drama until after he had already left.

"Damn!" John Riley swore, after the gambler stepped through the front door. "That card cheat is getting away with our money!"

John started for the door, but two men and two women, laughing among themselves, entered at just that moment, and by the time John got around them and out front, the gambler had disappeared into the night streets of St. Louis.

"Yes, sir?" a cabbie asked, pulling on the reins of his horse. "Do you wish a ride?"

"A man just ran out through this door," John said. "Did you see him? Which way did he go?"

"I'm sorry, sir, but I'm afraid I saw no one," the driver replied.

John looked up and down the street, but other than the normal movement of people and conveyances on a typical evening, he saw nothing. He let out a loud, frustrated sigh.

"Would you like a ride, sir?" the cabbie asked again.

"It was a ten-block walk from the hotel to the river where he could catch his boat. A cab would be a most desirable method of getting there, particularly with the baggage John had to carry. But thanks to his bad luck at cards, he would have to walk.

"Thank you, no," John said. "It's such a nice evening, I think I shall walk."

"Have it your way," the driver said. He clucked to his horse and his shay pulled away, empty.

It's my own fault, John thought. I had no business gambling so heavily. Whatever I have to go through now, I deserve.

John reached into his inside jacket pocket again, and he felt an envelope. He pulled it out and examined it, and as he did so, an idea came to mind. Here was first-class passage on the *Missouri Mist*, from St. Louis to Fort Benton, Montana. If he could persuade the captain of the boat to take the first-class ticket back and reissue him a deck-class ticket, then John would have enough money to get back. Barely enough, but enough.

The first thing John would have to do, though, was check out of the hotel. He had not yet made arrangements for this night, so he owed nothing at the desk, he was glad to say. If he went down to the river tonight, perhaps he could sleep aboard the boat. After all, it would be leaving early the next day.

John went back inside the lobby of the hotel and stood just inside the door, looking at the crowd of people. St. Louis, like Philadelphia and Washington, the two other cities he had just visited, was crowded with people. It seemed to John as if the people in these cities had no other purpose in life than to laugh and have a good time. Everywhere he went in those cities he saw men and women dressed in fine clothes, dancing, laughing, eating and drinking. Nowhere, it seemed, did anyone earn their keep by the sweat of their brow. John Riley had a great distaste for cities, and his present circumstances only enhanced that distaste.

John was laden down with baggage, as he was

returning with several presents for the Indians. That excess baggage was causing him difficulty now, for he discovered that the ten-block walk with three heavy bags was quite an ordeal.

After several blocks John was away from the nightlife of the city, and was passing through the warehouses and railroad yards. Here, he finally saw the face of the working city, for here were many men toiling mightily to load and unload train cars, wagons, and warehouse docks with items for tomorrow's commerce.

"Here, mate, where be you goin' with such a load?" one of the warehouse men called to John as he struggled along under the weight of the three bags.

"I'm going to the *Missouri Mist*," John replied. "I have passage for tomorrow's departure."

"A gentleman dressed as fine as yourself ought not to be walkin'," the dock hand said. "You ought to be ridin' in a fancy carriage."

"Don't let the clothes fool you, friend," John said. "I'm as broke as they come."

"That be a fact?"

"Would I be walking like this, if I could ride?"

The dock hand chuckled, then pushed a two-wheel cart over toward John.

"Here," he said. "Put your tack on this truck. It'll make your job a mite easier, I'm a'reckonin'."

John was pleasantly surprised by the man's action. "Why, thank you," John said. "You're a trusting

31

soul to lend me the truck. I'll return it as soon as I have put my luggage aboard."

"No need," the friendly warehouse man said. "The cart belongs to the *Virginia Dare*, a Mississippi boat tied up by the *Missouri Mist*. You'll be doin' me a favor by leavin' it there."

John Riley loaded his three bags onto the car, and, thanks to the kindness of the warehouseman, had a much easier time of it for the remainder of his journey.

When John reached the cobblestone levee, he stopped the cart and looked down at the river, and at all the boats which were tied there. It was nine-thirty in the evening, but the boats, like the railroad yards and warehouses, were hubbubs of activity. Lanterns burned along the levee and on the boats themselves, as stevedores and deckhands loaded cargo. Only the *Missouri Mist* seemed quiet, but as its decks were already laden with cargo, John assumed that the work was all done and the vessel was just awaiting tomorrow's departure.

As John stood there looking down at the *Missouri Mist*, a buckboard stopped behind him and four people got out. It was three men and a woman, and the woman, John noticed, was the same woman he had seen at the museum.

"There she is," one of the men said, pointing to the *Missouri Mist*. "I tell you, lads, seeing her like this, poised as it were for her long sojourn into the wilderness, 'tis sufficient to bring tears to the eyes of the most black-hearted man.

As the three men and the woman started down the levee, they passed close to John.

"Pardon me," John said.

They looked at him, and the woman gasped, and raised her hand to her mouth. John smiled. He thought she had seen him today. In fact, he believed she had even stared at him. Her reaction to him now merely confirmed that belief.

"Yes, sir, what can we do for you?" one of the men asked.

"Are you from the *Missouri Mist*?" John asked.

"Aye, that we are, and proud of it, too," the man said. His eyes narrowed. "You wouldn't be about to pass some unkind remark about her now, would you? For if such is your intention, be advised, sir, that you shall have Willie Parsons to contend with, that gentleman being none other than myself."

Willie cocked his fist.

"No, no, nothing like that," John said. "I've come to report aboard, that's all. I've booked passage for tomorrow. My name is John Riley."

"Mr. Riley, it is customary for the passengers to report on the day of departure," the young woman said, speaking for the first time.

"Oh," John said, obviously crestfallen by the information. "Yes, well, I see."

"Are you without a place to stay the night, lad?" Willie asked.

John grinned sheepishly. "As a matter of fact, I am," he admitted.

"Well, we couldn't turn the lad out now, could we, Miss Crystal?" Willie said.

"No," Crystal said. "We couldn't do that. I suppose you could come aboard tonight if you wished." The young woman smiled at him then. "My name is Crystal Lee. My father is the captain of this boat. If you wish, I can speak to him for you."

John smiled broadly. "Thank you, Miss Lee," he said. "But the truth is, I should like to speak to your father, not only about accepting me tonight, but, about changing my first-class accommodations, as well."

"Changing your first-class accommodations?" Crystal asked. "But why would you want to do that? They are all equal. None are any better than any of the others."

John smiled sheepishly again. "Miss Lee, I am certain that the first-class accommodations are wonderful," he said. "It is not to better my accommodations that I wish to speak to your father, but to lessen them."

"Lessen them?"

"Unfortunately, yes. I suffered a financial reversal earlier this evening. I'm afraid I have no money left. Or, so little money that I must find some source of income. I hope to convince your father to allow me to trade my first-class ticket in for passage on the deck. The difference in money will see me through."

Crystal looked at John, and at the fine clothes he was wearing.

"You'll excuse me for saying so," Crystal said, "but I'm not at all sure a dandy like yourself would survive deck passage. It can be most arduous."

"A dand——" John started, then he stopped. She had been fooled by his clothes. He decided to go along with her. "Yes, well," he said, clearing his throat. "It might be interesting to try such a journey."

Crystal sighed. "Mr. Riley, I don't know the nature of your financial reversals, and whatever they are, you have my sympathy. But please understand that if we get halfway there and you find you are unable to continue the journey, then you only cause more difficulty for the rest of us. I've seen your kind before, and I know what I'm talking about."

"My kind?" John said. "And tell me, Miss Lee, just what is my *kind*?"

"Your kind," Crystal said. "City dandies in fine clothes who have never had to earn their keep by work, and who think a trip up the Missouri is some fine adventure. It's not just some fine adventure, Mr. Riley. It's a most trying journey, even under the best of conditions, and in the finest accommodations. If I were you, I would just go back to the museum and enjoy the Egyptian Exhibit, before even trying this journey."

"Then you did see me," John said, and he smiled broadly. "I thought you did."

Crystal felt her face burning. Why had she said that? She had realized from the moment she saw him tonight that he was the one she had seen at the museum. It was probably that realization which was causing her to be so hard on him now, for in truth, she didn't want him to come on the boat. She didn't want him to, because she was frightened by the prospect of it.

"Yes," she finally managed to stammer. "I saw you there. Perhaps you should have stayed there, rather than get into a card game and lose all your money."

"What makes you think I lost all my money in a card game?" John asked.

"Didn't you?"

"As a matter of fact, I did. But I didn't mention it to you. How did you know? Or, were you secretly watching me there, as you were in the museum?"

"I was not secretly watching you," Crystal said hotly. "I just happened to see you, that's all. And as far as knowing that you lost your money in a card game, you didn't have to mention it, and I didn't have to see it. With a dandy like you, it sticks out all over."

"I see."

"Now, would you like me to ask my father to give you a complete refund? I'm sure the wilds of the Missouri Breaks are no place for someone such as yourself."

"You are most kind to be concerned about my well-being, Miss Lee," John said. "But I do wish passage on your boat."

"Very well, Mr. Riley. If you would come with me, I will talk to my father."

"Thank you," John said. He started for his luggage, but Willie waved him away.

"No need for that, sir," Willie said. "Since you are a paying passenger, even if it is deck passage, then by rights we should handle your baggage for you. Bear a hand there, lads," he said to the other two men with him.

Crystal led the way down the cobblestone levee toward the riverbank. She could feel John's presence behind her, and she could feel him looking at her. The back of her neck burned under the intensity of his gaze.

Unfortunately, she was paying too much attention to his presence, and not enough attention to her footing. She slipped on one of the rocks and pitched herself backward, to keep from falling. She fell right into him, and his arms went around her. His hands covered her breasts, and even though it was an accident of the moment, she was acutely aware of it, and she gasped.

"Are you all right?" John asked, helping her to regain her balance, if not her composure.

"Yes," Crystal said, more sharply than she intended. "I'm quite all right, thank you."

John kept his hand on her elbow, as if to help her the rest of the way down the levee. She pulled away from him.

"I told you," she said. "I am quite all right."

Quickly, and in order to get away from his disquieting presence, Crystal stepped onto the gangplank. Unfortunately, it was slippery wet, and she was incautious. As a result she slipped again, and this time, because she had opened up some distance between them, she fell before John could get to her. She hit the water with a splash.

Crystal let out a little scream as she went down, and John was there instantly, pulling her back up. Now she was soaking wet, and the dress hung heavily, and clung to her, revealingly.

"Are you all right?" John asked again.

"Will you quit asking me if I'm all right?" Crystal said. "I was all right until you came along."

"I'm sorry, I just wanted to. . . ."

"Willie!" Crystal called, interrupting John's apology.

"Yes'm,"

"Take this . . . this passenger to my father," she said, as she stood there dripping water, not only from her clothes, but from her hair. "I must get changed."

38

"Yes'm," Willie said. "Right this way, lad. Beware the gangplank, it's a might slick."

"Ooohh!" Crystal said, and she went on board, then up the stairs to her compartment.

A moment later, Willie was standing with John at the foot of the deck ladder, on board. John looked over toward the ricks of firewood.

"I could bed down there, I guess," he said.

"No good, lad," Willie said.

"Oh? Why not?"

"This is the main deck," Willie said. "And the main deck is awash half the time. You would fare better by finding yourself a place on the boiler deck."

"The boiler deck?"

"Aye, lad, that's the next deck up. The lowest deck, you see, is the main deck. Then comes the boiler deck, then the top deck, which we call the hurricane deck."

"I see," John said. "Very well, then I shall find a place on the boiler deck."

"Willie, are you back?" a voice called from the top of the stairs.

"Aye, Cap'n, I'm back," Willie said. "And a man more full of contrition you are not likely to see in this lifetime." Under his breath, Willie spoke to John. "Come on up, lad, an' meet the cap'n. Though I'm that ashamed of my actions, I wish I could avoid it this night."

"I see Crystal managed to get you boys out of

jail," the man at the top of the steps said as Willie and John reached the boiler deck.

"Aye, that she did, sir, at the cost of one hundred and fifty dollars for the lot of us."

"Hmmph," the captain said. "Time was when a man could throw himself a good drunk, get into one hell of a fight, and cover everything with a ten-dollar fine and costs. Who is this?"

"Miss Crystal didn't tell you?"

"Crystal didn't say a word. She just stormed by me like she was mad or something. Look here, Willie, was she wet, or did I just imagine that?"

"She was a mite wet," Willie said. "She fell into the river."

"How could she do a damn-fool thing like that?"

"She just slipped on the gangplank," John said.

"This here is John Riley," Willie said. "He's a passenger."

"I'm Captain Marsh Lee. I suppose you were told that the passengers don't generally report until the day of departure?"

"Yes, sir, we told 'im that," Willie said. "But the lad has a problem."

"Oh?"

"Captain Lee, I would like to trade in my ticket."

"You mean you won't be going back with us?"

"Yes, I want to go back with you, but I fear I can't afford to go first-class. I'm afraid I shall have to convert my ticket in order to save a little money."

"He had the misfortune to engage in a game of

40

chance earlier today," Willie said. "Cards, I believe. He lost all his money."

Captain Lee chuckled. "I see. Lady Luck deserted you, did she? Well, I'm sure we can work something out, Mr. Riley."

"I'd like to take deck passage," John said.

"All right, I shall inform the purser to refund you the difference in money first thing after we get underway in the morning," Captain Lee said. "And again, you have my condolences on your poor turn of luck in the card game."

"I thank you," John said. "Though in truth, I must inform you that luck had very little to do with it."

"Oh?"

"No, indeed," John said. "Unless you consider my misfortune to meet a four-flusher and card cheat as bad luck. He took the hand dishonestly, and when I called him out for it, he pulled a gun, took the money, and left."

"Then you were probably lucky that you weren't killed," Captain Lee said. "Often a card cheat will kill the man who finds him out, covering it by claiming it to be an affair of honor. In fact, it is no such thing. He merely wishes to preserve his dirty secret for a while longer, that's all. It is strange, though, that the proprietor of the gaming establishment did nothing."

"There was really nothing they could do," John

said. "The card cheat was that cool that he had his money and was gone before anyone was the wiser."

"Do you know his name?"

"No," John said. "But I won't soon forget him. He was a pale-looking man, with light hair and pale eyes. And there was a mark on his cheek."

"A mark, you say? Was it a scar of some sort?"

"No," John said. "I don't think it was a scar. It was more like a birthmark. It was shaped like a. . . ."

"Diamond?" Captain Lee asked in a quiet voice.

"Yes," John said. "Yes, it was. Why, do you know this man?"

"Yes," Captain Lee said. "I know him."

"Then you have had run-ins with him, too?"

"Yes," Captain Lee said without elaboration. "Uh, Mr. Riley, suppose I refund the entire cost of your ticket, and yet allow you to keep your stateroom. What would you think of that?"

"What would I think? I think I couldn't do it, that's what I think. Why would you offer something like that?"

"I don't know," Captain Lee said. "Perhaps I am merely trying to make up to you in some way for the misfortune which befell you tonight."

"Captain Lee, that's very decent of you," John said. "But, it was my misfortune, and none of your own. No, thank you very much for your kind offer, but I cannot do that."

"Then perhaps you would care to work your

passage so that it would be free," Captain Lee suggested.

"I must confess to you, I know nothing of riverboats."

"There is nothing to know," Captain Lee said. "I will merely ask that you position yourself near the smokestacks. If sparks start to fly, then there is the danger of a fire. I would expect you to keep alert for such a danger. Do you feel you could do that?"

"Of course," John said. He smiled broadly. "And, I thank you, sir, for providing me with this opportunity."

Marsh Lee turned and started to leave, then he looked back at John.

"I know who you are now," he said. "You used to scout some for the army, didn't you?"

"Yes," John said.

"And didn't you just undertake some sort of mission for the Indians?"

"I'm just completing that mission now," John said.

"Well, you are very welcome on my boat, John Riley. I must confess, however, that your fancy clothes threw me somewhat, for a moment there."

John chuckled. "You aren't the only one to be fooled by my clothes," he said. "I will be glad to get back into something more to my style."

Chapter Three

When David left the hotel with the money, he knew that the man he had cheated would be coming after him. It was a big man too, and from the look of the shoulders and arms which were just barely concealed by his jacket, the man could have pulled David apart limb by limb.

David shuddered at the thought. If the big man caught up with him, the only way David could hope to stop him would be to shoot him. David really had no qualms about shooting someone. He had done it before—and he could do it again. Before, however, it had been in open country and no one found out about it. It would surely cause some difficulty if he shot a man in downtown St. Louis. After all St. Louis was the fourth biggest city in the United States. The authorities might

44

take a dim view of anyone who killed someone inside the city limits. David giggled at the thought.

As soon as David got outside the hotel, he ran down the steps which led to a basement entry service access. There were some old barrels there, and he hid behind them. He wanted to laugh out loud when the well-dressed giant ran outside just behind him to look up and down the street, and wonder where David had gone. He must have thought David had the power to disappear into thin air.

David heard the man ask the cab driver if he had seen anyone run out. He heard the cabbie say no, then he heard the cabbie try to solicit a fare. He declined the ride, and David knew that it was because he didn't have enough money for cabfare.

So, he was cleaned out in the game, huh? Well, he had no business playing cards, if he couldn't handle it. Of course, the thing with the Ace of Spades was a foolish move on his own part. David realized that he should have palmed it before the hand started.

David stayed where he was for a few minutes longer, then, when he saw the big man walking toward the river carrying his three bags, he realized he would be safe, so he came out. He started down the street looking for another game, or for some amusing diversion.

He didn't find another game, but the amusing diversion presented itself a while later.

"What's a nice gentleman like you doin' out all alone?" a woman's husky voice asked.

David looked into the shadows of a nearby building, and saw her standing there. She was dark-haired, heavily made up, and she reeked of perfume. She reached up to her blouse, then unbuttoned it to reveal her plump jutting breasts. The white flesh of her breasts gleamed in the light from the nearby gas lamp. David felt a pressure in the front of his pants, and he rubbed himself.

She woman saw it, and she smiled victoriously, pushing her hair back from her face.

"Oh, my, you *are* ready for a good time, aren't you?"

David felt a quick flash of anger over her easy confidence with him.

"What makes you think an old cow like you can give me a good time?" he asked.

His question didn't even phase the woman.

"Because I know just what a young man like you wants," she said, jutting her breasts forward.

"What do I want, whore?"

The woman smiled, knowingly.

"Come with me," she said. "I'll show you what the likes of you wants. I know how to please you like no one else has."

David felt his pulse quicken and his breath shorten. The woman was at least twenty years older than he was, and any attractiveness she may have possessed was so disfigured by the heavy application of makeup as to be almost bizzare. And yet, despite that, he felt a lust consuming his insides. He wanted her so bad.

David followed her into an alley, then through a door which opened into the side of one of the buildings. The door was small and the stairway beyond, narrow. It was dank and dark and smelled foul from the scatterings of hundreds of chamber pots, and the obvious emptying of bladders against the walls.

"Here we are, dear," the woman said, opening a door at the top of the stairs. "My room is inside."

"My god, woman, how can you stand this foul air?" David asked. "Is there a window to open?"

"Of course," the woman said easily. She lifted the window, then turned and smiled at him as she started taking off her clothes, first her blouse, slowly.

The woman knew she was much older than he was, but she knew also, all the tricks her years in the profession had taught her. She enticed the young man who was about to become her lover by using a shadow here, a soft light there, a subtle positioning of her body so that, miraculously, the aged whore became a sensual creature. She could tell by David's reaction that she was accomplishing her purpose.

"You do want me, don't you, dear?" she asked, as she lay back on the bed, and spread her legs seductively.

47

"Yes," David answered in a husky voice.

"Come," the woman said, reaching for him and pulling him onto the bed with her. "Come, let me make you feel good."

Less than one mile away from the foul and fetid walk-up flat where David was rutting out his lust in the well-practiced arms of the dark-haired woman was the Mississippi River. There, tied up with the many other boats, was the *Missouri Mist*.

On the *Missouri Mist* there was a small cabin, located in the base of the wheelhouse on the hurricane deck, which served as quarters for Crystal and her father. When Crystal was much younger, her bed was in the same room as her father's. But as she grew older and her body began changing from that of a little girl into a young woman, her father provided her with some privacy by hanging a curtain to divide the cabin into two rooms.

Though the room was separated by a curtain divider, nothing could drown out the sound of her father's snoring, and on this, the last night before they were to leave St. Louis, Marsh Lee's snoring seemed particularly loud. Crystal tossed and turned and pounded at her pillow in a fruitless attempt to get to sleep.

Crystal told herself that it was her father's snoring which was keeping her awake. That seemed a little surprising to her though because she had always managed to sleep through his snoring in the past. Why was it so destructive tonight? Finally, realizing that sleep was an elusive quarry, Crystal got out of bed, and walked through the door, out on to the hurricane deck. She didn't bother to put anything on over her sleeping gown. After all, it was in the wee hours of the morning, and no one would be awake to see her. Besides, only her and her father's cabin opened onto the hurricane deck. No one ever came up here unless they had ship's business to attend to.

Crystal looked out over the city of St. Louis. It was quiet and dark, and she could hear a dog barking way off in the distance somewhere. The city was so peaceful that the loudest sound to reach her ears was the gentle lapping of the river itself, and the creaking of the boats and hawsers as they rode the current at anchor.

Crystal walked forward on the hurricane deck and stood against the railing, looking down over the bow of the boat. She could see the neat stacks of cargo, and the long ricks of firewood which would have to be replenished several times during the long journey upriver.

Crystal looked down at the boat. She admired the neat compactness of the *Missouri Mist*, and actually thought it, and the other Missouri River boats, were far more attractive than the gaudy Mississippi River boats.

The bow of the *Missouri Mist* was shaped like a spoon to allow it to slip easily over shoals and sandbars. It was one hundred and sixty feet long, with a beam of thirty-two feet. From her lower deck to the top of the wheelhouse, she rose forty feet. It was nearly sixty feet to the running lights at the very top of the twin, fluted smokestacks.

The *Missouri Mist* could carry two hundred and twenty tons of freight and thirty-six cabin passengers through water no deeper than a man's waist. She had a large paddle-wheel at the stern, eighteen feet in diameter and twenty-six feet wide. The wheel was rotated by two steam engines at a rate of twenty revolutions per minute. It was designed specifically for use on the Missouri, and though Willie Parsons was exaggerating when he said it could make five knots on a heavy dew, it could proceed, when unloaded, through water that was no more than twenty inches deep.

Crystal heard a sound . . . no more than a quiet bump or scrape, but she moved quickly and quietly to examine it. At first she saw nothing, then, just at the base of the smokestacks, a shadow within a shadow, she saw him: John Riley was moving around, doing something. At first, Crystal nearly called out to him, then she decided to wait for a moment to see what he was up to.

John stepped out of the shadows into a square of soft, silver, but illuminating light from the moon, and Crystal gasped. John Riley was in the middle of changing his clothes, and he was stark naked. Crystal knew she should turn and walk quietly away, and yet, though her mind willed it, her body refused to respond. Instead, she stood there, rooted to the spot, mesmerized by the scene which was unfolding before her.

John was tall and angular, with wide shoulders, a deep chest, narrow hips and flat buttocks. He turned once, to reach over for his shirt, and when he did she saw him full-front. The lower part of his body was dimmed, though not entirely hidden by shadows, and she stared, ashamed of her action, but driven by a curiosity that had grown even stronger by the opportunity thus presented.

She felt a sudden heat in her breasts, then she remembered the feel of his hands when she had fallen against him. The heat moved down from her breasts, and she had to bite her lower lip to keep from gasping out loud.

Finally John reached for a pair of trousers and, as he pulled them on, Crystal found the strength to step back from the railing. She felt a weakness in her knees and a hollowness in the pit of her stomach. The palms of her hands were sweating and her breathing was restricted. Those dark, bittersweet feelings she experienced when she stood at the stern of the boat to watch the engines, were reawakened. But now those throbbing feelings were brought on, not by the engines, but by her view of the handsome young man on the boiler deck. The warmth which had begun at her breast, now spread throughout the rest of her body, and her knees grew weak.

Crystal knew that she had never before physically reacted to a man in this way. Why was she responding so strongly now? She wasn't sure where such strong reactions might lead her, and she didn't want to find out.

When David awakened the next morning, he looked around at the room, and then at the woman who was in bed with him. The harsh light which came through the window was cruel to the woman's features, and David saw the crusted layers of old makeup applications competing with the dirt and wrinkles in her face. Her mouth was open and she was snoring. Her breasts, which had seemed so enticing to him last night, now mocked him obscenely, and he dressed and left as quickly as he could.

David hurried down the stinking stairway, through the alley, and finally back onto the street. He flagged a cab as it came by. The horse was early-morning lively, tossing its head as if proud of the hat its driver had put on it.

"Yes, sir. Where to, sir?"

"Anyplace where there's sporting blood, and I can get into a game of cards," David said, settling back in the seat.

"I'm afraid I'm not a gaming man, sir," the driver said. "I wouldn't know where to take you."

"Never mind," David said. "I know a place. Just go where I tell you."

"Yes, sir," the driver said. He slapped his reins, and the horse surged ahead.

A few moments later they were driving down First Street. David looked at all the boats which were tied there, and when he saw one in particular, he reached up and touched the driver.

"Stop here for a moment," he said.

"Whoa, boy," the driver said to his horse.

"The *Missouri Mist*," David said.

"I beg your pardon, sir?"

"The *Missouri Mist*," David said, pointing to the boat. "I didn't know it was in town."

"Who can keep up with them, there are so many of them?" the driver said.

"I can keep up with them," David said. "Yes, sir, I can keep up with them."

They sat there for another long moment, while David studied the *Missouri Mist*.

"Would you like me to drive down there, sir?"

"No," David said. "Take me to Union Station."

"Union Station?"

"Yes," David said. "I'm going to take a train."

"Where to, sir?"

"Anywhere," David said. "I don't really care."

"Have you given up looking for a game?"

"I have in this city," David said.

*   *   *

Union Station was a beehive of activity. In the depot itself hundreds of people milled about under the huge, domed ceilings. Their feet made hollow sounding echos on the marble floors. A huge clock was on the wall beneath a sign which read: "To Trains."

Agents, using megaphones, announced the imminent arrivals and departures of the trains, and the tracks on which the activity was taking place.

David bought a ticket to Philadelphia, choosing it over Chicago because the next train leaving was heading East.

The car shed was even more busy than the depot. There were at least a dozen trains in the car shed, and from fifty to a hundred people around each train. Conductors and porters were shouting, children were squealing and laughing, and the engines were venting steam. David hurried to his train, was shown to his car, then found a seat. He had taken parlor-car class, so he was most comfortable. Comfort would not take care of boredom, however, and he knew that it was a long trip to Philadelphia.

Three businessmen got on the train then, laughing, and talking to each other in that self important way that David had noticed businessmen had about them. One was bald, one was fat and bearded, and the third, who had no particular distinguishing physical trait, wore a gold watch stretched across his vest. He pulled out his gold watch and studied it for a moment.

"Gentlemen, I make it twenty-four hours to Philadelphia," he said.

"Anybody have any ideas about what we might do?" the bald one asked.

"I brought some cards," the fat one said.

"Pshaw, three-handed is no fun," the bald one said.

"Perhaps we can impose upon this gentleman to play with us," the one with the watch suggested. He pointed to David. "How about it, sir? Would you care to play some cards with us?"

"No, I don't think so," David said.

"Come on, it's going to be a long trip."

"I'd really rather not," David said.

"Oh, leave him alone, Carl. Not everyone is willing to play for our stakes," the fat one said.

"He can probably afford it," the man with the watch said. "If he couldn't, he wouldn't be traveling first-class."

"Come on, be a sport," the bald-headed one said. "Play some cards with us."

David sighed. "All right," he finally said. "You talked me into it."

Chapter Four

The *Missouri Mist* left her mooring place before dawn and moved over to one of the docks which would facilitate passenger loading. Marsh Lee had paid fifteen dollars for the privilege of tying up there for two hours. Prospective passengers were advised by circulars and by advertisements placed in the city newspapers to "board between the hours of seven and nine in the morning."

John, dressed now in buckskins and denim, stood at the railing on the main deck and watched with interest as the passengers began to stream aboard. He studied each of them, and though he said nothing aloud, he made a mental appraisal of each person as they boarded.

The passengers who were in family groups, such as a husband and his wife and two or three children, were the kind of passengers John welcomed, because they were the people who would bring stability and growth to the upper Missouri. Generally they settled in the agricultural areas, areas where the Indians had no interest at stake. In fact, these people were welcomed by the Indians, for they were a source of ready trade.

The others though, the gold hunters and the adventurers, were far less than welcome. They raped the land, and trespassed on sacred Indian grounds, killing game and damming up streams and rivers for hydraulic mining. Often, when they didn't find gold they turned to other enterprises, such as gambling or poaching or rustling. Those people were detrimental not only to the Indians, but to the peaceful white settlers as well. Fortunately, John saw very few passengers who seemed to fit that mold. Most appeared to be families.

"Oh, Papa, look how big this boat is!" one little boy exclaimed as he stepped on board with his family. "Why, I bet this is the biggest boat in the whole world!"

"I wouldn't say that," the boy's father said. "But it certainly is a nice, big boat."

The boy's mother looked around and held onto her husband's arm, and John could read in her face the changing expression of all her feelings: excitement, hope, fear, determination and courage. John hoped everything worked for the them.

John heard raised voices, and looked toward

the stern of the boat, the direction from which the voices came. He walked down that way to see what was going on.

"And I say I *will* bring it with me!" one man was saying. "I paid thirty dollars freight for it, and, at fifteen dollars per hundred-weight, that authorizes me two hundred pounds."

"Yes, you have impressed me most favorably with your arithmatical abilities, sir," Willie was saying. "For thirty dollars would indeed purchase two hundred pounds of freight. But it will do you no good with black gunpowder, for that substance we cannot carry."

"And why not?" the man asked angrily.

"If you have to ask, sir, then I wonder if you have the brains to be associated with the stuff at all. You must know that the slightest spark can set that powder off, and we're carrying passengers. Perhaps you don't realize it, sir, but 'twas just such an explosion which doomed the *Arabian Princess* last spring. There were twenty-two people aboard who were killed in that explosion."

"Yeah? Well, I'll tell you this, friend. I don't give one tinker's damn about the *Arabian Princess*, or the people who were killed. All I care about is making certain that I get this powder out to my mining claim, and it is going by boat."

"No, sir, not on this boat it isn't," Willie said.

"Willie, what is the problem here?" Crystal asked, arriving on the scene at that particular moment.

"Good morning, Miss Lee," Willie said. He pointed at the blustering passenger. "This . . . gentleman . . ." Willie set the word apart from the rest of the sentence, as if it were an affront to use the word in reference to the man. He cleared his throat and went on. "This passenger is attempting to transport two hundred pounds of black gunpowder on board the *Missouri Mist*."

"Two hundred pounds of black gunpowder?" Crystal said.

"What are you tellin' her for? This here is men's business; there ain't no need in gettin' a snot-nosed little girl into it."

"She's the . . ." Willie started to say, but Crystal held up her hand to interrupt him.

"That's all right, Willie, I'll handle this," she said sweetly.

"Ha! You'll handle it? Who the hell are you?" the bellicose passenger asked.

"I am the one who is going to tell you to get your powder off this boat," Crystal said. "I am the first officer."

"Yeah? Well, either you take my powder, or I will get a refund. Now, I don't reckon the cap'n of this vessel is gonna be any too pleased to hear that you're sendin' away a payin' customer, do you?"

"Willie, escort this man to the purser," Crystal said. "Tell the purser I said to refund his money. He is not going with us."

"What?" the man sputtered. "See here, I'm not

goin' to take this lyin' down. There ain't an ounce o' guts among the entire crew if they let themselves be bossed by a girl. Now me'n my powder is both goin'—unless the cap'n hisself tells me I ain't!"

"You heard the first officer," Willie said. "That's all the authority you need."

"I tell you, I ain't leavin'!"

"Escort this gentlemen to the purser, and then off the boat," Crystal said again. "Willingly, if he will go that way. By force, if it is required."

The prospector suddenly pulled a pistol and took a couple of steps back from Willie.

"I told you," he said. "I ain't leavin' here 'till I've talked to the cap'n." He pointed his pistol toward Willie and Crystal and waved it about, menacingly. "You," he said to Willie. "Go get the cap'n and bring him to me, or I'm going to fix it so's your first officer ain't so pretty." He laughed, wickedly.

John had been watching everything from the railing, and when he saw the man pull a pistol, he stepped toward him in two quick, silent steps. He reached out from behind the man and snatched the pistol away from him as cleanly as picking up a glass from a table.

"Hey, what the?" the man sputtered, surprised by John's sudden move. "You heard Mr. Parsons and the first officer," John said. "Get off this boat."

"Hank, Pete," Willie called, and as the two men came over, Willie pointed to the passenger. "Take

60

this unpleasant gentleman to the purser, refund his passage and then push him off the boat." Willie smiled. "If he gives you no more trouble, you can push him off on the side of the boat nearest the bank."

"You ain't heard the last of ole' Angus Pugh, I can tell you that," the man blustered.

"We've heard the last of you on this voyage," Crystal said sweetly.

Willie laughed at the passenger's frustrated, blustering anger, then he looked over at John.

"I want to thank you, lad," he said. " 'Twas a courageous thing you did, snatching away that gun like that."

"Not so courageous," John admitted. "I was standing at the rail behind him. He didn't even know I was there."

"Nevertheless, for a passenger to step forward like that when a crewman is in danger, why, that's a rare thing, sir, and Miss Lee and I are truly in your debt."

"I'm not exactly a passenger," John said. "I signed onto the crew last night."

"Did you now, lad?" Willie asked. He smiled broadly, and extended his hand for a warm shake. "Well, 'tis pleased I am to be welcomin' you aboard. The *Missouri Mist* is the best boat on the river, aye, 'n manned by the best crew too. 'Tis only to be expected of course, for Cap'n Lee is the finest officer afloat, approached only by Miss Lee."

"Yes," John said, looking at Crystal. "I'm glad to see there was no damage done by your falling in the river last night."

"No damage done," Crystal said shortly. "Though I would just as soon not discuss it, if you don't mind."

"As you wish. I heard you tell the passenger that you were the first officer. Is that true?"

"I wouldn't have said it otherwise," Crystal replied.

"Isn't it a bit unusual to have a woman as a first officer?"

"I assure you, sir," Crystal said. "My status as a first officer is not as surprising as the news that you are a member of this crew."

"Yes," John said. "Well, your father was kind enough to take me on, in order that I could book passage. My duties are somewhat limited, however. My main purpose, as I understand it, will be to keep a sharp eye out for fire. As you can see, however, I am now at least dressed for the part."

"Yes," Crystal said, and at that particular moment, she recalled the incident of the night before, and she blushed mightily. "Well, I'm afraid it takes more than a change of clothes to adjust to the rigors of life on board a Missouri riverboat."

"That's strange," John said. "Last night you seemed to show an inordinate interest in my change of clothes."

"Last night?" Crystal asked in a quiet, choked

voice. Had he realized she had watched him change clothes?

"You did comment about my suit, as I recall," John said. "In fact, if memory serves, you called me a dandy, I believe. Surely my clothes today can bear as much witness to my value as what I was wearing last night."

Crystal let out a sigh of relief. So, he hadn't seen her last night, after all.

"Is something wrong?" John asked. "You are acting rather strangely."

"No," Crystal said. "No, nothing is wrong. Uh, perhaps you are right. Perhaps I did act too hastily. I shall reserve judgment until you have had an opportunity to prove yourself, one way or another."

"If you ask me, girl, the lad has already proven himself," Willie said. "Anyone who saves the neck of Willie Parsons, is jake by Willie. Lad, I've expressed my feelings to you, and that's a fact. I'll be making a point of keeping you company later. Now I have my duties to attend to, and I beg your pardon for going on."

"I'll see you later, Willie," John said.

"I, too, have duties," Crystal said. She smiled, almost shyly. "I do hope things work out for you, Mr. Riley."

"Thank you," John said.

About half an hour later, Captain Marsh Lee pulled on the chain which blew the boat whistle, and its deep-throated tones could be heard on both sides of the river. Marsh put the engine in reverse and the steam boomed out of the steam-relief pipe like the firing of the cannon. The wheel began spinning backward and the boat pulled away from the dock, then turned with the wheel going downriver and the bow pointing upstream. The engine lever was slipped to full forward, and the wheel began spinning in the other direction, until finally it caught hold, overcame the force of the current, and started moving the boat upstream.

For the first part of the journey they were on the Mississippi, and they beat their way against the current, around a wide, sweeping bend, with the engine steam-pipe booming as loudly as if the city were under a cannonading. Finally they reached the mouth of the Missouri, turned into it, and the trip was begun.

For the rest of the day the *Missouri Mist* beat its way up river, with the engines clattering and the paddle wheel slapping and the boat itself being enveloped in the thick smoke which belched out from the high, twin stacks.

Crystal was in the wheelhouse, though for the moment her father was at the wheel, and she was standing to one side, looking down toward the bow. There, she saw John and Hank, busily restacking bundles of empty bags. By the terms of John's limited-duty employment, he was not required to engage in such labor, but he had been pitching in and helping all day and Crystal couldn't help but admire him for that. Perhaps she had been mistaken about him. Perhaps he was not quite the dandy she had believed him to be. Or, perhaps she hadn't really believed it at all, but had merely created the idea, as a means of protecting herself from what she was really feeling about him.

"Didn't you hear me?" her father suddenly asked, and Crystal realized that he had spoken to her, though she had no idea what he had said.

"I'm sorry, Dad," she said. "Were you talking to me?"

Marsh chuckled, and made an exaggerated point of looking around the wheelhouse. "Well, now, I don't really know, girl. Is there anyone else here?"

Crystal laughed with him. "I guess not," she said.

"I asked you if you would mind taking a turn at the wheel. I need to go down to the engine room."

"You go ahead," Crystal said. "I'll take over up here."

Marsh started to leave the wheelhouse, but just before he left, he stopped in the door and lit his pipe. He took several reflective puffs, and let the smoke wreath around his head before he finally said something to Crystal.

"Darlin'?"

"Yes, Dad?"

"Darlin', don't be lettin' yourself get attached to

Mr. Riley. He doesn't exactly fit into the plans I've made for you."

Crystal forced a laugh. "Dad, what on earth makes you even suggest such a thing? Why, I have no ideas at all toward Mr. Riley."

"I don't know," Marsh said. "Maybe you are attracted to 'im, without even realizin' it. It's obvious that you find him a handsome man."

"What makes you say that?" Crystal asked. "Have I said as much?"

"Darlin', you don't have to say it with words," Marsh said. "It's written on you, as clear as chalk on a slate. You do find him a handsome man, don't you?"

"I suppose I find him handsome enough," Crystal said. "But city slickers and drawing-room dandies simply aren't my cup of tea."

"City slickers?" Marsh replied. "Darlin', we are talking about John Riley, aren't we?"

"Yes," Crystal said. "I'm talking about John Riley. Didn't you see the way he was dressed when he first came aboard? He was all done up in fancy silks and fine clothes. I'm afraid I'm just too much of a pioneer girl for the likes of him."

"Don't you know who that is?" Marsh asked. "Do you mean to tell me you have never even heard of him?"

"No," Crystal said. "Why? Should I have heard of him?"

Marsh chuckled. "Now he is doin' some trapping

66

on his own. Sometimes he guides wagon trains, other times he hunts for the railroad, and in the past, he scouted for the Army. Why, he was one of General Custer's finest scouts, and folks say that if Custer had listened to John Riley, he'd still be around. He's on his way back from Washington, now. He went there on a mission for Angry Wolf and the Mandans. They say John Riley is about the only white man the Mandans will trust. Call John Riley what you will, but you sure can't call him a city slicker."

"Oh," Crystal said in a quiet, surprised voice. "Oh, I didn't know."

"No, sir," Marsh went on. "He is not a dandy. What he is, is one of the most dependable and knowledgeable men in the Northwest. But, despite all that, he doesn't fit into the plans I have made for you. So, if you want to please me, you won't be lettin' yourself fall in love with him."

"Don't worry, Dad. I certainly have no intention of doing that," Crystal said.

For the next couple of hours Crystal was lost in her task. She had no time to think of John Riley, nor to consider the new facts she learned about him from her father. She could do only one thing, and that was steer the boat.

To the novice it might not appear to be such a difficult job at this point on the river. But already the river was beginning to show why it was the most dangerous navigable river in America. It was broad here, and deceptively peaceful looking. But the flat surface of the water covered the shoals and sandbars, the rock outcroppings, the eddy currents and whirlpools, which were all through the river at this point. Crystal knew much of the river and could avoid some of the hazards that were permanent, simply by relying on her memory. But many of the hazards of the river were temporary in nature; a new bar of sand shifted into what had been the channel just a short time before, or a submerged log waited to take out the bottom of the boat.

It was this talent, being able to find and avoid those new, uncharted hazards, which made Crystal so valuable to her father. Crystal was able to determine by the slightest discoloration of the water, or by the smallest ripple, if there was some danger lurking ahead. She could read the river as easily as most educated people could read a printed page.

By nightfall they were near the town of Washington, Missouri. As the crow flies it was a distance of no more than forty-five miles, though the *Missouri Mist* had already come ninety miles through the twisting river. A railroad track ran alongside the shore at that point, and the train they saw heading for St. Louis would be there in an hour. One hour, by rail, to cover the same distance it had taken the river boat twelve hours to traverse. That was graphic evidence, if such evidence were needed, that riverboat traffic on the Missouri would soon come to an end. Already there were fewer trips than there were last year, and one of the largest riverboat companies had just announced that it was halting service altogether.

Willie relieved Crystal at the wheel after a while, and Crystal came down to the main deck to stand, unobserved, behind a stack of cargo, and watch the starboard engine in its labor. Her neck and shoulders were tense from the hours at the wheel, and she reached around with her own hand and tried to massage the aching muscles. The cool air made her shiver.

"Here," a man's voice said. "Let me do that."

Before Crystal could protest, strong hands and gentle fingers went to her neck and shoulders, and began kneading her flesh expertly, skillfully, spreading a soothing sensation throughout the pounding ache which had started there. Her benefactor was none other than John Riley.

"You ... shouldn't ... be ... doing ... this," Crystal tried to protest, but his hands were having such an amazing, relaxing effect, that she found it impossible to resist strenuously. And now she had goosebumps caused by his proximity, not the cool evening.

John laughed, softly. "You don't really want me to stop, do you?" he asked. He continued to massage as he spoke.

"No," she admitted. "That feels so good. Where did you learn to do that?"

"It's a parlor trick," John said. "After several hours of playing cards, drinking tea, and being engaged in perfectly useless information with other wastrels and dandies, it is sometimes necessary to get a massage to relax."

"You . . . you let me make a fool of myself," Crystal said. "Dad told me about you, about how you were a scout for General Custer, and how you are a trapper and wagon train guide. You aren't a city slicker at all."

"Perhaps not," John said.

"Why didn't you say something?"

"I don't know," John teased. "You seemed so positive, that I was beginning to wonder myself. Here, turn this way and hold still."

From the back John put his arms around Crystal, locking his hands just beneath her breasts. He pulled her against him, then leaned back and lifted her feet from the floor. Miraculously, it seemed, her muscles quit hurting.

"That's an old Indian trick," he said. He turned her toward him, and looked into her face for a long moment, then he put his arms on her shoulders. "And this," he added, "is a trick of my own."

John pulled Crystal to him, and before she realized what was happening, or could react in any way, he crushed her lips beneath his. His hands

70

left her shoulders and his arms wound around her tightly, pulling her soft body to his.

When the surprise passed, Crystal tried to resist, and she began to struggle against him. But the harder she struggled, the more determined he became to hold her, until finally she abandoned the struggle and let herself go limp in his arms, the smell of his manliness overwhelming her.

As she stood there in his arms listening to the pumping of the steam piston, her surprise changed to surrender, then to curiosity, and finally to sweetness. The secret, hinted-at pleasure she often felt during those moments of formless fantasy came over her now. John's lips opened on hers and his tongue pushed into her mouth. It was shocking and thrilling at the same time, and she let a moan of pleasure escape from her throat, like the sigh of escaping steam. Her blood heated and her body flushed with a warmth she had never before experienced.

She wondered how long the kiss could go on, and she gave herself up to it, losing herself in its hold until her head grew so light that she abandoned all thought except this intimate pleasure. After an eternity that was too short, John pulled his lips away and Crystal felt herself leaning against him, as limply as steam-wilted grass.

Finally sanity returned and she realized what she had allowed to happen. With that realization was also the knowledge that she had enjoyed it . . .

and he *knew* that she had enjoyed it. Her cheeks flamed in embarrassment, and she felt a rush of anger, not only with herself, but with him, for taking advantage of her weakness. She slapped him.

"You had no right to do that!" she said, angrily.

"Perhaps not," John said, smiling as easily as if she had just shook his hand, rather than slapping him. "But it was an opportunity I didn't intend to let pass. After all, one doesn't get opportunities like that too often."

"I assure you, sir, you shall not get this opportunity again!" Crystal said, and she turned abruptly and moved quickly to the bow of the boat to get away from his insolent gaze and disturbing presence.

Chapter Five

"All right, stand clear!" Willie called. He was out on the bow. "Everyone stand clear!"

"Willie, the cap'n wants to know if we are ready?" Hank asked, calling down from the hurricane deck.

"Tell the cap'n we are ready," Willie replied, and the message was relayed back up to the wheelhouse.

Every Missouri riverboat carried two very long poles, called spars, at the bow of the boat. Whenever the boat got stuck on a sandbar, those two poles would be put down in the water to the river bottom at about a forty-five-degree angle, then driven back by cables attached to a steam capstan. The resultant action was a very powerful polling of the boat. That action was technically known as sparring, though as the poles looked like grasshopper legs when in the water, it was often referred to as 'grasshoppering.'

"Willie, the cap'n says, 'Very well, Mr. Parsons, please proceed','' Hank called back down.

The *Missouri Mist*, which was now four weeks out of St. Louis, was stuck on a sandbar. It wasn't a bar they had blundered into as a result of poor piloting. It was a bar which covered the entire river channel, and thus could not be avoided. Now, their only hope lay in attempting to traverse the sandbar at its most advantageous part. And the traversal of such a sandbar could only be accomplished by grasshoppering the boat across.

Hank was on the forward part of the hurricane deck, relaying messages back and forth, Willie was in charge of the actual sparring, and Pete was on the capstan engine. At a signal from Willie, Pete moved the lever to start the operation.

The poles dug into the river bottom, then strained and bent slightly. The boat crept forward, croaking and groaning under the exertion. Finally the poles were fully extended, and the boat was as far forward as it could go.

"All right, hold it Pete," Willie called. "We've got to rewind the capstan and set the poles now. You men, bare a hand."

John helped the other crewmen as the poles were reset and the capstan rewound for a second sparring.

"Ready?" Pete called.

"Ready," Willie answered, and Pete moved the lever to start the second operation.

Again the poles strained backward, and again the boat started sliding forward. The poles bent, as before, but then, suddenly, one of the cables snapped, and it whipped back around with a loud *whoosh*.

"Look out!" Willie shouted, and everyone on the bow deck dropped down to avoid the whistling lash of steel.

The cable smashed through the flagpole, breaking it off as cleanly as if it were no more than a matchstick.

Though everyone had ducked, only Pete was in any real danger, and he had the good fortune to dive to the deck just in time to avoid it.

Though Pete managed to avoid the cable on its first swing around, it continued to whip and flay about, smashing everything in its path. Pete was in the unfortunate position of not being able to stand up, because the cable was whipping over his head. As he was unable to stand, that also meant he couldn't get to the throttle lever to shut down the engine, and as long as the engine went, the cable would continue to whirl about madly.

"We've got to get that engine shut off," Willie warned. "If that cable flies loose and hits the boiler, we are going to have one hell of an explosion!"

The cable continued to whirl, but as some of the steam pressure was used up, it wasn't whirling quite as fast as it had at the beginning. That was little consolation though, because it was still moving with enough force to make a shambles out of the bowdeck. It took down the flagpole on its very first revolution, then it smashed through the railing, and now Pete was still trapped beneath the slashing steel line.

John watched it spin for about two more revolutions, then, when he had it timed just right, he leaped up, ran to the bowdeck, ducked at just the right moment, and reached the engine throttle lever. He pushed it shut, and the cable, without the whirling momentum of the capstan, fell, whistling, into the river.

"Great job, lad!" Willie congratulated, and Pete, a bit shaken, but otherwise all right, stood up and shook his hand. Soon even the passengers perceived what had happened, and what John had done, and all of them came forward to congratulate John on his act of bravery. Only Crystal was a bit reserved in her praise, though she, like everyone else, did tender her congratulations.

The incident with the cable was but one of a series of things John did during the journey upriver. When the meat they had brought from St. Louis proved to be contaminated, John led a hunting party ashore and returned with a buffalo and two deer. He organized fishing parties and showed the youngsters aboard how to build Indian-style fish traps so that there was nearly always a fresh supply of fresh catfish. He did all this without boastful bravado, a common trait in too many other men along the river.

Willie, who was generally quite reserved, made no secret of the fact that he admired John greatly. It also seemed to Crystal that Willie spent a great deal of his time singing John's praises to her.

"Willie, for heaven's sake," Crystal finally said. "If I didn't know better, I'd swear you were a matchmaker, trying to marry me to Mr. Riley."

"Believe me, lass, you could do a lot worse in your life," Willie insisted.

"Yes, well, it just so happens that Mr. Riley is not interested in such an arrangement, and neither am I. Besides, I have already been admonished by my father against such a thing. So, you can see that any ideas you may have along that line are without hope of success. You may as well forget them now."

In fact, Crystal's father had cautioned her again, and yet again, not to fall in love with John Riley. Perhaps that was Marsh Lee's mistake. Perhaps he had, in some way, placed a desire for the forbidden fruit in Crystal's mind, for, despite his warnings, or maybe, because of them, Crystal felt that she may be doing just what her father had cautioned her against doing. She did know that he had awakened feelings in her that she had never felt before.

Perhaps it was love.

She really didn't know, and she wished she had someone she could discuss it with. She certainly couldn't talk to her father about it! He had been constantly warning her against just such a thing. But she had to speak to someone.

Crystal smiled then, for she knew just the person to go to. In three more days they would stop at Trenton Town. Trenton Town wasn't really a town. It was just a trading post owned by Eb Trenton, and named Trenton Town in hopes that someday it might really become a settlement.

Eb Trenton's trading post was on one of the most remote parts of the river. Perhaps it was the remoteness and the joy of seeing someone out here which caused Crystal to gravitate toward Eb. Or, perhaps it was because Eb was, outside her own father, the finest man she had ever known. In the past she had thought about it sometimes and she felt a little guilty, for it seemed that Willie, or Hank, or Pete, should hold that distinction. And yet, for all that she loved those three men, she was none-the-less acutely aware of their shortcomings, and their propensity for drink, which would forever place a burden upon those who cared for them.

Eb Trenton didn't seem to have any such shortcomings. He was always ready to lend a helping hand . . . in fact, there were times in the past when the *Missouri Mist* had run into such difficulty that they called upon Eb Trenton for supplies when they had no money to pay for them. Eb had never turned them down, nor, had he ever made them self-conscious about taking help.

Eb was about fifty, and he and Crystal had been friends for as long as she could remember. She called him "Uncle Eb" and she always looked forward to visiting him. Eb regaled her with exciting stories, and presented her with trinkets when she was a child. Now, he was someone she could talk to as an adult, and she discovered that she could tell him things that she wouldn't even tell her own father.

He was the one she would discuss John with.

Trenton's trading post was built right out on the riverbank, with a long, well-built pier extending into the water. It was in a wide part of the river, and, as much as possible, Eb kept the channel dug out so that the boats which called there would have an easy time docking and departing.

There were two boats there now, the *Annabelle* and the *Susan B*. The *Annabelle* was going downriver, but the *Susan B*. was coming up, and so Eb sought out the captain of the *Susan B*. to ask news about the *Missouri Mist*.

"She was just comin' into Omaha as I was leavin'," the captain said. "I suspect she'll be here sometime."

Eb smiled. "Good, good," he said.

"You'll have three boats tied up here at the same time," the captain of the *Susan B*. said. "Why, if you don't watch it, this place'll get as busy as St. Louis, and you'll have boats tied up for a mile along the bank."

"Ho," Eb said. "Wouldn't that be glorious, though."

"Cap'n, one of the passengers has a complaint," someone told the captain, and the captain, with the long suffering sigh of his trade, excused himself and went to attend to the matter. Eb was left alone for a moment, so he walked outside the large, wooden building which was the trading post and onto the porch. He stepped up to the railing and looked out at the river.

"It was right here," he said, speaking aloud, though no one was near him to listen. "Right down there in those rushes. I knew from the moment I did it, that I shouldn't have. And yet, it has probably worked out for the best."

Eb looked at the river for a while, and listened to the soft whisper of its power. Behind him, in the part of his trading post which served as a saloon, there was a burst of laughter as someone finished telling a joke. At the opposite end of the building there was a ladies tea-room to provide a nice place for the ladies to gather. More than one woman had expressed their appreciation to him for providing them with a place they could socialize without having to go into the saloon with the men.

Some of Eb's friends had laughed when he put

in the tea room. And, in fact, that part of his trading post accounted for very little of the profit in his business. But it provided the femininity the trading post needed, the softness Eb needed, and had been without, since his wife died.

As Eb thought of Mary, he went inside the trading post, through the saloon where he smiled and exchanged greetings with half a dozen customers, and finally, back to the two rooms which were his living quarters. He opened a trunk and looked inside. He had no likeness of Mary, only a few dresses, a quilt she had made, and a small cameo broach that had belonged to Mary's mother and had been her proudest possession.

Eb picked up the broach and held it in his hands. He felt close to her when he did that.

"Will you be going to the jamboree this spring?" Mary had asked him. It was mid-winter, and they were sitting by a fire in their little mountain cabin. Outside there was six feet of snow on the ground, but in a lean-to behind the cabin, there was a winter's supply of fur pelts. The jamboree was the annual meeting of fur trappers, traders, merchants, Indians, scouts, soldiers, and adventurers. It was not only a way of selling furs, it was also a great social occasion.

"Of course," Eb answered. "We'll both be going."

"No," Mary answered. She smiled, wanly. "I don't think I'll be up to it."

"Nonsense," Eb said. "Why, half the fun of the jamborees is to see all the new babies. You wouldn't want to cheat the others out of that fun now, would you?"

"No," Mary said. "I suppose not. But Eb, I . . . don't think this is going to be an easy birth."

"Why do you say such a thing?"

"I don't know. It's just a feeling I have. Women know about such things."

Eb laughed. "Don't go givin' me any of that 'women know' kind of talk, like as if you're havin' this baby all by yourself. I had a hand in it, you know. 'N come birthin' time, why I'll be right here to see that ever'thin' goes all right."

"I hope it's a boy for you, Eb. I hope it's a nice, big, healthy boy to help you with the trapping."

"Trapping nothing. Why, this country is fillin' up so that soon the fur creatures are going to be plumb to hell 'n gone. This'll be my last year of trappin', I reckon."

"What will you do?"

Eb smiled.

"I've been waitin' to surprise you," he said. "But I reckon this is as good a time as any to tell you. We've got quite a bit of money saved up now. The trappin' has been good for the last few years. How'd you like to go back to Virginia and buy a farm?"

"Oh . . . oh, Eb, do you mean it?"

"Yes, I mean it," Eb said. "We've got enough to

buy just about any farm we want. Yes, and stock it too."

"Oh, I'd love that." She reached up and touched the broach she was wearing. "I'd love to go back to where my parents are buried."

"We'll go this summer," Eb promised. "Right after the jamboree."

"And we'll raise our son in Virginia," she said. Her face clouded. "Oh, but Eb, are you sure you aren't just doing this for me?"

"It's what you want, isn't it?"

"Yes."

"Then don't question my motives."

For the rest of the winter, Eb and Mary sustained themselves with their dreams and plans of returning to Virginia to build their farm. Eb would tell Mary about the crops he would grow and the way his fields would be planted, and Mary would tell Eb about the plans she had for the house.

"Curtains," Mary said. "Oh, Eb, I want curtains in every room of the house. And real wallpaper . . . blue in our bedroom, and bright yellow in our son's bedroom. Yellow is a happy color, and I want our child to be happy."

"How can he help but be happy with you as his mother?" Eb asked.

"A garden," Mary said. "I want a garden. Not just potatoes and carrots, but flowers . . . roses, sweetpeas. . . ."

"You can have the biggest flower garden in the state if you want to," Eb said.

Eb thought of that flower garden later, when the spring wild flowers were in full bloom. He wished Mary could have come with him, for surely no flowers in the world could be more beautiful than these. Mary was back in the cabin, just days away from her delivery, and he had gone out on the last trap run of the season. Actually, it was so late in the spring that the season was over. There had been only a couple of animals in the traps, and they had poor pelts. Eb took in his traps. They were good traps, and he expected to clean them up and sell them at the jamboree.

With the money he got for his equipment, and the winter's catch of furs, plus what he already had saved he would have enough for a farm. Perhaps the farm wouldn't quite come up to the grandiose plans he and Mary had been making, but he would be able to buy a good farm.

Ed gathered an enormous bouquet of wild flowers and took them back to the cabin.

"Mary, you talk about your flowers," he said as he pushed open the door to the cabin. "You've never seen flowers like . . . Mary!"

The last word was an agonized scream, for Mary was lying on the floor in a pool of blood. She had been alone when the baby came, and there had been problems.

Mary was dead.

*   *   *

"Eb! Eb, you in there?"

The call brought Eb back, and he noticed with some surprise that there was a lump in his throat and tears in his eyes. After all these years, the pain of that moment had never subsided.

"Yeah," Eb said. "Yeah, I'm in here."

"There's smoke downriver," the voice said. "It must be the *Missouri Mist.*

"All right, fine," Eb answered. "I'll be out in a moment."

Eb put the broach back in the trunk and closed the lid. They were private memories, and he didn't want to share them with anybody.

Chapter Six

When they were within three miles of the trading post, excitement on board the boat began to grow, not only among the passengers, but among the crew as well. The boat whistle was blown several times, long, deep, haunting sounds to disturb the tranquility of the surrounding breaks. After a moment or two, it would be answered by the whistle of two other steamboats already tied up in Trenton Town. Two whistles would answer, also in the same, deep-toned, haunting notes.

"Oh, the *Annabelle* and the *Susan B* are here!" Crystal said excitedly.

John looked at her in surprise. "You mean you can tell just by the sound of the whistles?" He asked, impressed by her feat.

Crystal was at the bow of the boat, plotting their

course through the channel, and John, whose duties had been expanded considerably as he had proven himself capable, was sounding.

"Sure," Crystal said easily. "Every boat whistle has its own tone. Why it's as distinctive as a person's voice, and as easy to distinguish."

"How many boats do you know?" John asked. "I mean that you can identify just by the sound of the whistle?"

"I know about thirty, I suppose," Crystal said. "Oh, oh, it looks like some sand has shifted, John. You'd better sound over there," she added, pointing to a spot on the water.

John looked in the direction Crystal had pointed.

"Over where?" he asked, confused by her request. All the water looked alike to him. "I don't see anything."

"Right there," Crystal said. "Can't you see the difference in the water? There, it is flat and glassy, but beyond, it has more color."

John looked closely, and, after having it pointed out to him, he was able to discern a very small difference in the texture of the water surface. He cast his weight into the flat, glassy area, it splashed and fell quickly to the bottom.

"You're right," John said. "I make it no more than two feet there."

"Willie!" Crystal called.

"Aye, Willie standin' by."

"Come to starboard!"

"Come to starboard!" Willie repeated, and then, one more time between Willie and the wheelhouse, the order was repeated. Marsh, who was at the wheel, responded, and the boat moved a little to the right.

John pulled the weight back, coiled the line, then cast it far in front of them. It sank almost straight down, showing the effect of Eb Trenton's work in keeping the channel open.

"Eb has been doing a lot of work," John said. He chuckled. "He must want people to stop by and see him."

"He has a lot of people here right now," Crystal said. "Oh, maybe we can have a dance. Wouldn't that be nice?" She asked, her voice colored by excitement.

"Now that all depends," John replied.

"Depends on what?"

John smiled. "On whether or not you save any dances for me. If you save some for me, it will be nice. If you give them all away to someone else, it won't be much fun. So, what will it be? Are you going to save a few dances for me?"

"Maybe I will," Crystal said, smiling at John coquettishly. The smile suddenly left her face as she spotted something in the water. "Come to port!" she shouted, and Willie relayed the call up to the wheelhouse. John looked in the direction Crystal was looking and saw, barely, a submerged log.

"If you could read trail sign the way you can read this river, you'd make one fine scout," he said.

"Thank you," Crystal replied, beaming under his compliment.

The *Missouri Mist* came around the last bend, then glided majestically up to the dock of Trenton Town. The passengers of the *Annabelle* and the *Susan B.* were all standing out on the docks, waving and shouting, and the passengers of the *Missouri Mist* crowded to the rail and returned the waves and shouts. Children laughed and ran excitedly up and down the dock, while those on the deck of the *Missouri Mist* ran just excitedly about the deck. One little boy almost tumbled overboard, and John had to grab him to keep him from falling.

"The children are certainly excited about coming here," John said.

"Yes," Crystal replied. "This has always been my favorite stop along the river."

"Why?"

"Well, for one thing, I have always loved Uncle Eb," Crystal said.

John's eyes reflected his surprise at her statement, and Crystal smiled.

"He isn't my real uncle. I just call him that."

"Eb is a fine man," John said. "Even if he is a bit sad."

This time it was Crystal's turn to be surprised.

"You've noticed that too?"

"Yes," John said.

"I didn't think anyone but me had ever felt that way," Crystal said. "I've always sensed that, but I've never been able to explain why. And no one else seems to have noticed."

"I can't explain it either," John said. "It's nothing he says or does. There's just a feel about him, like some immense sadness he suffered long ago, and from which he has never recovered."

"His wife died a long time ago," Crystal said. "She is buried out behind his place."

"I know," John said. "But a lot of men lose their wives, and a lot of wives lose their husbands. They eventually get over it."

"Maybe Uncle Eb really loved Mary," Crystal suggested. "I mean really loved her, so much that he has never recovered."

"Perhaps," John said.

"She was a lucky woman," Crystal said, and when John questioned her with his look, she added; "I mean to have someone who loved her the way Uncle Eb obviously did."

"I would say then, that Eb is a lucky man to have found someone he could love that much," John said.

They were silent for a long moment after that, each lost in their own thought, each frightened to share that thought with the other.

Could you love me that much? Crystal was thinking, and yet, she dared not think such a thought, even

90

in the secret recesses of her own heart. She sought to change the subject somewhat, to get it on more comfortable ground.

"It isn't just because of Uncle Eb that I like to come here," Crystal went on, speaking in a lighter tone of voice. "It's this place. I love this place, too. It's so wildly beautiful."

"Yes," John said. "It is especially popular with all the passengers. But it's beauty has nothing to do with it."

"Oh? Then what does account for its popularity?"

"I guess, coming as it does right in the middle of nowhere after miles of desolation, it reminds everyone that there are still other people in the world, their fellow-kind. In that, I suppose, it is not too different from a desert oasis."

Crystal smiled.

"Why, John Riley, if I didn't know better, I'd say you were a bit of the philosopher."

"Perhaps I am," John agreed. "Such thoughts come to a man when he spends a lot of time alone."

"And you spend a lot of time alone?"

"I spend most of my time alone," John said.

"Do you like that?"

"Yes," John said. "I like it very much, and I wouldn't trade it for any other kind of life."

"Oh." Crystal wasn't sure she knew what she wanted to hear, but she didn't think that was it. If he preferred to spend all his time alone, then that meant he wouldn't be that interested in spending time with her. Oh, why was she thinking such thoughts, anyway? What did she care how he wanted to spend his time? It certainly didn't mean anything to her, did it?

"What are you thinking?" John asked innocently.

Crystal looked at John. Wouldn't he be surprised to know what she was really thinking.

"Nothing much," she lied. "I was just thinking that if you feel that way, then it probably won't bother you so much when we push on, will it? I mean if you like being alone, you won't have the same sense of attachment to this oasis as the rest of us."

"I won't be going on with the rest of you," John said easily.

"What?" Crystal asked in a soft, quiet voice.

"I'm leaving the boat here."

"But why? I don't understand. Is there something wrong?"

"No, nothing is wrong," John said. He looked at Crystal, and, for just a moment, the barriers were down in both sets of eyes. Each could look through to the soul of the other, if they wished. "Crystal, I thought you knew that Trenton Town was my real destination. I had a ticket to Fort Benton, but I intended to get off at Trenton Town, all along."

"You mean you live here?"

"No," John said. "But I must return to the Mandan Camp to give them a report on my trip to

92

Washington. This is the best spot on the river for me to leave the boat in order to get to their camp."

"I . . . I see," Crystal said. She was unable to keep the disappointment from her voice, off her face and out of her eyes. She had neglected to raise the guard she had, inadverdently lowered.

"I'm sorry," John said when she saw her reaction to the news. "I thought you knew about my mission for the Indians."

"Yes, of course I knew," Crystal said. "I guess I just wasn't thinking, that's all."

"You aren't upset, are you?" John asked.

"Upset? Of course not. Why should I be upset? After all, this is your destination, isn't it? This is where you are supposed to get off."

"Yes," John said. "But you do seem a little bothered by it."

Too late, Crystal raised her guard. Her defenses had already been breached. John knew what she was thinking, but she had to go on, to pretend that she was still in control. "Sir, you presume too much," she replied haughtily. "It is a matter of supreme indifference to me whether you leave this boat now, or whether you continue on board until the Missouri runs dry. Why should I be interested in your comings and goings?"

"Yes, why indeed?" John asked. He put his arm out and touched her shoulder, gently. "Crystal, maybe we could. . . ."

"Stand by to secure lines!" Willie shouted.

*　　*　　*

Crystal, hearing the call for docking, summoned all her strength and pulled away from him.

"I have work to do," she said importantly. She left the bow of the boat and hurried away to attend to her own duties.

John stood there and watched her leave. She made an effort to feign indifference, but she wasn't able to turn away before John saw something in her eyes which thrilled him.

Crystal was upset that John was leaving the boat! That could only mean that she cared about him. Could he dare hope she cared for him as much as he did for her?

Chapter Seven

Two banjos, two guitars, and a fiddle swung into a rousing rendition of "Shucking the Corn." The women managed to dig out their brightest dresses from trunks they had packed away on the boat, and the men came up with their cleanest denims. Such attention to personal appearance attested to the importance they all placed on this opportunity to find a few hours of pleasant escape from the long, difficult weeks of their journey.

The young, unmarried men were emboldened by the excitement of the occasion, and they paid court to the young, unmarried women much more openly than they would have in the polite society back East. The young ladies laughed and feined surprise over the boldness of the men, but they, just as emboldened, eagerly accepted the invitations.

In a very short time, there were several squares formed, including one square which John and Crystal joined.

Eb Trenton was the dance caller, and he shouted and clapped his hands and did intricate dance steps as if he had his own square. The dancers were caught up, not only by the excitement, but in the music and Eb Trenton's expert calls. Thus inspired they bowed and whirled and moved and glided as adroitly as if they were on the finest dance floor in the biggest city of the East. None of them gave a second thought to the fact that they weren't really at such an establishment; rather they were dancing on a rough-hewn plank floor on the banks of the Missouri River, two thousand miles deep into the great Northwest wilderness.

Even those who weren't dancing, those who were too young, and those who were too old, were greatly enjoying the proceedings. They sat around the dance floor and clapped in rhythm with the band, and watched the couples who were dancing, and, vicariously, became one of them.

To one side of the room sat a large punch bowl, providing the dancers with refreshment. Some of the guests, deciding that the punch needed some help, provided that help by spiking the drink rather liberally with strong whiskey. As a result, more than a few young men got drunk. Later on in the evening a couple of young men from the other boats grew jealous over the attentions of one of the young ladies, and a fight developed. The fight was over quickly enough, with no damage done, but it did provide a chance for the dance to break up, and the musicians, pleading for the opportunity to take a rest, went over to enjoy some of the punch themselves.

Crystal had danced a few dances with John during the evening. She would have willingly danced all of them with John, but, because her father had warned her several more times not to fall in love with John, and had mentioned again his mysterious plans for her, she thought it would be better if she didn't give in to her wishes. She accepted dance invitations from a dozen other young men from the three boats, and enjoyed herself thoroughly, though, a small part of her heart yearned to dance only with John Riley.

When the dance finally did break up, she looked around the room for John, but she didn't see him. It had been several minutes since last she saw him. In fact, John was nowhere around. At least, he was nowhere in plain sight, and Crystal couldn't very well ask about him. She had to accept his absence.

Crystal wandered over to the punch bowl and poured herself a cup, but when she tasted it and realized how strongly laced with whiskey it was, she put it down and walked outside.

It was night, and as she walked away from the lights of the trading post, she could see how bright the moon was tonight. The river winked and danced under the moon, and the trees, sighing softly in the night breeze, waved against the moonbeams, scattering silver in the night. In the near distance crickets chirped, while a bit farther away, frogs added their own serenade. Lightning bugs flashed in winks of brilliant gold.

Crystal found a tree stump which was flat, and just the right height for a good seat, and she sat down to let the cool breeze move through her hair. The exertion of the dance and the closeness of the crowded dance floor had caused her to perspire slightly. Now, in the breeze, she felt a delightful coolness. The same breeze also managed to keep away any mosquitoes which might have been out, so that the overall effect was pleasant.

As Crystal sat there for a moment or two, she became aware that she wasn't alone, and when she looked around, she saw Eb standing a short distance away. He appeared to be looking down at something, and then Crystal realized that he was looking at the grave of Mary, his wife. Crystal knew about Mary's grave, of course. She had seen it several times before. She knew that Eb visited it frequently, and took comfort from it. She wished now that she hadn't come back here. She didn't want to intrude on him.

Eb stood quietly for a few moments longer, then he looked up and saw Crystal, though Crystal got the impression that he knew she was here all along.

"Well, well, well," Eb said. "If it isn't the prettiest girl on the Missouri. Or, in the whole country, for that matter."

"Uncle Eb," Crystal said. She stood, and as Eb walked over to her, they embraced.

"I was wondering when we would get our chance to be alone for a while," Eb said. "I was afraid you would get back on your boat and go away without even talking to me."

Crystal laughed. "Uncle Eb, you know there's no chance of that," she said, "You are the only friend I have on the entire river."

"Ah, girl, you are saying that just to please old Eb. But as sweet and as pretty as you are, I know that you have friends at every stop."

"No," Crystal said. "None like you. No one I can talk to like I can talk to you. Oh, Uncle Eb . . . I can't even talk to Dad the way I can talk to you. And I need to now. I need to so badly."

Suddenly, and unexpectantly, tears sprang to Crystal's eyes, and Eb, seeing that, took her in his arms again.

"What is it, darlin'?" Eb asked. "Tell me what's botherin' you?"

For some, strange, reason, Eb Trenton had always held sway over Crystal with his strong, but gentle ways and words. There was a tenderness in him, a concern which Crystal knew was genuine.

"Why is it, Uncle Eb?" Crystal asked. "Why is it I could always come to you with my troubles? Even when I was a very little girl, you could kiss away my hurts and talk away my fears. I love Dad, and he loves me, and no girl could ever want for a more wonderful father, but. . . ."

"Shush now, girl," Eb said, putting his finger to her lips. "There are no buts about your pa. He's the finest man I've ever known."

"He is," Crystal said. "Oh, Uncle Eb, he is, and I don't mean to take anything away from that. Maybe it's because he is my father, that I can't always talk to him. Like now, when I have something tearing at my heart and I can't get it out."

"Get it out now, girl," Eb said softly.

"Uncle Eb, I'm in love," Crystal said.

Eb smiled. "You are in love, are you? Why, girl, that should be a joy to the heart, not a pain. Why are you suffering so?"

"Because of *who* I am in love with," Crystal said.

"Oh? And who might the lucky fellow be?"

"John Riley," Crystal said. "Oh, Uncle Eb, I've never met anyone like him before. He is strong, but gentle, courageous but quiet, and so wonderful that you can't believe it, but. . . ."

"But he hasn't noticed you yet? Then you should add 'blind,' to your description of him."

"Oh, no, that isn't it," Crystal said. "That isn't it at all. He has noticed me, and I think he feels about me the same way I feel about him. In fact he . . . he . . ." Crystal paused and her face flushed red.

"He what?" Eb asked.

"He . . . kissed me," Crystal said. "Only it wasn't just a kiss, it was. . . ."

"Crystal, darlin', did John Riley compromise you in any way?" Eb interrupted with concern in his voice.

"Compromise? I don't know exactly what you mean," Crystal said.

"Did he do anything other than kiss you?" Eb asked. "Did he go further?"

"No," Crystal said. "But . . . I wanted him to," she added, very quietly. "Oh, Uncle Eb, does that make me very wicked?"

Eb pulled Crystal to him and put his arms around her. "No, darlin'," he said. "That doesn't make you wicked at all." He chuckled. "That just means you have grown into a woman. Now, has John Riley told you he loves you?"

"No," Crystal said. "But I know he does. I can tell when I am around him. He tells me with his eyes, and with his actions, and with his voice. But he hasn't told me with words."

"Have you told him?"

"No, I haven't told him," Crystal said.

Eb chuckled again. "Well, is that what's causin' all the pain? You love him and he loves you, but neither of you have told the other? I can fix that for you real simple. I'll just go to John and. . . ."

"No!" Crystal said sharply, putting her hand quickly on Eb's. "No, Uncle Eb, you can't do that! You mustn't! He must never know that I love him."

"What? Why not?" Eb asked.

"Because of Dad," Crystal said. "He has told me, time and time again, that I should not let myself fall in love with John."

"Your Dad has said that?" Eb asked.

"Yes. So, you can see, Uncle Eb. I can't love John, for it would displease Dad so, and I could never displease him."

"I don't understand, girl," Eb said. "Why would marryin' John displease your pa, so? I know John Riley well, and I know him to be as fine a young man as anyone would ever hope to meet."

"Dad has plans for me," Crystal said.

"Plans? What sort of *plans*?"

"I don't know," Crystal said. "I just know that he has plans . . . plans which would be destroyed by my loving John."

"Perhaps if your pa knew you were already in love with John, he would change his plans," Eb suggested. "Or, at least accommodate them to that fact."

"No," Crystal said sadly. "No, I don't think so. I don't know what he has in mind, Uncle Eb. But I am sure that it is unalterably opposed to my loving John Riley. That's why John must never know. And that's why I have such a hurt in my heart.

Oh, Uncle Eb, what will I do? How can I ease this pain?"

Eb reached down with his finger and put it under Crystal's chin. He raised her head so he could look directly into her eyes.

"You think you are broken-hearted now, darlin'?" he said. "Someday, perhaps, I'll tell you my own story, and then you'll learn what it's like to have a real broken heart. I've lived with a pain in my heart which would drive most men crazy, and yet I've gone on, and managed to fetch some sweetness out of life besides. The world doesn't come to an end over a little heartbreak, girl, though I know your sufferin' is none the easier for my tellin' you all this. Just know, darlin' that you can bear up under most anything, if you've a will to. That's the bitter lesson I've learned."

"Uncle Eb, you've had heartbreak? I knew it," she said.

"You knew it?"

"Yes. You've never said anything, and yet, I've always known there was a sadness, buried somewhere deep inside."

"Bless you, darlin'," Eb said. "You're a girl with a sensitive soul to know that."

"But, how could anyone break your heart?"

"It couldn't be helped," Eb said. "It was somethin' that was none of her doin'."

"Her? It was a woman?"

"Yes."

Crystal walked toward Mary's grave, and Eb followed her. Crystal reached it and looked down at the well tended mound.

"Was it Mary?" Crystal asked.

"No," Eb said. "It wasn't Mary. Though it sore broke my heart when she died."

"You mean . . . it was another woman?"

"Yes."

"Uncle Eb, there was another woman in your life besides Mary?"

"There still is," Eb said.

"But she's never taken Mary's place in your heart," Crystal said. "I mean, you seem to love Mary so, even though she's gone."

"No, darlin', she's never taken Mary's place in my heart. But she occupies a mighty big place of her own."

Crystal saw a tiny weed growing from the grave mound, and she kneeled down and pulled it out, then smoothed away the earth with her fingers.

"Tell me about Mary," Crystal said. "Was she beautiful?"

"Oh, she was very beautiful," Eb said. "She had hair as red as the blaze of sunset."

Crystal looked around in surprise. "She had red hair?"

"Yes. As red as yours."

"Maybe that's why you like me," Crystal said. "Because I have red hair."

Eb chuckled. "I must say that you do remind

104

me of her. You are every bit as pretty as she was. Maybe you are a little stronger."

"Is that why she died? Because she wasn't very strong?"

Eb kneeled on the opposite side of the grave, and he, like Crystal, began pruning very small, nearly invisible weed sprouts, as he talked.

"She would have been strong enough if we had stayed in Virginia," he said. "That's where we were from."

"Is Virginia beautiful?"

"Yes," Eb said. "A different more gentle and tame kind of beauty, but beautiful in its own way. Virginia is very old country, you know. There are towns and farms and families there who have been there for two hundred years. It's all very civilized, and you can take a train or a boat or a stage to anywhere you want to go. They have magnificent roads, and telegraph lines to send messages, schools, churches, most anything you can imagine. And not just in the cities, but all over the state."

"Why did you leave Virginia?"

"The war," Eb said. "The Civil War. He sighed. "Mary's family supported the South. Her father was an officer in the Confederacy and her brothers were both soldiers. I believed in the Union. I couldn't fight against the Union, and I wouldn't fight against Mary's family. There was nothing for Mary and me to do but leave Virginia, and once we left, we had to get far enough away that we wouldn't get involved at all."

"Did Mary's father ever forgive you?"

"He was killed at Gettysburg," Eb said. "One of her brothers was killed at Fredricksburg, and the other at Franklin. Her mother died soon after. There was no one left to forgive us."

"Oh, poor Mary," Crystal said, as she felt an overwhelming wave of sympathy for the poor woman who lay buried in the grave at her knees.

"That may have contributed as much as anything to her . . . her inability to survive out here," Eb said.

"Did you have the trading post then?"

"No. We lived in a cabin not far from here. I trapped furs, and I made a lot of money. We were going to go back to Virginia and buy a farm near where we used to live. She was really looking forward to returning. She wanted to be with her folks, even though they were dead." Eb stood up then, and sighed. "I reckon she's closer to them now than she would have been had we gone back."

Crystal also stood up, and moved to Eb and put her arms around him. They embraced for a long, quiet moment, and, never in her life had she wanted to comfort someone more than she wanted to comfort him at that moment.

"You stayed out here because she's buried here, didn't you?" Crystal finally asked.

"That's partly the reason," Eb said.

106

"Oh? What's the rest of the reason?"

Eb looked at Crystal, and then he smiled and held his finger up and wagged it back and forth.

"No, girl, you don't get all my secrets," he said. "Certainly not at one tellin', anyway."

"All right," Crystal teased. "Keep your secrets, see if I care."

"You'll learn them all some day," Eb promised. "In the meantime, why don't you go on back to the party? I have a feelin' that things are goin' to work out all right for you in the end."

"Oh, Uncle Eb, do you really think so?"

"Yes, darlin'," Eb said. "I really think so."

Chapter Eight

It wasn't a pleasant laughter. Instead, like the shattering of fine glass, the laughter had a harsh, brittle edge. The laughter had come from David Lee, and his mirth was at the expense of one of the serving girls in the hotel gaming room. The girl had stepped back quickly to avoid David's attempt to grab one of her breasts, and as she did so her skirt, the hem of which was securely and purposefully held down by David's foot, was ripped off. Now she stood before the crowd in her undergarments, trying without success to cover her breasts and thighs.

"You find that funny, do you?" one of the other men at David's table asked. It was obvious from the tone of the man's voice that he disapproved of David's action.

David's laughter died on his lips and he looked at the man who had spoken. He brought his finger up to his cheek and rubbed the diamond-shaped mark which was there, though in fact he wasn't even aware of doing it. Rubbing that mark was a nervous habit brought on in moments of stress.

"Yes," he said. "I find it funny. Do you not think it humorous?"

"I find it childish," the man said. "And I'm certain the lady finds it offensive."

"Lady?" David asked with a raised eyebrow. He laughed, again the harsh, brittle laugh, and he looked around the room with his eyes falling pointedly upon the girl he had just de-frocked. "What *lady* are you talking about? I see no ladies in this place. Does anyone see a lady?" he asked, facing the others.

Suddenly David's face was wet with the unexpected splash of a drink. He looked back around in surprise to see the woman in question. She was standing there holding an empty glass in her hand. She had just thrown a drink in David's face and her eyes were flashing her anger and challenge to him.

"I'm a lady, you bastard," she spat at him.

The crowd in the room laughed and David, who had thought to be playing the joke, suddenly found himself the butt of one. It was definitely not a situation to his liking, and his skin burned as he realized all eyes were now on him.

"What do you think of that?" the girl asked, enjoying this opportunity to turn the tables on her adversary.

"I'll show you what I think," David said menacingly, and he drew his fist back, preparatory to hitting her, but the cold, metallic click of a cocking revolver stopped him. David looked back across the table at the man who had chastised him earlier.

"Uh, uh, uh," the man said in a quiet, sing-song voice. He wagged his finger back and forth as one does when one is chastising a naughty child.

"What are you doing?" David asked.

"I feel compelled to warn you, friend, that if you touch that lady, I shall be obliged to lodge a lead ball in your brain."

David smiled, but the smile got no further than his mouth. "You didn't really think I was going to hit her, did you?" he asked. He shrugged his shoulders. "I was teasing. I was just having a little fun with her, that's all."

"I'm sure you were," the man said. "But you see, the question is, was she having fun with you? Now, I know I wasn't, and I have my doubts about her. Tell me, Miss, were you enjoying the raving antics, of this raving buffoon?"

"Indeed I was not!" the woman replied with all the self-righteous indignation she could muster.

"Ah, I see," the man with the gun said. He

looked back at David with eyes that were cold and gray. They were eyes which David knew would never blink if he shot him. "It seems she was not having fun. That being the case, if you don't mind, sir, you would do us all a great favor by leaving this establishment."

"Leave?" David blustered. "You want me to leave this place? Not on your life, sir."

The man with the pistol smiled a cold smile.

"You seem to misunderstand the situation here. It isn't my life that is in question, it's yours." He raised the pistol. "Now, sir, you may walk out, or you may be carried out. It really does not matter to me."

"But . . . but I have the winning hand, here," David protested. "The game isn't over."

"I just raised your bet," the man said. "And you folded."

"But I didn't fold," David started, though he got no farther in his protest, because the man interrupted him.

"Yes," the man said. "You folded. Ask anyone you wish and they will tell you that. They all saw you fold."

David looked around the table hoping to elicit support from one of the other players. He knew without having to look, though, that no support would be forthcoming. After all, he had been winning steadily for the last hour or so, and he couldn't possibly have made any friends among these men.

They probably enjoyed seeing him run out of the game. All right, to hell with them. He had already won over one hundred dollars tonight anyway. He certainly didn't need help from the likes of these people. They were all boorish oafs anyway.

David sighed and started to pick up the pile of chips from in front of him.

"Leave them," the man with the gun said.

"What?" David gasped.

"I said leave them," the man said again. "Before you folded, you bet everything in front of you."

"But I. . . ."

"You've been cheating all night, friend, only you're good. You're so good that I haven't been able to catch you at it. Now I figure we'll just divide up what you have there 'n it'll ease our losses somewhat."

David stood up, looked at the man's smug smile, and fixed it in his mind. He would want to remember it later.

"All right," David said calmly. "I never argue with the winning hand."

"I had a feeling you would see things my way," the man said.

"Gentlemen," David said. He looked over and saw the woman. She was still standing in her undergarments, though now she was so interested in the deadly byplay between these two men that she was no longer aware of her immodest condition.

112

David smiled at her. "And Lady," he added sarcastically. "I bid you farewell."

The fresh air outside nearly gave him a headache, so accommodated had he become to the smoke, whiskey, and heavy perfume-scented air of the gambling salon. He was surprised to see that it was dark, though he may have been just as surprised if it had been light. The fact was he spent so much time at gambling tables that he frequently lost track of time altogether, and rarely did he have the faintest notion of the hour, be it day or night.

As David thought back on it now, it sometimes seemed as if he had been born in a smoke-filled, whiskey smelling room. And yet, nothing could be further from the truth. He was raised, in the words of his father, a 'God-fearing' young man, no stranger to clean living and fresh air.

How different his life was now from the life of his youth. And how much more he enjoyed it now. Let the poets and the preachers sing the praises of virtuous living and the great outdoors. Who needed mountains and trees and rivers? Give him the seamier side of city living. Gambling, women, and whiskey were the things which kept life from becoming a monumental bore.

A team of horses pulled a closed-body wagon by. The sign on the side of the wagon advertised the *Philadelphia Enquirer*.

"All the latest news from the capitals of the

world, brought to the readers of Philadelphia," it boasted proudly.

David smiled. So, he was still in Philadelphia, was he? He remembered coming to Philadelphia from St. Louis. He had happened onto a stroke of good luck on the way, because he managed to clean out three businessmen in the twenty-four-hour long cardgame. He won well over one thousand dollars during the trip.

For the first three days in Philadelphia, David did nothing but spend the money he won in a totally hedonistic search for pleasure. He bought women, sometimes two at a time, and discarded them immediately afterward. He bought champagne and drank it straight from the bottle until it started to go flat, then he bought more. He ate quail, and veal and lobster in the finest restaurants in town.

Then, when his money began to dwindle, he started looking for more card games. During the past week there had been a succession of card games, one after another. He had no hotel room. He ate at the gaming tables, and the only sleep he got was the naps he managed to grab on sofas or in chairs. Finally he lost track, not only of time, but even of where he was

It was not unusual for David to be unsure of where he was. In the past year he had been in Chicago, Cleveland, Cincinnati, and, of course, most recently, St. Louis. It was his habit to make the rounds of the most promising gaming establishments of the cities until he had worn out his welcome. Then, and only then, would he depart for more fertile territory elsewhere. Sometimes he was able to stay longer than other times, but always he would eventually overstay his welcome, and when he did so he would be forced to quit the city. That was because he would not be allowed in anymore card games anywhere, and without the card games, he had no means of support.

Whenever it was necessary for David to leave a city, he would go to the railroad station and purchase a ticket on the very next train, regardless of where it was going.

David was almost ready to leave Philadelphia now, but, not quite yet. He was still stinging from the insult paid him by the man with the gun, and the woman the man had defended. David intended to make the man pay for his insult.

David walked across the street from the hotel where there was a quiet park. He chose a bench under a flowering mimosa tree, which would afford him a view of the front door of the hotel. There, he sat and he waited. It was a wait of more than two hours, but David was a patient man. At last the wait was rewarded, for finally, the man left the hotel.

There was a woman on his arms, and for a moment, David was angered by the fact that there was someone with him. Then, he noticed who the woman was. David smiled at his good luck. Here was a golden opportunity to take care of both the people who had insulted him, for the woman on his arm was none other than the one the man had defended.

David stayed in the shadows and watched and listened. He could hear everything as clearly as if he were standing alongside them.

"Oh, you silly thing," the woman said, with a high-pitched giggle. "You didn't actually hope to find a carriage at this hour of the night, did you? Or, should I say this hour of the morning?" she added again, with a high-pitched, laugh.

"Madam, you forget who I am," the man said.

The woman laughed yet again. "Oh, you are the silly, aren't you? I haven't forgotten who you are. I've never known. You haven't told me your name."

"You are quite right, madam, I didn't tell you my name," the man said. He was obviously intoxicated now, for he spoke the words slowly and distinctly, as if making a concerted effort not to slur them. It was good that he was drunk. That would make David's job much easier.

"Aren't you. . . ." the woman started, but because she, too, was drunk, she had to start again. "Aren't you going to tell me who you are?"

"No," the man said. "It's better this way. I don't know you, and you don't know me. We'll just be two strangers who met in the night."

"We'll do a sight more'n meet, my love, if you

get my meanin'," the woman said. She laughed again, but this time the giggle was replaced by a more ribald sound. The man put his arm around the woman's shoulder and pulled her to him. He slid his hand under her blouse and cupped her breast.

"Oh, aren't you the anxious one, though?" the woman asked, her voice husky.

"Why don't we go back into the hotel?" the man asked. "I could get us a room there and we wouldn't have to look for a carriage."

"Oh, no, love, I'm afraid we can't go in there," the woman said. "You wouldn't want me to be arrested for solicitin', now, would you?"

"No, of course not."

"That's what'd happen if we was to go back. The hotel detective knows me, you see."

"Then, how about over here, in the park?" the man asked. "It'd be awful romantic."

The woman laughed. "I'm game if you are," she said.

David got up from the bench and moved behind a large stand of honeysuckle. The fragrance of the honeysuckle in the soft, summer night was almost stifling, and he felt his heart pounding as he waited. He smiled cruelly. In a few moments the man and the woman would be half undressed and very occupied and that would make his job so much easier.

They crossed the street and walked by David

without noticing him. They went into the middle of the park, then ducked into the shadows of a large tree. David walked behind them, moving so quietly that they had no idea he was there. Even though he was less than thirty feet away, the shadows were so deep he lost sight of them. He waited for a few minutes, then he heard them. The moaning sounds of the woman gave evidence of what they were doing. David smiled again. Now he could move with absolute impunity. There was no way the man would notice.

Boldly, David stepped into the shadows under the tree and walked right up on them. They were writhing in lustful pursuits on the ground, totally oblivious of their surroundings. At first David thought he would get rid of both of them. Then a delicious idea came to his mind. He would take care of the man, only, and leave the woman. That way she would know how close she had come and the fear of it would stay with her, and haunt her, for the rest of her miserable life. Too, she'd find herself coupling with a corpse—another once-in-a-lifetime experience.

David slipped a dagger out of his belt, and without a second thought, he plunged it into the man's rib cage. He stabbed the man three times, pulling the knife out and pushing it in again and again. As the knife went in, the man made a grunting sound, and he jerked convulsively with each stab. The woman beneath him had her eyes closed, and she heard only the sound of his grunting, and felt the jerkiness of his movement. She totally mistook what was happening.

"Oh, honey," she said. "Oh, yes, honey, oh yes!"

David turned and walked away as silently as he had arrived. Within a few seconds he was swallowed up by the shadows of the park, and the woman never even knew he'd been there. He was almost a hundred yards away before he heard her first scream.

The woman's screams alerted a policeman somewhere, and the policeman blew his whistle. Another whistle blasted shrilly, very close to David, and then he heard the sound of running and a policeman hurried by.

"What is it?" David asked. "What's wrong?"

"Didn't you hear it, sir?" the policeman called back. "A lady is in distress."

"Then hurry, officer. You must do your duty," David called encouragingly to him. David stood there for a moment until the running police officer had disappeared into the darkness.

David's walk had brought him to the banks of the Schuylkill river, and he stood there for a moment, watching the water rush by. When he was absolutely certain he wasn't being observed, he tossed his dagger into the water. His little adventure had gone perfectly thus far. There was no sense in blundering by keeping the dagger and possibly having it discovered on him.

David walked away from the river and, a few moments later, he had the good fortune to encounter an empty cab. The driver was asleep and the horse was returning to the barn on its own, its hooves clopping along on the cobblestones.

"Cab!" David called.

The driver sat up with a start and pulled his horse to a halt.

"I was just goin' in for the night," the driver said. "I'm off duty."

"Please," David said. "I have to catch a train, and I'll make it worth your while."

"Eh? Catch a train, did you say?" the driver asked. "I don't see any luggage," he added, looking at David with narrow, distrusting eyes.

"My luggage has already gone to the station," David said. And in that he wasn't lying, for he had long ago developed the habit of leaving his luggage in the baggage room of the depots in order to facilitate a quick withdrawal.

The driver sighed, then motioned for David to get in. As they pulled away they heard the clatter of running hooves and the ring of steel-rimmed wheels. An ambulance was rushing toward the park.

"Must have been an accident," the driver said. "Poor beggar. I wonder what happened?"

David settled down in his seat and smiled to himself. He knew what happened. The poor beggar, as the driver called him, had signed his own death warrant when he insulted David in public. And now, the woman was paying too.

David thought of how the woman had reacted as he had stabbed the man. She thought he was in the throes of passion, and she urged him on, like a good little whore should. David laughed out loud.

"What are you laughin' at, mister?" the driver asked, surprised to hear laughter in conjunction with the sound of an ambulance.

"Oh, uh, nothing," David said. "I just thought of something, that's all. Something I found rather amusing."

"Humph," the driver said in a disapproving grunt. He clucked at his horse and urged it on. He was clearly ready to go home and go to bed, and this stranger in the middle of the night was an unwelcome fare.

Chapter Nine

Crystal climbed the ladder which led to her room. It was not an ordinary room, but one which had been built on to the Trading Post long after the main building was completed. It looked a little like the wheelhouse of a riverboat, for it was a cupola which extended above the roof line. Surrounded with windows, the room offered a panoramic view of the river and the green countryside around the trading post. Eb had made the offer of the room when Crystal was just a little girl, and Marsh consented to let Crystal stay ashore, anytime they were docked there.

At first, Crystal's brother, David, was a little jealous. Why would Eb make a special room for Crystal, but not for him?

"Because she is a girl," Marsh tried to explain to his petulant son.

But David perceived it as just one more example of Crystal having everything her way, and one more excuse for his bad behavior.

Crystal felt badly that David believed as he did, and she tried to be friends with him, but he had always made it difficult. David stayed on the borderline of trouble all the time he was a boy, and, once he became a man, he crossed over that line. Finally, Marsh had taken as much as he could take, and he sent David away.

Crystal knew that it was a sin to think so, but, when David left she was glad. Her life was much easier now that she didn't have to apologize for David all the time. He was her brother, and she knew she *should* love him. She tried, she really tried. But it was hard, because David found so many ways to hurt Marsh and everyone around him. Wherever he was now, Crystal hoped he was happy. And she hoped he would stay there.

The moon was shining in through the windows which wrapped around the cupola, and Crystal sat on her bed and looked out, enjoying the scenery the bright moonlight illuminated. The river was a flowing stream of molten silver, and the rolling hills of the breaks which came down to the river, were delineated in shades of silver and black, under the great, glowing pearl in the sky.

As Crystal sat there enjoying the beauty of the

scene, she thought of her conversation with Eb. She was glad he had shared some of his heart-break with her. For some, strange reason, she had an idea that her being there provided a comfort to him.

She also remembered that he had told her things were going to work out for her in the end. She hoped that was true.

Crystal sighed, and began to get ready for bed. She looked around the room and saw many of her possessions there. They were favorites which stayed here all the time, for Eb had told her this was her private room, and no one else would ever use it. As a result, some of the toys, her best doll, that she had since outgrown were still here. Crystal smiled as she took her doll down off the shelf. Willie had bought her that doll in Omaha, when she was only eight-years-old. She had seen the porcelain-faced doll in a window, and she thought it was the most beautiful in all the world. She knew that if she asked her father for it, he would probably complain, not that it was too expensive, but that it would get in the way around the boat. So, she never said a word about it. Then that night, as they were leaving Omaha, she discovered it in her bed. Later she learned that Willie had bought it for her, just because he had seen her looking at it.

Crystal hugged the doll, then put it back. There were a couple of books on the shelf next to the doll, and she touched them, and remembered the pleasure she had received from reading them when she first got them. Propped up behind the shelf was a theater programme signed by Lillie Langtry. These were things which would just be in the way on board the *Missouri Mist*. If just as a storage place for the things she considered important, she welcomed this room. But it wasn't only that. Here, in this room, Crystal enjoyed the luxury of total privacy. That was something she never had on board the boat.

Crystal took a nightgown from the closet, slipped into it, then lay down on the bed and watched the moon floating through the sky, as she waited for sleep.

But sleep didn't come.

She sighed, fluffed the pillow, turned over, and tried again.

No success.

After what had to be several sleepless hours, she sat up in bed and looked outside again. She could see the three boats tied up to the dock, all totally quiet as everyone aboard was sound asleep.

The trading post was quiet too. Even the saloon had grown quiet a couple of hours earlier.

"Perhaps a walk will make me sleep," Crystal said aloud.

Crystal started to get dressed, then she decided against it. If the walk did do its job, when she came back she didn't want to have to get completely changed for bed again. Instead of dressing, she just pulled a wrapper around her, put on her shoes, then started cautiously down the ladder.

The trading post was big and dark. The floor where the dance had been held was wide and empty. Through a door she could see into the saloon, equally as dark, and equally as empty. There was a faint smell of whiskey and beer in the air, though it wasn't overpowering.

Crystal walked quietly across the wide-planked floor, then she let herself through the door and out onto the porch. She could hear the breeze in the trees, and the whisper of the river. Someone, somewhere, was snoring, and for all its raucous intrusion, it, too, seemed a natural part of the night.

Crystal walked down the porch steps, then out onto the bark-strewn paths. One of the paths led down to the dock, another she had followed earlier today, led back to Mary's grave, which was actually a small, well-kept garden. The third path, Crystal knew, led to a small, but swiftly flowing, mountain stream which emptied into the river. It was that path Crystal chose to follow.

Crystal could smell the pine needles and the bark as she walked. Her feet made soft, crunching sounds, and she disturbed an owl, who hooted at her in defiance.

Ahead on the path, there was a small ridge, and on the other side of the ridge, the stream. There were trout in that stream, and on a few occasions in the past, she had come here with Eb and her father to sit on the side while they fished.

Crystal crossed the little ridge, then sat down on a cushion of grass and watched the black stream break into silver and white froth, as it tumbled over rocks on its way to the river. She pulled her knees up and wrapped her arms around her legs while she looked at the water.

"If ever there was a more lovely scene, I have not beheld it."

Crystal gasped and looked up to see John standing there.

"John!" she said. "Where did you come from?"

"I'm sorry," John said. "I didn't want to frighten you. I saw you walking down the path alone. I couldn't resist the opportunity to be with you."

"It isn't an opportunity," Crystal said. "You have no business. . . ."

"Crystal, why do you fight everything?" John asked.

"What do you mean?"

John sat down beside her and took her hands into his.

"Are you going to tell me that you feel nothing for me?" he asked.

"Yes, I . . . I mean no, I . . ." Crystal started, then she stopped. "John, this isn't right," she said.

"It is right, and you know it," John said. He moved his hands to her shoulders, then, lightly,

127

with the tips of his fingers, up from her shoulders to her neck. She tensed.

"John, you're making it so hard for me," she said. Her breathing became audibly more labored. "I can't keep on fighting you, I . . . I get dizzy."

John moved his fingertips from her neck up to her face, then with the slightest amount of pressure, he pulled her face toward his.

"No," Crystal murmured quietly. "No."

But though she resisted him with her words, she let her lips be drawn to his, and when their mouths came together, she knew that it was all so right.

In the back of Crystal's mind, she knew she had just abandoned all pretense. They were alone, in the middle of the night, and she was practically undressed. He would be able to do with her as he wished, and she couldn't stop it, nor did she intend to try.

John's lips were like fire and ice. Never had anything tasted sweeter, and yet, been so fraught with danger. Never had anything frightened her so, and yet drawn her so powerfully to it.

John's fingers left her face and moved down to the tiny buttons of her nightgown. A second later the buttons were open, and she felt the cool, night air on her naked, burning flesh. His hand cupped her breast, and her nipple strained upward. He bent his lips to her nipples, then, with his other hand, raised the hem of her nightgown and moved across her naked thighs into the moist, heated center from which all pleasurable sensations were flowing.

"I love you, Crystal," John whispered in her ear. "I love you, and I want you. I want you now."

"Yes," Crystal answered in a whimpering voice, knowing now that she couldn't deny herself, anymore than she could deny him. "Oh, yes, yes, yes."

John pulled the hem of Crystal's nightgown all the way up to her waist, and she felt a delicious sensation of cool air and soft grass against her naked skin. The top buttons of her gown were open so that both breasts were exposed, and aching in sweet agony from the supplications of his lips and tongue.

"John! John, lad, where've you gotten yourself to?"

The sound of Willie's voice hit Crystal with the impact of a slap in the face, and she jerked in convulsive fear.

"Shh!" John hissed quietly.

"John, lad. This bein' your last night, surely you've no wish to leave your friends to drink alone? I know you're out here somewhere."

Willie's voice was getting closer, and it was obvious that he was coming toward the creek. John rolled away from Crystal, then pointed toward a large bolder which was just a few feet away. Crystal crawled to the bolder and got to the other side of it, just before Willie crested the ridge. Thankfully, he didn't see her.

"Ah, there you are," Willie said. "Come on, lad. Do come back to the boat. We've a fifth of good scotch to drink, yet."

"I'd rather stay here," John said.

"All right, we'll stay here," Willie said. "Hank, Pete," he called.

"No, no, wait," John said. "On second thought, you're right. My last night, I should come to the boat."

"Now you're talkin', lad," Willie said.

"Come along, then."

"You go ahead," John said. "I'll be right there."

"Don't be long, I don't know if I can keep the others out of the whiskey," Willie said. "You know how it is."

"Yes," John said. "I know how it is."

Crystal, with shaking hands and nervous fingers, rearranged her nightgown and wrapper as Willie and John were talking. Finally she heard Willie leave, but still, she didn't move.

"You can come out now," John said softly.

Cautiously, Crystal emerged from behind the rock. She looked up toward John, and he was holding his hand out toward her, offering to help her up the bank.

"I'm sorry," John said. He tried to laugh. "Willie must have the worst sense of timing in the world."

"No," Crystal said. She took a deep breath. "No, I'm glad he came when he did."

"You're glad?"

"Yes. I . . . that is, we . . . nearly did something we would regret."

"No, Crystal," John said. "I would never have regretted it. I told you, *I love you.*"

"No," Crystal said. "Don't say that, John. Please, don't say that."

"But I don't understand. Why can't I say it, if it is true?"

"I can't explain it," Crystal said. "Please don't make me try."

Crystal started to run then, and, though John called after her, she didn't look back. She ran all the way up the path to the trading post, and, once inside, she moved quickly up to her room.

"Oh, Dad, what is it?" she sobbed into her pillow, once she was in bed. "What are the plans you have for me which would deny me this happiness?"

Sleep did come rather quickly after that, but not for the reason she wanted. She went to sleep quickly, because she tired herself out crying in her pillow.

Chapter Ten

David took the train from Philadelphia to Louisville. He laughed at the impotence of the police in Philadelphia, and congratulated himself on his brilliance at defeating them.

Louisville, he thought, would be a perfect place for him. He had never been there before, so he wouldn't be known. That meant that he should have little trouble getting into games . . . especially as Louisville had had a reputation for gambling, which was well deserved. But it wasn't a reputation which would do David any good, for it was centered around horses. David hung around the racetracks for almost a week, but he was unable to figure a way to turn the odds in his favor. And if the odds weren't in David's favor, then he had no interest in the game. He tried to get some card games going, but he wasn't very successful. Finally, because he found the place inhospitable, he left.

The next train out of Louisville was bound for Chicago. David took it. He had been to Chicago before, and he knew he could find games there. Chicago turned out to be as inhospitable as Louisville, though for a different reason. There were games in Chicago, but David wasn't welcome. He had left bad blood there his last visit, and the word was out. David couldn't even get a game which would pay enough to cover his room and board. There was nothing for him to do but leave Chicago and try to find more fruitful ground, elsewhere.

From Chicago, David went to Omaha. David had avoided Omaha in the past, because it was right on the river, and too close to old memories. The result was he wasn't known in Omaha, so there were many games available. David did very well, and enjoyed several winning nights in succession. Then, about a week after he arrived, he was caught cheating, so he was forced to leave this game, just as he had left the game in St. Louis. He had to pull out his pepperbox pistol, take the pot, and leave at gunpoint.

As always, a narrow escape excited David sexually. He remembered the woman he had found in St. Louis, and he wanted another one just like her. He prowled around the back streets of town until he found what he was looking for.

She was standing in the doorway of an old building with her hip provocatively thrust out. David walked by her once, looking at her out of the corner of his eye. Her face was covered with powder, and her cheeks were heavily painted with rouge.

David got to the end of the block, then he stopped and came back, passing her a second time. The woman smiled at him.

"I'm not goin' away, love," she said. "If you want me, all you have to do is pay."

"What makes you think I want a whore?" David asked.

"Honey, you've got the look," the woman said. "I know the look, and you've got it."

"What if I do?" David replied. "I can certainly find someone better and younger than you."

The woman laughed. "Honey, there ain't nothin' better 'n me." She thrust her pelvis toward him.

David started to walk away.

"It's gonna be a long, cold night for you, honey, if you don't take what I got to offer you now."

David reluctantly turned and came back to her. She reeked of perfume. He put his hand out and let it rest on an ample breast, partially exposed by the low-cut neckline.

"You can have it, dear," the woman said. She pulled down her bodice, exposing flesh until she reached the nipple. David reached for it, and the woman pulled her dress up back over it. "But . . . you're gonna have to pay."

"Where?" David asked.

"Oh, listen to that, will you? Not how much, but where? Honey, you need it bad, don't you?"

"Where?" David asked again.

"Come with me, love. I have a grand salon, just up these stairs."

David, with his heart pounding and the palms of his hands sweating, followed the woman up the stairs.

One hour later David's terrible lust was satisfied, and he got up from the whore's bed.

"You don't have to leave now, honey," she said to him. "You paid to spend the whole night."

"Madam, I've no intention of spending an entire night in a sty like this," David said. "I'll lie with the pigs, but I won't sleep with them."

"You've a cruel streak about you, you have," the woman said in a hurt voice. "You oughtn't to talk to a lady like that."

"If I ever see a lady, maybe I won't," David said. "That is, *if* I ever see one."

"You mean you've never seen a lady? You don't have a mother or a sister?"

"I have a sister," David said.

"Would you want people talkin' to her the way you've been talkin' to me?"

David laughed. "Yeah," he said. "Now that you mention it, I think I would."

David was still laughing over that thought, as he stepped out into the alley behind the building, when a rope suddenly dropped around him.

"Hey!" he shouted in fear and surprise. "What's this?"

David was jerked roughly to the ground, and though he managed to free himself, there were two men on him by the time he stood up again.

"What's going on?" David asked in a frightened voice. "Who are you two men? What do you want?"

"We're bringin' a message to you, gambler," one of the men said.

"A message?"

"Yeah," the other one said. "Our boss don't like gettin' cheated in card games."

"I didn't cheat. . . ." David started, but before he could get the words out, he was hit in the face by a punch that brought blood to his lips.

"Our boss said you did, 'n we don't get our pay this week, 'lessen we get it outta you."

"But I tell you . . ." David started, but this protest, like the other one, was terminated by another solid punch to the face.

David was, basically, a coward. But even a coward will fight back when all other avenues of escape are blocked. David swung wildly, and had the sudden, gratification of feeling his fist crash into flesh. One of the two men let out a sharp exclamation of pain.

David's pathetic victory was short-lived, and his effort futile, however, because both men began pummeling him at the same time.

David fell under the rain of blows, but that didn't stop the beating. He was hit and kicked until, mercifully, he passed out.

When David came to, he wasn't lying in an alley, but on a cot. He groaned and sat up.

"Well, I see you are still alive," a voice said. The voice seemed to come from just beyond a fog which had wrapped itself around David's head.

David looked beside him and saw a somber, gray, cement wall.

> *A few lines wrote on a jailhouse wall,*
> *That's all folks know of Bob McCall.*

David saw bars. He was in jail!

"What am I doing in here?" he asked.

"What are you doin' in here?" the voice beyond the fog asked. The fog cleared, and David saw that it was a policeman. "You're stayin' alive, that's what you're doin'."

"There were two men," David said. He put his hand gingerly to his head and felt a split lip, a swollen eye, a crusty patch of dried blood on his ear. "They attacked me."

"Yeah," the policeman said. "Your girlfriend

saw it all happen, just outside her window. She screamed for the police. It was your good fortune that a couple of officers were just passin' by."

"My girlfriend?" David scoffed. He took a handkerchief from his pocket, licked it, and touched it gingerly to his ear. "She's not my girlfriend. She's nothing but a whore."

"I'd say she lowered herself somewhat by bein' with you," the policeman said. "Folks in this town can put up with whores. They don't care a whole lot about card cheats."

"I wasn't cheating," David said.

"There are seven witnesses who are willin' to swear that you were."

"And you believe them?"

"You got 'ny witnesses on your side?" the policeman asked.

"I have these bruises."

"I know. That's why you're here."

"I see," David said. "I get beat up, so I go to jail."

"You might say you was took into protective custody. You ought to be thankin' us instead of moanin' and groanin'."

"I don't feel like thanking anyone for putting me in jail, no matter what the reason. I want out."

"I'll let you out, on one condition."

"What condition is that?" David asked. He took the handkerchief down from his ear and looked at it. There seemed to be as much dirt as blood.

"You gotta leave Omaha on the next conveyance."

"Is that all?"

"That's all."

"That's no problem. I never liked Omaha anyway. When's the next train leave?"

"No, that's not what I said."

"What?"

"I said the next conveyance. That'd be the *Far West*, a riverboat that's leavin' up river in about . . ." the policeman pulled his watch out and looked at it, then snapped the case shut again. "In about thirty minutes. If you want out of jail, you're gonna be on it."

"Up river you say? Up the Missouri?"

"That's it."

David chuckled. So, it had come back to this. "All right," he said. "I'll be on it."

"I thought you would see things my way," the police officer said, pulling a ring of keys from his pocket and inserting one of them into the cell door lock.

One week later, David stood at the railing of the *Far West*, watching the muddy water slide by the hull. Behind him the engine clattered and clanked, and the steam relief valve boomed like cannon fire. On the shore he saw nothing but rocks and grass and desolation. It was all familiar to him, because he had been raised on this river. His earliest memories were of watching the tediously unchanging riverbank slide by for mile after unbroken mile.

David had stayed in his cabin for the first week. He didn't even leave it to eat, but paid to have his meals delivered to him. Only when his cuts and bruises had gone down, did he venture out on deck. This was his first day.

"David? David Lee, is that you?"

David turned to look at the speaker, and saw that it was Captain Arnold Harris, master of the boat. David had known Captain Harris for many, many years. In fact, David knew most of the Missouri river captains.

"Yes, sir, it's me all right," David said.

"Well, my word, boy, did you just get on board? I haven't seen you before this very moment."

"I got on in Omaha," David said. "But I wasn't feeling too well."

"How are you now?"

"I'm doing just fine, now," David said. He stuck out his hand. "How are you doing, Captain Harris?"

Captain Harris stared at David's hand for just an instant, then he reached out and took it.

"There was a time when I didn't figure I'd ever want to shake your hand," Captain Harris said "But that's been a while, and I'm hopin' you've changed since then."

"Yes, sir, Captain Harris. I've changed. The truth is, I've changed a lot," David said.

"Well, I reckon if ever' a man needed a lot of

changin', it was you. But ever'one has a second chance comin' to 'im," Captain Harris said. "And that goes for you too, I reckon. I'm hopin' your time away has been good for you, especially for the sake of your sister 'n your pa."

"It has been good for me, Captain Harris," David said. "I've learned a lot."

"Uh, huh," Captain Harris grunted. "Have you learned to put aside your wild ways?"

"Yes, sir," David said. "All I want to do now is get back up river and be of some help to my pa."

"It's about time you started thinkin' of helpin' your pa," Captain Harris said. "It's a well known fact that you been nothin' but heartbreak to 'im so far. For him and your sister."

David rubbed the diamond-shaped mark on his cheek. "There was heartbreak all around," he said. "But that's all goin' to change now. By the way, where is my pa? Do you have any idea?"

"I passed him goin' up river when I was comin' down," Captain Harris said. "Like as not, he's already started back down this way. I reckon we'll meet up again in a couple of weeks."

"If you don't mind, Captain Harris, when we do meet up with the *Missouri Mist*, I'd like to transfer over."

"I don't reckon I mind," Captain Harris said. Captain Harris rubbed his chin and studied David closely. "I just hope your pa don't mind."

"He'll be happy to see me," David said. "I promise you that. Believe me, I've turned over a new leaf. All I want to do is put all that's past, behind me. I'm going to learn the river and be as good a boatman as my pa."

"Boy, that you can never be," Captain Harris said. "Marsh Lee is the finest master ever to command a vessel on this or any river. You'll never match him."

"No," David said. "But I can at least try."

"You'll be doin' good if you can keep up with your sister," Captain Harris went on.

"My sister?" David said. "What are you talking about?"

Captain Harris chuckled. "Haven't you heard? She has her pilot's certificate now. They say she's as good as any man, and better'n most."

"Yeah? Well, I can't say as I'm surprised. My sister always was an extraordinary girl." David replied.

"I know your pa has always set a great store by her," Captain Harris said.

"Yes, he has, hasn't he?" David replied.

"Cap'n," one of the hands called down from the hurricane deck. "Cap'n, you're wanted at the wheel house."

Captain Harris looked up and waved with a sigh. He looked back at David. "Truth is, I could use someone as good as your sister on my boat. Everytime we get into the slightest whirlpools or jetties, I have to go up to the wheelhouse and take over."

David watched Captain Harris climb the stairs, then he started to turn back to the railing when something caught his eye. He looked back around and saw that a newspaper was lying on a box near the boiler. What caught his eye about it, was the fact that it was from Philadelphia. When he picked it up, he saw that it was nearly two months old. That would be just about the right time. He found the story he was looking for at the bottom of the sixth column on Page Eight.

NO ADVANCE ON PARK
MURDER

PHILADELPHIA, JUNE 15—

Although the authorities are reluctant to admit it, it is reported that scant advance has been made in locating the perpetrator of the crime of murder committed in Azelia Park on the night of the 7th, inst. The murder victim was a well-known railroad heir, Sam Andrews, late of this city. As he was with a lady of the evening when he was stabbed, the authorities are speculating that it was a crime of jealous passion. They suspect it may have been one of the 'lady's' earlier customers, and they are questioning each of them, in the hopes of making an early arrest.

David folded the paper up and put it back where he had found it. He smiled, smugly. It would appear he had gotten away cleanly.

Chapter Eleven

The first pink fingers of dawn touched the juniper trees and the light was soft and the air was cool. John liked it best early in the morning. He was camped in the cool shadow of Citadel Rock. The last morning star made a bright pinpoint of light over the sandstone bluffs that lay in a ragged line along Beaver River, far to the east.

The coals from his campfire of the night before were still glowing, and he threw chunks of wood on it and stirred the fire into crackling flames which danced merrily against the bottom of the suspended coffeepot. A rustle of wind through feathers caused him to look up just in time to see a golden eagle diving on its prey. The eagle swooped back into the air carrying a tiny mouse which was kicking fearfully in the eagle's claws. A lizard scurried beneath a nearby rock and impaled a fly on its quick, lethal tongue.

John poured himself a cup of coffee and sat down to enjoy it. It was black and steaming and he had to blow on it before he could suck it through his lips. He enjoyed its bracing effect, as he watched the sun peak above the sandstone bluffs, then stream brightly down onto the high plains floor.

John thought of Crystal. Crystal Lee. It was a beautiful name, and the beauty of the name fit the beauty of the girl.

Of course, John had heard of her, even before he met her. He had heard of her because she was the only woman pilot on the river, and it was a good story to tell, of a woman who was as good as a man in a job which was as demanding as that of a riverboat pilot. John had even heard that the woman pilot was pretty. But nothing he had heard prepared him for what he encountered.

Crystal was a beautiful woman. He would grant that the storytellers had at least warned him of that much. But Crystal was so much more than just pretty. There was something else about her; something John couldn't understand, nor even begin to describe. Perhaps it was something which effected only John, but whenever he was around her, he experienced a type of euphoria unlike anything he had ever experienced before.

Then, his last night at Trenton Town, when he had seen her walking down the path in the moonlight, he knew that he must have her. Never in his life had he been moved by such an irresistable force as that which caused him to follow her. And, glory of glories! He discovered that she felt the same way about him, for indeed she was a willing and eager participant for as far as they went. It was only the unexpected and totally exasperating appearance of Willie, which stopped them from consummating the love they both felt.

And yet, even then, with all commitment out in the open, and with the obvious fact that had it not been for Willie nothing would have stopped them, Crystal made a pathetic claim that it was wrong. Why? Why did she insist upon denying that which was so evident to both of them?

John stood up and stretched to work out the aches of spending the night on the ground. It had been three days since he left the *Missouri Mist* at Trenton Town, and he was just begining to get used to life in the wilderness again. He tossed out the last dregs of coffee, cleaned out his mess kit, then slipped it and the coffeepot into the saddle-bag on his pack horse. John had two horses; a saddle horse and a pack animal, both of which he had left with Eb Trenton during the time he was in Washington. As a result, the animals had a long rest and plenty of good food. Now they were both very strong and ready for the trail. Normally, John enjoyed being on the trail, and if it hadn't been for the fact that he had to quit the river and leave Crystal, John would have looked forward to this time in the mountains, with as much eager anticipation as before.

"You're good company, horses," John said to his animals. They were used to hearing his voice on the long, lonely treks through the wilderness, and one of them nuzzled him, comfortably, happy to be restored to the life he knew.

"But neither one of you are as pretty as a girl named Crystal Lee."

John was being watched. He didn't realize that he was being watched, but he was, and he had been since before dawn. An Indian, his face lined with age and wizened with experience, sat quietly behind a rock outcropping, studying him. After the Indian was convinced that no evil spirit had come to inhabit John's person, he stood up and walked out to greet him. His sudden appearance didn't seem to startle John in the least, for John looked at him and smiled broadly.

"Angry Wolf," John said. "It is good to see that you still have the ability to walk without your feet touching the ground."

"You did not hear me?" Angry Wolf asked.

"No."

"You did not see me?"

"No."

"And yet, you were not frightened by my appearance," Angry Wolf said. "Why is it you were not frightened by my appearance?"

"I was expecting you," John said. "I knew you would come soon. You should have come sooner. I had some coffee, but I drank it all."

"Have you more coffee?" Angry Wolf asked, pointing to John's saddlebags.

"Yes," John said.

"Then at our evening meal you will make some coffee—and I will drink it. Have you tobacco?"

John chuckled. "Angry Wolf, would I take such a long journey and not bring tobacco for my friend?" he asked. He opened one of the saddlebags and pulled out a small pouch. "Here," he said. "There is enough tobacco here to keep your pipe filled all winter. Oh, and also, I brought you this." John handed a small envelope to Angry Wolf, and Angry Wolf looked inside.

"Little white papers?" Angry Wolf said, confused by the gift. "You have brought Angry Wolf little white papers? What shall Angry Wolf do with little white papers?"

"Here," John said. "Let me show you."

John took one of the papers from the envelope, held it crooked, then reached down in his shirt pocket and pulled out a small, cloth bag of tobacco. He pulled the bag string open with his teeth, and poured a little tobacco in the paper, closed the bag and put it back in his shirt pocket. Then he licked the edge of the paper and rolled it over until he had a small white tube of paper filled with tobacco.

"It is called a cigarette," John said. He put it in

his mouth and lit it, then took a puff. "It is what many men smoke, back east."

"A cigarette?" Angry Wolf said. He reached for it and John gave it to him. Angry Wolf held it to examine it, but he crushed it between his fingers and all the tobacco spilled out. "A paper pipe," he said. "No good. It is too easy to break."

John laughed. "It's easier than a pipe," he said. "And when you are finished, there is nothing left. You don't have to take care of it as you do a pipe."

"It is good to be able to take care of a pipe," Angry Wolf said. "I have a pipe which belonged to my grandfather's grandfather, and I will give it to my grandson's grandson. You cannot do this with a pipe which is made of paper."

"That's true," John agreed. "That's very true. He looked around. "Is your horse near?"

"Yes," Angry Wolf said.

"Come," John invited. "We will ride together."

Typically, Angry Wolf did not ask John to give him an early report on what happened during his trip to Washington. John would provide all that information at a council meeting which would be held in Angry Wolf's village. Then, Angry Wolf and the others would be free to ask as many questions as they wished, and all would hear the news at the same time. It was a peculiar, but stringently enforced aspect of the particular type of fairness practiced by the Mandan Indians.

They rode through the breaks for most of the

day, taking a noon meal of jerky and water without leaving the saddle. When they camped by a swiftly flowing stream for the night, Angry Wolf disappeared while John built a fire and started a pot of coffee. A short time later Angry Wolf returned and dropped two rabbits on the ground near the fire.

"We have meat," he said simply.

John and Angry Wolf skinned and cleaned the rabbits, then spit them on a long, green twig. With the forked limbs as support, they suspended the rabbits over the fire, and a short time later the mouth-watering aroma of cooking meat permeated the campsite.

"Is Washington a great distance?" Angry Wolf asked, tearing off a piece of the meat with his teeth.

"Yes," John said. "It is a very great distance."

"How far?"

"Well," John said. "First, one must go to Omaha or St. Louis by river boat, and then. . . ."

"Omaha? Is that an Indian city?"

"No," John said. "It is a white man's city, but it is a city with an Indian name. In America there are many cities and states with Indian names."

"Why is this?" Angry Wolf wanted to know

"It is a way the whites have of paying honor," John said. "They honor the Indians by naming their cities and states after them."

"I think it would be better to honor the Indian

by not taking away his land," Angry Wolf said simply.

"I agree with you," John said. "Unfortunately, it is not that simple."

"How many days' travel does it take to reach the place called Washington?"

"It is four weeks by boat to reach Omaha. It is one more week from Omaha to Washington, if you go by train."

"In Washington, are there many houses?"

"Yes."

"I would like to see this place called Washington," Angry Wolf said. "I would like to see men who are chief of a land so big it takes many weeks to go from one end to the other, and yet, they wish for even more land. They must be men with very big bellies."

"Big bellies?" John asked with a little laugh. "Angry Wolf, why would you think that?"

"They are men who are never satisfied. They always want more. Perhaps they eat more than they need."

John laughed again. "My friend, I wish I had taken you to Washington with me," he said. "Perhaps the men with the big bellies could have learned something from someone who is as wise as Angry Wolf."

It was nearly noon the next day before John and Angry Wolf reached the village. They came down off the mountain with the village dogs barking in front of them, and as they approached, John was able to see the entire village laid out before him. It consisted of several lodges and tents scattered on both sides of a small creek. The creek was a narrow stream which flowed down from the high country, then broke into white water as it bubbled across the tiers of rocks just above the village.

When they reached the bottom of the bluff and started into the village, everyone came out of the dwellings, or away from the cooking fires, which were the community gathering places, and came to meet them. A group of nut-brown children ran to the village edge and laughed and ran in circles as they welcomed the small party. Many of the adults joined the children, and as John and Angry Wolf walked to the center of the village they formed a small, but greatly excited procession. An old woman greeted them.

"Old woman, have you prepared a lodge for this man?" Angry Wolf asked.

"Yes," the old woman answered. She pointed to a tipi near the side of the stream.

"How can I thank her properly?" John asked, when Angry Wolf pointed out the tipi the old woman had prepared for him.

"Do you see the medal and ribbon she wears?" Angry Wolf asked.

John looked on the old woman's shawl and saw

a faded ribbon, now gray, but once, obviously, blue. The ribbon said, "First Prize."

"Yes, I see it," John said. "What is it?"

"This old woman made a shawl for a white man. The white man took it to a place where such things were judged, and the shawl won a prize. The man brought back the ribbon to this old woman, and she has worn it ever since. If you would thank her, you would tell her that the ribbon is a wonderful prize. It means much to her."

"Old woman," John said, looking at the woman who had heard and understood every word of the conversation between John and Angry Wolf. John was a little self-conscious about it, but he saw from the expression in her eyes, that she was expecting it to be said. "You have a wonderful prize. It brings you much honor."

The old woman beamed. "First Prize," she said. "Blue Ribbon. The best." She turned her forefinger around and jabbed it into her own chest. "Me."

When John went into the tipi, he saw that all his needs had been provided for. There was a bed of skins stretched over straw; there were clay pots for water and food; and there was even a pipe with a small amount of tobacco, an exceptional gift, as tobacco was very dear to the village. John, as was expected of him, stretched out on the bed to rest from the long journey. No one would ask a question of him until the council meeting tonight.

It was dark when John woke up some time later.

He could hear the drums and songs of the villagers, and he knew that they were gathering for the council meeting. He knew, also, that part of the reason for the songs and the drums, was to make certain that he was awake, without having to be so rude as to wake him directly.

John sat up, ran his hand through his hair, then stood up and prepared himself to go to the council meeting. He hoped what he had to tell them would be acceptable. He wished he could have brought them better news, but from the mood in Washington, he knew how easily it would have been for him to bring them less. Still, they were not likely to be very happy with the results of his trip.

There were several gathered around the council fire when John went outside. The Indians were formed into a circle, leaving the center of it open.

Inside the open part of the circle, a smaller group of Indians were already sitting and passing a long-stemmed pipe back and forth. The pipe was passed to Angry Wolf, and when Angry Wolf saw John, he held it out to him, inviting him to sit with them and smoke. John joined them, and they smoked in silence for several moments. Then, Angry Wolf picked up a feathered stick, his symbol of authority, and he looked at John.

"You have traveled far, my friend," he said. "This is the message you were asked to take to the great chiefs in Washington. You were to tell them this land belongs to the Mandan people. We were born on it and we will die on it. Look at us. Are we clouds to disappear on a sunny day? We are people. We must be somewhere and the Great Spirit put us here. The Great Spirit did not put the White Man here, and they must build no more villages for the white man. They must not send more white men into our land to dig for the thing you call gold. They must build no more soldiers' forts on our land. This is the message you were asked to deliver to the great white chiefs in Washington. Did you do this?"

"Yes, Angry Wolf, I delivered the message," John said.

"And how did the great white chiefs in Washington reply?"

John looked around the council into the eager faces of all who were gathered there. He understood their plight, perhaps more than anyone. He had seen the steady encroachment of the white man, and he had seen, first-hand, the Indians' game being taken. Often, the white men slaughtered buffalo and took only the prime, rumpsteaks. Sometimes special hunting expeditions were organized and entire hunting clubs would come from the East, go on a five-day buffalo killing binge, then return to the East with only trophies from the hunt, leaving the meat to rot on the plains.

"You must realize," John began, "that the great

white chiefs in Washington, and all the soldier chiefs still recall the battle you call Greasy Grass."

"Sitting Bull's victory over Yellow Hair," Angry Wolf said.

"Yes," John answered. "There are many civilian and soldier chiefs who wish to punish all Indians for Custer."

"But you were a scout for Custer," Angry Wolf said. "I see no such hate in your heart."

"It was a battle, fairly and bravely fought," John said. "I cannot feel hate for that."

"The battle of Greasy Grass was fought by the Sioux and the Cheyenne," Angry Wolf said. "Do the soldier chiefs and the great white chiefs not know we are Mandan?"

"Yes, they know," John said. "But to the great white chiefs in Washington, all Indians are the same. They do not know the difference between the Sioux, the Mandan, the Apache, or the Mohawk."

"The Mohawk? What are Mohawk?"

"An Indian tribe which lives back East," John said. "Once, many winter counts ago, they were fierce warriors."

"They make war no more?"

"No. Many Mohawk died. Many others live with the white men."

"Then we are not like the Mohawk, because we will never live like the white man. And if the white man wants war, we shall give him war."

"The white man does not wish war," John said quickly.

"That is good. If they do not wish war, they will give us what we ask for."

"Angry Wolf, there are some in Washington who would have the soldiers come and destroy all Indians," John said. "If they had their way, there would be no more Mandan, Sioux, Cheyenne, Apache, or anything else. Then the white man would be right. All Indians would be alike, because all Indians would be dead."

"And many whites would be dead as well," Angry Wolf said.

"Yes, this is true," John said. "That is why I hope that Angry Wolf and the Mandan people will be very wise and listen to the proposal of the white man."

"What is the proposal of the white man?" Angry Wolf asked.

"The Mandan people will be given all the land south of the Missouri, between the Musselshell and the Judith Rivers," John said. "Nothing east of the Musselshell, and nothing north of the Missouri."

"But our land goes to the Yellowstone River," Angry Wolf protested. "The land west of the Musselshell already belongs to us. There are no whites there. This is not a gift, for one cannot give what one does not have."

"My friend," Jonn said. "The first offer was to

157

keep the Mandans twenty miles south of the Missouri. They were afraid to have Indians living along a river which handles so much river boat traffic. I talked to them and made them remove that restriction."

"The land north of the Missouri has always belonged to us," Angry Wolf protested.

"This I know," John said. "But I also know that the best game is south of the Missouri. This, the great white chiefs in Washington did not know or I fear they would not have given you that land either."

Angry Wolf thought for a while, then he spoke again.

"I believe you spoke to the great chiefs in Washington with the heart of a Mandan," he said. "For this, you have the thanks of the Mandan people. But the offer of the great white chiefs is a bitter one, and it must be discussed by the council. Go, now, and return to your tipi. We will discuss this and tomorrow we will have the answer."

John got up and walked through the crowd of concerned, sitting Indians, back to his tipi. There was nothing more he could do now. It all depended on the decision of the council.

John wasn't sure what awakened him. It may have been a sound, but if so, it was so quiet that even its memory had faded. Perhaps it was just some extra sense that alerted him that he was not alone. But if so, he felt no danger, just an awareness that someone else was in the tipi with him.

John looked toward the open flap of the tipi and he saw her there. A young Indian woman, standing in a shaft of silver moonlight, looking toward John's bed. She was nude, John could see that by the moonlight, but, though it disclosed her nudity, it did so in a subtle way. Her body was highlighted and made all the more mysterious and intriguing by the shadows and lighting of the night.

John sat up and when he did, the girl walked softly toward him. She didn't say a word, but merely came into his arms, offering herself to him. She was, John knew, a gift from Angry Wolf. She was one of the necessities Angry Wolf had provided for him, like the tipi, food and water. It would be a terrible breach of etiquette if John sent her away, and under ordinary circumstances, it was something he would never even consider. But now, for some inexplicable reason, even as the girl came to him, John thought of Crystal. When he thought of her he felt guilty, somehow, as if by being with this girl he was violating some unspoken promise to Crystal.

But no, there had been no promises . . . on the contrary, she had gone to great lengths to deny what was between them. And the love they had almost shared was interrupted before it could come to sweet fulfillment. That didn't leave anything for John to hold onto. At least, not yet. Especially when a young, beautiful, warm girl was here, in his arms, offering in the flesh that which, thus far, he could only imagine with Crystal.

John rolled over onto the girl who had come into his tipi. And as he felt her beneath him, his mind cleared of all thoughts and doubts, to be replaced only by a quickly rising tide of passion. He took her then, and discovered an amazing amount of passion in the quiet girl, as she reacted eagerly, hungrily, to his thrusts. John felt a warmth in his body, building into a heat, and finally erupting into lightning surges of energy as a sudden rapture burst over his body.

Later, when the heat receded and there was only the pleasant relaxation afterward, the girl, who had still not uttered a word, got up and left as quietly as she had come. John had no idea who she was, nor did he think he would ever find out.

It was better that way.

Chapter Twelve

The *Missouri Mist* was headed downriver, and the beat of the giant sternwheel, plus the current of the river, combined to give her a brisk pace. Rocks and trees on the shoreline slipped by quickly as she maintained as steady and as rapid a speed as the twisting turns and shifting sandbars of the channel would allow.

Captain Marsh Lee was at the wheel, while Crystal polished the brass bell in front of the wheelhouse. Crystal was not only a licensed pilot, but also the First Officer of the boat. That made her second-in-command only to her father, so it certainly wasn't necessary that she polish the bell. She was doing it, because it was a job she enjoyed doing.

Keeping the bell polished was the very first job

Crystal had ever been given on the boat. As a little girl, she had taken a great pride in keeping the bell shiny. As she grew older, and more and more responsibility was given her, she never forgot that early pride of accomplishment, nor did she relinquish that first job.

Crystal enjoyed the still youthful excitement of putting a shine on the bell that was so deep it seemed to go on forever. But it wasn't just the physical aspects of the work which she found rewarding. She also appreciated those quiet moments of reflective contemplation she enjoyed while polishing the bell. It was an opportunity to be gainfully employed, while at the same time allowing her mind the freedom to think of other things. In fact it was just such an opportunity for reflection which drew her to the bell this morning.

It was now obvious to Crystal, if it hadn't been obvious before that she was in love with John Riley. No matter that she tried to deny it, no matter that her father cautioned her against it, what she felt for John wouldn't go away. She was in love with him, and she was going to have to tell that to her father. Why had he so often cautioned her against falling in love with John? Was there some terrible secret about John that she didn't know? Surely there couldn't be, or Uncle Eb would have cautioned her about him when she was talking to him. Uncle Eb said nothing against the notion of her loving John. On the contrary, he told her that John was one of the finest men he had ever known. Perhaps if her Uncle Eb spoke to her father for her, to plead her case, her father would relent from his, what seemed to her, arbitrary decision. She knew that her father respected Eb's opinion on things. Perhaps he would listen to him on this.

Crystal wondered, though, if Eb would speak on her behalf if he knew about the last night she had seen John. If he understood how close Crystal had come to losing her innocence with John, would he condemn her, or would he still speak for her? That had been a dangerous few moments, and yet, even now, as Crystal thought of it, her blood warmed, and her skin flushed as hot as when it was happening. All that had occurred three weeks ago.

A lot had happened in that three weeks. They had reached Fort Benton, taken on a new load of passengers and cargo, turned around, and now were headed downriver again. It had been three busy weeks, but the intensity of that last night with John had not decreased, and the memory had not faded. In fact, with the greatest of ease, Crystal could reconstruct every sight, sound, smell, taste and feel of that experience. Every moment of that time with John had been so filled with exquisitely silken sensation, that she had only to close her eyes, to have it all back. It could be with her now, with the slightest effort on her part. Even as she thought of it, she closed her eyes to recapture the rapture.

"Darlin', you're goin' to polish the ring right out of that bell," Marsh suddenly teased.

"What?" Crystal asked, reacting to her father's comments. She had been so absorbed in her thoughts that she wasn't paying attention to what she was doing, and she discovered that she was rubbing the same place over and over again.

"The bell," Marsh said. "Don't you think you've polished it enough?"

"To tell the truth, Dad, I wasn't paying much attention to it," Crystal said.

Marsh chuckled. "That's pretty obvious," he said. "If you don't mind sharing with an old man, just what could a pretty young girl find to think about so seriously?"

Now, Crystal thought. Now was the time to tell him that she was in love with John. Now was the time to get it all in the open. She drew a deep breath.

"Dad, there's somethin' I want to talk to you about."

"Oh?"

"It's important," Crystal said.

"I thought it might be," Marsh said. "You look like you been workin' it up all mornin'."

"I suppose in a way, I have," Crystal agreed.

"What's it about?"

"It's about John Ril. . . ."

"Cap'n, smoke comin' up!" Willie shouted from below. His call interrupted Crystal in midsentence.

"Looks like we're about to meet another boat," Marsh said. "I wonder who it is?" He pulled on the whistle cord, and the deep, dualtone of the *Missouri Mist* rolled out across the river, and then came back from the nearby bluffs.

The distant boat answered with its own call.

"That'll be the *Far West*," Marsh said, recognizing the whistle. "I think we have some mail for them, don't we, darlin'?"

"Yes," Crystal said.

"Well, we'll hail 'em, and pass over the mailbag. Also, we'll see if they have any news from downriver." Marsh pulled on the whistle cord again, and again the heavy bleat of the *Missouri Mist* whistle rolled out from the boat.

The *Far West* answered again.

"Oh, I'm sorry, darlin', you were about to tell me somethin'," Marsh said.

At first, Crystal had resented the interruption. Now, she was glad she had been interrupted, for the amount of courage she had gathered to speak had left her. She couldn't tell him about John Riley. Not yet. She would have to wait until another time, until the opportunity was just right.

"Nothin, Dad," she said. "Nothing important."

"I thought you said it was important."

"Not really," she said. "Let's meet the *Far West*."

The two boats closed the distance between them

rather quickly, then they maneuvered to come side by side. Finally with the skillful application of power, and a deft adjustment of rudders, the boats were together. Mail was exchanged, and, along with the mail, one passenger.

Crystal looked at the passenger as he stepped from the *Far West* onto the deck of the *Missouri Mist*. She gasped. The passenger was David Lee, her brother.

"Dad!" Crystal said.

"Yes?"

"Look! Isn't that . . .?"

"David!" Marsh said.

"What's he doing here?"

"I'm not sure," Marsh said. "I can only hope that my prayers have been answered."

"Your prayers?"

"About David, and you," Marsh said. He looked at Crystal. "You remember I told you that I had plans for you?"

"Yes."

"You will soon learn what those plans are. Now, if you'll excuse me, I'm going to see David."

Crystal watched as her father moved quickly to the rail where the young man stood. Marsh and his son looked at each other for a long moment, then, when Marsh opened his arms, David went to them, and the two men embraced.

"Crystal! Crystal, come, quickly!" Marsh called. "Come and greet your brother!"

Crystal went hesitantly, and stood back a small distance. David looked at her and smiled.

"Well, don't you share father's enthusiasm in welcoming back the prodigal son?" David asked. "Where's your biblical sense of obligation?"

Crystal returned his smile, and went to her brother and embraced him.

"I haven't lost it," she said. "I'm very glad to see you David."

"I must confess," David said, looking around the boat. "I never thought I would say this, but I'm happy to be back. Even this old barge looks pretty good to me right now."

"Are you here to stay?" Marsh asked.

David looked at his father. "That depends on you," he said. "Will you let me stay?"

"If you are truly sorry," Marsh said. "And if you think you have changed."

"Oh, I've changed, all right," David said. "I have really changed."

"Then, of course you can stay. Willie, Hank, Pete, what do you think? David has returned! My son has returned!"

"I think it calls for a celebration," Willie said.

They did celebrate. That night, Pete cooked them a fine dinner of fried chicken and fresh biscuits, and there was good wine for all. Even though there was a lot of home cooking, there was even more wine, and as the evening wore on David drank more and more. Gradually, he changed from the grateful prodigal to a vindictive young man. Crystal saw it coming, but she refused to admit it. She had so hoped that David's first words were true ... that he had changed. It was soon obvious that David hadn't changed at all.

"Like an unwanted cat," David said, morosely. "You may as well have put me in a bag and dropped me over the side, for all the support I got from you after I left."

"Son, it was to force you into becoming a man that I put you ashore without support," Marsh said. "I did what I did for your own good."

"For my own good, you say?" David sputtered. "If you knew what all I've been through ... what I've had to do just in order to survive ... you would never have treated me that way."

"Maybe not," Marsh agreed. "Maybe not. Anyway, what has happened has happened. It's time now that we tried to make a new life. I have plans for you, son. Plans that I hope you agree with."

David had long sinced passed the wine, and was now drinking whiskey straight from the bottle. He turned the bottle up and drained the rest of it with long, adams-apple-bobbing swallows. He let the bottle down, and wiped his mouth with the back of his hand.

"Tell me about your plans," he said, staggering.

"Not now," Marsh said.

"Now."

168

"No, tomorrow. Tomorrow, when you are sober. Then I'll tell you."

David laughed, and reached for another bottle.

"You're going to wait until I'm sober?"

"Yes."

David laughed, a high, shrill laughter. "Then I may never learn of your plans," he said. "For I don't intend to ever get sober again."

The discussion ended on that note, for David drank more and more. Marsh became more and more morose, as he saw that his son really hadn't changed as he had hoped. Soon, David staggered drunkenly to bed, while Marsh went sadly to his own. And Crystal, who watched them both leave, wondered now if the opportunity ever would present itself to talk to her father about her own problem.

Crystal had been fourteen years old when Marsh sent David away. Because Crystal was only fourteen, everyone tried to protect her from what was going on. But Crystal knew the truth, and she could still remember standing behind the door, watching in frightened curiosity as her father had paid off Mr. Moore.

"I caught 'em together, red-handed, I did," Moore said angrily. "My wife, and that wild, young buck you call a son. I caught 'em together, ruttin' aroun' like a couple o' hogs in heat. And I want to know what you are gonna do about it."

"Mr. Moore, I'm not at all sure what you expect

me to do," Marsh replied. "What, exactly, do you want me to do?"

"To begin with, you could try makin' it up to me," Moore said.

"I see," Marsh said. "And just what way do you have it in mind that I could make it up to you?"

"It seems to me like some sort of restitution is in order," Moore said. "I mean, after all, she is my wife. She belongs to me. A man ought not to have his possessions used, 'lessen he's paid for it in some way."

"Paid for it?" Marsh asked.

"That only seems right."

"Tell me, Mr. Moore, what is the fair compensation for using someone else's wife these days?"

"Fifty dollars ought to be about right," Mr. Moore said.

"Fifty dollars?" David interrupted. He laughed. "I could have every whore in St. Louis for fifty dollars!"

"This is my wife you're a'talkin' about!" Moore said angrily. "And iffen I wanted to, I could have you hauled off to jail for adultry!"

"Well, we ain't gonna pay no fifty dollars for it," David said, but his father cut off his son's remark with a wicked, backhanded slap. The *pop* of Marsh's hand against his son's flesh was so loud that, even from her vantage point behind the door, Crystal had flinched. She had never seen her father hit her brother before, though there were times when even she felt he needed it. The expression in her brother's eyes as he glared at his father, frightened Crystal.

"I'll give you fifty dollars," Marsh told Mr. Moore. "But I want you and your wife to leave this boat at the very next stop."

"Cap'n Lee, for fifty dollars, me'n the wife'll get offen this son-of-a-bitch tonight."

"No," Marsh said. He looked over at David. "My son is leaving the boat tonight."

"Tonight?" David said. "What are you talking about? We aren't anywhere near a place to get off. What do you expect me to do if I leave tonight?"

"You can have a skiff," Marsh said. "Flag the next boat that is going down river. One will be along, soon."

David glared at his father again, then started to leave the wardroom where all this was taking place. When Crystal saw him coming toward the door, she left quickly, so as not to be discovered. That was the last time she saw her brother, until suddenly, and mysteriously, he reappeared today.

And now, David slept in a drunken stupor, on the deck below.

"Crystal?" Marsh called quietly through the curtain which hung down to make her room. His call interrupted her thoughts.

"Yes, Dad?"

"Crystal, are you all right?"

"Yes, Dad, I'm fine."

"We never did get around to talking about whatever was bothering you today."

Crystal lay in her bed and looked up into the darkness above. She sighed, quietly. "No, I guess we didn't."

"You want to talk about it now?"

"No," Crystal said. "It isn't important, now. Dad, David had no right to speak to you the way he did today!"

"You mustn't blame him, Crystal," Marsh said. "Perhaps he has more right than you think. I am his father, but I let him down in his time of need. He has to be hurt and confused by that."

"You would think that by now he would be grown up," Crystal said. "But it is quite obvious that he hasn't."

"Perhaps he just needs to settle down," Marsh suggested.

"Hmmph. If you ask me, he'll never settle down."

"Perhaps he will."

"When?"

"When the right woman comes along," Marsh suggested. "I've always thought that what he needed was a good woman."

"I pity the poor woman who would get my brother as a husband."

"Why?" Marsh asked. "Crystal, can't you find any admirable qualities in your brother? Can't you find anything a woman might be attracted to?"

"Attracted to? Of course," Crystal said. "David

172

is a very handsome man, but he knows it. He is terribly egotistical about that. He could probably have any woman he wanted."

"Could he have you?" Marsh asked.

"Me?" Crystal replied, laughing. "That's a funny question. I've never thought of him in that way."

"Why not?"

"David is my brother." Crystal was very uncomfortable. "Girls don't think about their brothers like that."

"But if David weren't your brother," Marsh suggested. "Suppose he was someone you just met. How would you feel about him then?"

"Why are you asking me this?"

"I'm just trying to judge how a young woman would view David as a potential husband. He simply has to settle down before it is too late."

"I don't know," Crystal answered. "But I'll tell you one thing. If he weren't my brother and if I did have him for a husband, I'd certainly take him down a notch or two. I could settle him down, you better believe that."

"I do believe that," Marsh answered from the other side of the curtain. "And that is the answer to my prayers."

Crystal pondered her father's strange response for a moment, but, just for a moment. It had been a long and eventful day, and soon she was asleep.

Chapter Thirteen

"Darlin'," Marsh called from the wheelhouse to Crystal the next morning. "Come on in here and give your ole' pa a kiss, will you? Just like when you were little, and my best girl."

Crystal had been standing on the hurricane deck, just in front of the wheelhouse, and she turned back toward her father and smiled. "Well, I'm not so little now," she said. "But I am still your best girl. Or at least, I had better be." She walked around to go inside and kiss her father.

"Are you really?" Marsh asked. "Are you really my best girl?"

"Of course I am," Crystal said. Then, when she saw that her father was serious, she looked at him with a puzzled expression on her face. "Pa, why would you even ask such a question? What's wrong?"

For a moment, Marsh didn't even answer. He just stood at the giant wheel, turning it gently to answer the currents and channel of the river. The breeze ruffled his hair. Finally he cleared his throat and spoke. "Sweetheart, there is something I want to talk to you about."

"Does it have anything to do with the plans you were talking about?"

"Yes," Marsh said. Marsh looked at Crystal. "Darlin', you are a fine girl. No man could ever want for a better daughter, and I want you to know that I love you more'n anythin' in this world. Your happiness is more important to me than anythin' else in this world. It's important for you to know that as you listen to what I'm about to tell you."

Crystal looked at her father with an expression of curiosity etched on her face. In addition to the curiosity, there was a slight concern reflected in her emerald eyes.

"Pa, what is it?" she asked. "What are you trying to tell me? You are frightening me."

"I don't want to frighten you, darlin'," Marsh said. "In fact, I hope what I'm about to tell you makes you happy, because it will open up a whole new life for you. And, it will make a lifetime dream of my own come true."

"What, Dad?" Crystal asked. "What is it?"

Marsh looked at Crystal and sighed, then rubbed his hand across his chin. A quick-building film of moisture covered his eyes. He was crying! Crystal had never seen her father cry before, and he was crying now!

"I . . . I want to tell you a story," he said. "It is a story about a most mysterious," he stopped to clear his throat, "and wonderful event," he said, going on. "It happened twice. The first time it happened was thousands of years ago, way off in the land of Egypt. A baby was put in a basket, and set adrift in the rushes to be found by a Princess. That baby was raised in the house of a Pharaoh, and he became . . ."

"Moses," Crystal said, smiling. "That was always my favorite Bible story when I was a little girl, remember? I would have you tell it to me over and over again," she said.

"Darlin', there's a good reason why that's your favorite," Marsh said. "You recall that I said this wonderous event happened twice? Once was thousands of years ago, in the time of Moses, and the other time was eighteen years ago."

"Eighteen years ago?"

"It happened right along here, not too far from where we are now," Marsh said. "I was master of the *Edmond Carter* then. You remember that boat, don't you, darlin'? I sold her to Captain Jason McCord, and he lost her in river ice, in '72."

"Yes, I remember," Crystal said.

"Well, I was master of the *Edmond Carter*, like I said. We come around a bend, and I saw fire on the water. I immediately signaled to stop engines, and I set a lookout forward to see what was wrong. We were drifting ahead slowly, when the lookout spotted a small canoe drifting out from the rushes along the banks. He called for a gaff, and pulled the canoe to the side of the boat. That lookout was none other than Willie Parsons, and a moment later, he come runnin' up to the wheelhouse, carryin' what he had discovered in that canoe. I was so astonished that you could have knocked me over with a feather.

"What was in the canoe?" Crystal asked, her curiosity now aroused by her father's strange and wonderous tale.

"You," Marsh said quietly.

"Me?" Crystal replied in a tiny voice.

"Yes, darlin'. It was you."

"But . . . I don't understand. Had I fallen overboard? How did I get there?"

"You didn't fall overboard, darlin'," Marsh said. "For, until that very moment, you had never been on board."

"Then, I'm not?" Crystal started, but she couldn't go on.

"You'd been set adrift," Marsh explained. "Whoever done it was worryin' about your welfare, because you were wrapped up good'n warm, and you were snug 'n dry in that little canoe. They must have set the fire when they heard us comin', then set you adrift when they saw us. We hung around there for a couple of days, but we never saw a soul. The fact is, we didn't even pick up any sign. But by then, I would have fought anyone who might have tried to take you back anyway, so we just moved on and I took you to raise as my own, even though my own wife had already been dead for over a year."

"Then you aren't my father?" Crystal asked quietly.

"Maybe not by blood," Marsh replied. "But darlin', I swear to you, no blood father could ever have loved his daughter any more'n I've loved you."

"I've never doubted your love for a minute, pa," Crystal said. "Even though I am adopted."

"Well, now, that's the next part of it," Marsh said. "You've never been adopted. That is, not by no legal means. I was always up in the wilds of the river 'n all, 'n I just never got around to it. Anyhow, it didn't really seem necessary to me. I mean no legal papers was going to change how I felt about you. And then, almost before I realized it, you grew up, and, I was afraid to, for fear you wouldn't understand 'n you'd be hurt by it. You've no idea what a burden this has been on my heart all this time."

Marsh wiped a tear from his eye, and seeing that, Crystal, too, began to cry. She went to him, and he took her in his arms and squeezed her affectionately. Finally, after several moments, Crystal managed to stop crying, and she stepped back away from him and rubbed her eyes.

"I'm sorry," she said. "This must seem very ungrateful of me."

"Not at all," Marsh said. "I'm sure it came as a shock to you, that's all. But honey, listen, nothing has changed. You are still who you always were, and I'm still who I always was, and we still love each other."

"I know," Crystal said. "I know. But, Dad, there's one thing I don't understand. Why did you think telling me this story would make me very happy? What did you mean when you said it would open up a whole new life for me?"

"It has to do with the plans I have for you," Marsh said. "I want to be able to leave this boat and any savings I may have to David. The fact is, as I never got around to adoptin' you, I don't know as I got any choice."

"I understand," Crystal said quickly. "Dad, you've done so much for me, believe me, I won't feel in the least left out if you . . ."

"No," Marsh said. "You don't understand. You didn't let me finish. I want to leave the boat and savings to David, but I want to leave them to you as well. I don't want it to be broken up. There's a way I could do that if . . ." he looked over at Crystal for a moment before he went on. "If the two of you were living as one."

"What do you mean?" Crystal asked, confused by the statement.

"It's really very simple," Marsh said. "And it would solve everything."

"What would?"

"Darlin', I want you to marry David," Marsh said.

"Marry David?" Crystal gasped. "Dad, do you realize what you are saying?"

"Yes, I realize perfectly what I am saying," Marsh said.

"Dad, I can't marry David! I can't believe you would even suggest such a thing. Why . . . it's . . . it's unthinkable!"

"No, it isn't," Marsh explained quickly. "Think about it, you are no blood relation to David at all. There is no reason—legal or moral—why you couldn't marry him. Crystal, David needs a *good* wife, someone who can love him and force him to settle down. And I think you are that woman. Besides, I wouldn't want to see him marry some other woman and let her move in here and start taking things over. Things which are rightfully yours."

"I don't know, Dad," Crystal stammered. "This is all so strange."

"You do love him, don't you?"

"Yes, of course, I love him," Crystal said. "But, Dad, I thought I loved him as a brother. I had no idea you expected anything else from me."

180

"Honey, love is love. And now that you know he isn't your brother, this other thing, the husband and wife thing, why, that can come along later. Darlin' I want this very, very much," he added.

"Dad, please, I. . . ." Crystal started.

"Honey, it isn't unusual for parents to arrange marriages for their children," Marsh said. "And most of the time it is with someone the daughter or son doesn't even know. You've known David all your life. It shouldn't be so difficult for you to adjust."

"What about David?" Crystal asked. "Does he know I am not his real sister? Does he know of this marriage you have planned?"

"He does know that you are not his real sister," Marsh said. "In fact, I've always considered that proof of David's basic instinct for goodness. He knew, but he never told you. He could have told you, and he could have hurt you deeply, but he never did. I have always been very proud of him for that. As far as the marriage is concerned, no, he knows nothing about it. I will have to tell him just as I have told you."

"He may not want to do it," Crystal suggested.

"I'll take care of him," Marsh promised. "But you are the one I am worried about, honey. I don't want to force this thing on you."

"Is this really what you want, Dad?" Crystal asked in a small voice.

"Darlin', more than anything else in the world,

this is what I want," Marsh said. "But," he added. "I only want it because I know it is going to be the best thing for both of you. I love you equally, even though you aren't my flesh and blood, and David, even though he has done many things to disappoint me. I love you both, and I want you to be happy, not only now, but in the later years, long after I am gone."

"If it is really what you want, then I shall do it," Crystal said.

"Darlin', remember what I said," Marsh replied. "I want you to do this, only if it will make you happy."

"It pleases me to make you happy," Crystal said. "I'll do it."

"Thank you, darlin'" Marsh said, pulling Crystal to him and squeezing her hard. He was so happy over how things had worked out for him that he didn't even notice the new tears spilling from Crystal's eyes.

Chapter Fourteen

That evening the *Missouri Mist* put into a slip and tied up. It was due to stay there for three days, replenishing its wood supply. This would also be an opportunity to hunt for fresh meat, and Marsh authorized a hunting party to go ashore the next day for just such a purpose.

Ordinarily, Crystal welcomed these breaks, and often she went with the hunting party. She was an excellent shot with a rifle, and bagged her first deer when she was only eleven years old. This time, however, she did not feel like hunting, and as the members of the hunting party talked excitedly and animatedly about the successes they planned to have, Crystal moved silently about the boat, attending to regular boat business.

David was planning on going along on the hunt,

and he was as full of braggadocio as the others. Before dark the hunters began drinking a little, just to celebrate the hunt, and by bedtime, David was as drunk as he had been the night before. This time, however, his drunkenness was not exacerbated by belligerency, and the crew and passengers were spared that unpleasantness. Finally, David went to bed in a drunken, though peaceful slumber.

Crystal had spent the entire day, from the time her father had told her of his plans for her wedding to David, waiting and dreading the moment David would be told. She didn't know how he would react, and she didn't know how she would react to him, when he approached her. When he went to bed that night without saying a word to her, she knew that he had not been told, and she breathed a silent prayer of thanks for the temporary relief.

The next day Crystal got up in the gray light of early morning, and she left the boat before anyone else had arisen. She scrambled up the bank, then climbed up a trail for a high bluff, overlooking the river. In the past, this bluff, known as Castle Rock, had been the scene of many happy picnics. This morning, it would be a place where Crystal could be alone with her own thoughts.

When she reached the top, she walked out to the overhanging ledge and stared down at the boat below. From up here it looked like a perfectly scaled model, and Crystal could see every inch of the *Missouri Mist*, from its proud bow, to the businesslike paddlewheel at her stern.

A wispy pall of wood smoke lay in a diaphanous haze over the boat. It came not from the engine boiler, but from the cookstove, and Crystal knew that Hank was awake and cooking breakfast for the hunting party. The hunters would just be beginning to stir, now, as the rich aroma of coffee and bacon would fill the decks of the boat.

The thought of breakfast made Crystal hungry, so she took some beef jerky from the knapsack she had brought along, and slipped the canteen off her shoulder. The canteen contained tea and the tea and jerky made a passable breakfast.

Crystal wondered when David would be told. She had not slept well during the night because the shock of what she learned had kept her awake. It was so strange to realize that the two men she had grown up knowing and loving as her father and brother were not even related to her at all! They may as well have been strangers. It made her rethink her entire past. And ponder life.

Crystal was ready to marry David. She was ready to do it, because it was Marsh Lee's wish that she do it. But though her lips told Marsh the words he wanted to hear, her very heart and soul rebelled against it, and the more she thought of it, the more she questioned whether or not she would be able to go through with it.

Crystal tried to put a positive light on it. After

all, some parents did arrange marriages, and they made such arrangements, often, with perfect strangers. At least, that wasn't the case here. David wasn't a stranger. David was her brother. Or, at least, he was a man who had been raised as her brother, and she had developed a sisterly love for him, despite his shortcomings.

Except for the last few years when David was away, they had lived together for as long as she could remember. What would change now? They would still live together, just as they always had.

No, Crystal thought. It would not be like it had always been. She was being asked to live with David now, not as his sister, but as his wife. She would be expected to share his bed.

Crystal blushed. There had been several times while she was growing up, that she had thought of sharing a man's bed. At first, she had thought of it in a way which was almost clinical, wondering from an intellectual standpoint, what it would be like. Then, as the changes in her body began to manifest themselves, the intellectual aspect of it dwindled, and she thought of sharing a bed with some nameless, faceless lover. Most recently, however, that man had been given a face and a name. Though circumstances had prevented it from happening, her body longed for, and her mind imagined, how it would have been had Willie not interrupted John and her on that last night at Trenton Town.

Crystal closed her eyes tightly to try to banish John Riley from her mind. There would be no John Riley now. She could never see him again, for to do so would make what she had to do even more difficult.

As Crystal thought of marrying David and sharing his bed, she suddenly recalled an incident which happened four years ago, just before Marsh sent David away. The boat had stopped on its journey downriver on a particularly hot day, and Crystal, knowing the location of a secret waterfall, left the boat as she did everytime they stopped there, and went to the waterfall to take a bath. Perhaps she wasn't the first one to discover the secret waterfall, but she had never seen anyone else there, and she had never told anyone about its location. It was a place she felt belonged to her, and to her alone, and she had no wish to share it with anyone.

When Crystal reached the waterfall she stood there, watching the water cascade down the side of the limestone bluffs, bouncing and tumbling across the rocks until it reached the bottom in a fine spray, there to fall into a pool so clear you could see the white pebbles shining brightly, even at its deepest point.

Crystal looked around, making certain no one else was here, then when she was sure she was alone, she took off her outer clothes and then her underthings. After all she was fourteen years old now, and she was well aware of a need for modesty. She stepped into the water and began splashing around happily, enjoying the refreshing coolness.

Suddenly her brother skittered down the side of a rock and jumped into the pool with her. He was as naked as she was!

"David!" Crystal screamed in a shocked voice. "What are you doing here?" She tried to cover herself, and she put one arm across her small, but well-formed breasts, and the other across her abdomen. Little droplets of water clung to her skin.

"I'm doing the same thing you are," David said, looking at her in open admiration. "I'm taking a bath." He began splashing water on himself.

"Have you gone crazy?" Crystal asked. "You get out of here! You shouldn't see me like this!"

"Why? I've seen you without your clothes," David said. "When you were a baby I watched you take your bath."

"Yes, but we were both young then. Now you're eighteen, and I'm fourteen, and things have changed."

"Oh," David said. "You mean you've grown here, is that it?" He reached out and touched her firm, young breasts. "Why are you so modest?" he asked. "You are a woman now. You should be proud. Look, it doesn't bother me for you to see me."

David turned to face her, and he grabbed himself and held *it* in his hand, a one-eyed serpent, ugly and revolting, yet, somehow fascinating too.

"You look like a woman," David said. "The question is, are you?"

"I . . . I don't know what you mean?" Crystal said.

"Let me show you," David replied. He stepped up to her then and took her in his arms, then pulled her against him. Crystal felt a pressure against the small triangle of wet hair at the junction of his legs. David tried to push in, but he couldn't do it.

"We can't do it this way," he said. "We'll have to lie down."

"No! What are you doin'?" Crystal screamed. She jerked away and ran back to the bank where she grabbed her clothes. "Stay away from me, David, or I'll tell Dad!"

"Come on, it'll make you feel good," David said. "You'll like it. I promise you, you'll like it. I've done it lots of times."

"No!" Crystal said.

David chuckled. "Is it because we're brother and sister? Don't worry about that. That's nothin' to worry about."

Crystal sat down on a rock and pulled her legs up, then wrapped her arms around her legs, rested her head on her knees and began to cry.

"Please," she said. "Please, just go away and leave me alone."

"All right," David said. "All right, I'll go. I guess I was wrong. You look like a woman, but you aren't. Ah . . . I don't have to mess with you anyway. There's a real woman on board now, and she's always glad to see me."

As Crystal recalled that incident, two things were clear to her now, which weren't clear to her then. One was David's strange statement not to worry about them being brother and sister. David knew, even then, that she wasn't his real sister, and that was what he was talking about. The other comment which became prophetic, was David's boast of knowing a real woman who was always glad to see him. That woman turned out to be Mrs. Moore, and her eagerness to see David anytime he wanted, resulted in the two of them being caught by Mrs. Moore's husband. That was what got David kicked off the boat, and that was why he was gone for the last four years.

Suddenly, Crystal felt guilty. Perhaps if she had allowed him to do what he wanted to do that time at the waterfall, he would not have gone to Mrs. Moore, and he wouldn't have been sent away. And if he hadn't been sent away, Crystal sighed. If he hadn't been sent away, what? Her father, that is, the man she had believed to be her father, would have still asked her to marry him. Perhaps, though, David would not have become as bitter had he stayed home, as he had become over the last four years.

Crystal watched the boat until the hunting party, six men including David, left the boat. They sauntered casually up the trail, carrying their rifles in a variety of ways, some with the weapon laid across the back of their neck with their arms folded over it, others with it across their shoulders, holding it by the barrel with the stock pointing up, while still others carried their rifles loosely, easily, in one hand, ready to raise them quickly, should game be suddenly encountered.

After the hunters disappeared, Crystal walked back down to the boat. Marsh was standing on the deck by the gangplank as Crystal stepped back on board.

"Where have you been?" Marsh asked.

Crystal glanced up at Castle Rock. "I was up there," she said.

"You must have left early."

"I left before dawn," Crystal admitted. "I had some thinking to do. I thought it would be a little easier if I could go off somewhere and be all alone for a little while. I hope you don't mind. Was I needed this morning?"

"No," Marsh said. "Nothing like that. It's just that, well, to tell the truth, I was a little afraid you might have left."

"Left?" Crystal said in a puzzled voice. "Left for where?"

"Just left," Marsh said. "For who knows where. After all, it must have come as quite a shock to you yesterday to learn the secret of your past. 'N seein' as I got no legal right to keep you aroun', why, I reckon you could leave near 'bout anytime you wanted to, 'n I couldn' do nothin' about it."

Crystal smiled, but, despite her smile, her eyes filled with tears.

"Dad, do you honestly think I could just go away and leave you? I don't care what you told me yesterday. As far as I am concerned, you are my dad. I know I couldn't love you any more if we were of the same blood, and I don't love you any less, now that I know. Don't ever worry that I'll just go off. I could never do that to you."

Marsh opened his arms and Crystal moved into them. The older man pulled the young girl against him, cushioning her head on his shoulders.

"Darlin', many is the time I've been proud of you in my life, but I don't know as I've ever been any prouder of you than I am right now."

They stood in each others embrace for a long moment, before Marsh finally dropped his arms and looked at Crystal. "Were you thinkin' about marryin' David?" he asked.

"Yes," Crystal admitted. "I was thinking about that."

"And are you still of a mind to?"

"I told you I would, and I will," Crystal said.

"Darlin', you've got no idea what a happy man that makes me," Marsh said. "To know that you and David'll be married, that at last you'll be a part of this family, not just in fact, but in name as well. Why, that means a lot to me!"

"David hasn't said anything about it," Crystal said.

"I haven't mentioned it to him yet," Marsh said.

A shadow came across his face then. What was it, Crystal wondered? Was it pain? Was it a slight worry that perhaps this was not the right thing to do after all?

"David hasn't quite . . . settled down, yet," Marsh went on. "I hoped bein' away all this time would change him. And I still hope that it has. Maybe the excitement of bein' back 'n all is still workin' on him. Anyway, I prefer to wait before I tell him. And I'd take it as a favor if you'd not mention anythin' to him until I've had a chance to talk to him."

"All right," Crystal agreed.

"Good girl," Marsh said, hugging her one more time before leaving to attend to some detail with the boat.

When the hunting party had not returned by noon, those who remained behind on the boat joked that they must have taken some whiskey with them, and were having a good time. By mid-afternoon, though, the jokes turned to worry, and by late afternoon, Captain Lee was putting together a search party. That was when Willie, who was on the hurricane deck, spotted them coming back.

"Cap'n Lee, Cap'n Lee, the hunting party is

returning," he called. "My word, there are Indians with them."

"Indians?" several of the passengers exclaimed in excitement. They crowded to the rails to watch the party return. Some watched the Indians out of curiosity. Others watched out of fear.

"Where are their guns?" someone suddenly asked.

"What?"

"Our men," the sharp-eyed observer said. "They all had rifles when they went out of here. Now none of 'em are armed."

"Oh, the Indians have the guns!" someone else said, and a buzz of apprehension passed through the boat.

That was when Crystal saw John Riley. He, like the Indians, was riding on horseback, whereas everyone in the boat's hunting party was on foot. John Riley, also like the Indians, was armed.

"It's all right, Dad," Crystal said. "There's John, and he is armed.

The crew of the *Missouri Mist* seeing that John was with the Indians, quickly calmed the rising fears of the passengers. Everyone on the crew remembered John from the passage upriver, and they knew that he was a good and trustworthy man.

"What is this?" Marsh asked. "Why are our hunters disarmed?"

Angry Wolf to give the deer to you as a gift. And, also, to make you a proposal."

"A proposal? What sort of proposal?"

"A trade," John said. "The Mandans will furnish you with fresh meat in exchange for a few items you might have."

"Please convey my thanks to Angry Wolf," Marsh said. "Tell him his gift is most generous."

"Generous?" David said. "You forget, I killed the deer in the first place."

"And you forget, that it wasn't our deer to kill," Marsh snapped back at his son. Marsh turned back to John. "Tell Angry Wolf, also, that we accept his offer, provided we have something he wants."

John took a piece of paper from his pocket and began to read. "Tobacco, coffee, salt, and, if you have them, some blankets."

"What is the rate of exchange?"

"Angry Wolf said he would accept my judgment on exchange."

"Then so shall I," Marsh said. He stuck out his hand and took John's, shaking it warmly. "Bring your meat aboard, and pick out whatever you think is fair."

"Don't do it, old man," David snarled. "You'll wind up lettin' that Indian lover steal us blind."

"From all I have been able to learn, you are the only one around here who steals," Marsh said. He pointed an angry, accusing finger at his son. "Now, you get some tobacco, coffee, salt and blankets up here. And you get good stuff, too. We're going to make a deal with Angry Wolf and the Mandans, and by God it's going to be a deal of honor."

"Honor?" David snorted.

"Yes," Marsh said. "I know that's a difficult word for you to deal with. But you're going to learn the meaning of it, if'n it kills me!"

"How long are you planning on laying up here?" John asked Marsh.

"About three days," Marsh answered.

John smiled. "In three days we could kill enough meat to get you all the way to New York."

"Thanks, John," Marsh said.

John smiled, then went back and swung up on his horse. Just before he turned to ride away, he looked over at Crystal and smiled again. She felt as if she had been struck in the heart. Never had she felt anything so sweet, and yet so bitter, as she thought of the love she felt for him. And yet, she knew that it was a love which would have to be denied.

Chapter Fifteen

The air was scented with the aroma of roast deer, and everywhere the boat men, crew and passengers sat around in contentment over the feast they had enjoyed, compliments of Angry Wolf.

The men who had been on the hunting party entertained the others with hair-raising tales of their adventurous encounter with the Indians, and as the hours wore on and the liquor flowed, the adventures became more dangerous with each telling.

David was on his way to becoming as drunk as he had on the previous two nights. It was not a pleasant drunk, for, whereas the others of the hunting party seemed to enjoy their adventure, David resented what had happened to him. He took John's intercession on their behalf as unwanted interference. He condemned the Indians, and John, and hinted darkly at what he would have done to the Indians if John hadn't come along, and what he still might do, if given the chance.

Crystal could take no more of it. She went to the part of the boat which would take her the greatest distance away from David and his drunken boasting, but she could still hear him, and the belligerency in his voice.

David had been on board for three nights, and he had drunk to excess each one. He drank to celebrate and he drank to get over his anger. Crystal was convinced that he also drank just for the sake of drinking. Maybe that was what her father meant when he said he wasn't ready to tell David about his plans, yet. For just an instant, Crystal had the irrational hope that her father would never find David ready for marriage and thus she could put off the dreaded moment forever.

Crystal looked down at the dark, winding water, then she looked up toward Castle Rock where she had watched the sun rise this very morning. She could see the dark, jagged outline of the rock, silhouetted against the star-dusted sky, and she got the sudden, irresistible urge to climb up there again. Let David continue to rant and rave at the others about his mistreatment today. She would be far enough away from him that she could put him completely out of her mind.

Quietly, Crystal walked down the gangplank until she was off the boat. Then, for the second time today, she climbed the path which led to Castle Rock.

The climb took about fifteen minutes, and when she reached the flat top of the rock, there was a soft carpet of moss under her feet. On impulse, Crystal slipped out of her shoes and ran across the rock like a child, with her hair streaming out behind her. She went to the edge of the rock and looked down over the river. She could see the same scene she had seen this morning, only instead of the golden hues of dawn, it was now displayed in the soft, night shades of silver and black. Only the boat itself escaped the unifying paint brush of evening, and it glistened a brilliant white, like a lily, clinging to the edge of a pond. It gleamed also from the several lamps which were giving out golden bubbles of light. From some part of the boat, someone was twanging a jewsharp, and the steady, monotonous beat intruded into the softness of the night.

Crystal heard footsteps behind her, and she turned quickly, to see who it was.

"I hoped you might slip away," John said. "I've been watching the boat, praying for the chance to see you alone."

"I . . . I have to go right back," Crystal said. She started to leave, but John reached out and grabbed her arm to stop her.

"No," he said. "You aren't going to leave yet. Not until we have had the opportunity to get a few things straight between us."

"We have nothing to get straight," Crystal said.

"We have everything to get straight," John said.

"You are hurting me."

John wasn't holding her tightly enough to hurt her, but she knew that as long as he was holding her at all, she was his prisoner.

"I'm sorry," John said. He let go of her, and she started to walk away, so he grabbed her again. "No," he said. "You aren't leaving. Not just yet. We have to talk!"

"What about?" Crystal asked.

"Crystal, do you remember the last time we were together? It was in the middle of the night at Trenton Town. A night just about like this one, and. . . ."

"I remember," Crystal said, blushing fiercely over his reminder. "You don't have to bring it up again. I remember."

"I not only remember," John said. "It occupies my every waking moment. It's all I think of. When I think of how close we came, only to. . . ."

"I don't want to talk about that," Crystal said.

"I love you," John said.

"I don't want to talk about that, either," Crystal said.

"Then I won't talk," John said, and suddenly he

pulled her to him and kissed her with hungry, burning lips.

Crystal felt her blood run hot and her skin flush and she knew that she was in danger of repeating the performance of Trenton Town.

"No," she finally said, breathlessly, as she broke away from the kiss. "No, we'll talk."

John smiled at her.

"That's more like it," he said.

"Do you have any parents?" Crystal suddenly asked.

"What?" John asked, surprised by the unexpected question.

"I want to talk about parents," Crystal said. "Do you have any?"

"No," John said. "My father was killed during the War Between the States. My mother died about ten years ago. Crystal, why do you ask such a question?"

"Because I've been thinking a lot about parents in the last few days," Crystal said. "I've been thinking, and I've been wondering."

"Wondering? Wondering what?"

"I've been wondering about my parents," Crystal said.

John chuckled. "What do you want to know about them?"

"The first thing I'd like to know is who are they?"

"Who are they? What do you mean? Captain Lee is your father, and. . . ."

"No," Crystal interrupted. "No, that's just it. I recently learned he isn't my father at all."

"I don't understand," John said. "If he isn't your father, then who is?"

"That's what I'd like to know," Crystal said. "I'm a waif, John. I was an unwanted baby, stuck in a canoe and set adrift in the river . . . just like Moses. Only, unlike Moses, no one from my family stayed around to watch after me. My real family doesn't know if I am dead or alive. They didn't care . . . they just abandoned me. I was lucky that Dad . . . that is, Captain Lee, came along when he did."

"That probably wasn't luck, Crystal," John said. "Don't you believe your real parents, whoever they are, planned it this way?"

"I don't know," Crystal said. "I just know that it is a hard thing to accept. To suddenly learn that I was abandoned, discarded like so much trash."

"I'm sure there is much more to the story than that," John said. "Anyway, you should look on the bright side of it. You did wind up with a family. I can't imagine a finer father for any girl than Marsh Lee. He has never treated you any differently than he would a natural daughter, has he?"

"No, never," Crystal said. "He has been marvelous to me, and I love him so. I could never love anyone else anymore."

"So, you see? You've lost nothing," John comforted. "Now, I can't say as I can speak too highly of your brother," he went on. "How he can be any relation to Marsh Lee is beyond me. Are you sure it was you he found in the canoe—and not David!"

"No, it was me!"

"Well, I don't suppose one man can be responsible for another, even if it is his own son. I'll not hold David Lee against the captain, though justice would certainly be better served if David would go away again. Only this time, it should be permanent. In fact, with very little encouragement, I could see to that."

"Oh, John, no," Crystal said. "Don't say that. You mustn't speak like that."

"Crystal, honey, look. I know you feel that you have to be defensive of him," John said. "After all, you have believed him to be your brother all this time. But now that you know the truth, you must realize you don't owe him a thing. You certainly don't owe him some misguided loyalty." John had called Crystal 'honey' and hearing him use that term of endearment just made it all the more difficult for Crystal. She was unable to stem the tears which began to flow.

"What is it?" John asked. He put his hand on her hair, touching it lightly, then he dropped his fingers down to her cheek and turned her head slightly, toward him. "Why are you crying?"

'Oh, John, you don't know," she said. "You

couldn't know what I told Dad I would do. What I *must* do."

John pulled his fingers away from Crystal's cheek, and looked into her face with an expression of apprehension, as if he knew what was coming next.

"What is it?" he asked.

"I . . . I promised Dad I would marry David," Crystal said quietly.

"You did what?" John asked. The question itself came out as a gasp.

"I promised Dad I would marry David," she said again, as quietly as before. "So you can see why, when you started to talk a moment ago, I had to cut you off. I had to stop you before you began to say words which could only mock us now."

"My God, girl, why would you do such a thing?" John asked. "Surely you can't love him? Surely you can't. . . ."

"Please," Crystal said, holding up her hand to stop him again. "Please, John, try to understand. I had to do it."

"Understand? No, I can't understand. I can't understand at all!" John said. "Crystal, do you love him? No, that is impossible, you couldn't love him."

"Yes," Crystal said. "At least, I have always told myself that I loved him. After all, I thought he was my brother, and. . . ."

"I don't mean *that* kind of love, Crystal, and you know it!" John spat. "I mean, do you love him as you love me?"

"As . . . I . . . love . . . you?" Crystal asked.

"Yes," John said. "You don't deny that you love me, do you?"

"John, please, don't ask me that," Crystal said. "You know I'm not at liberty to answer a question like that. I told you, I'm going to marry David. That is why I haven't let you get close to me. That is what I was thinking about before, at Trenton Town."

"Do you love me?" John asked again, saying the words slowly and distinctly, and setting the words apart to give equal emphasis to each one.

"John, I. . . ."

"Do you?" John asked again, more forcefully than before.

"Yes," Crystal said, very quietly. "Yes, John Riley. I love you."

"God, you don't know how much I have wanted to hear you say that," John said.

"John, I . . . I shouldn't have said it. I shouldn't have told you. I have no right to be speaking of such things to you, now."

"Yes, by God, you *do* have the right!" John said. "And I have the right to demand it of you. I'm taking the right for both of us. This is too precious a moment to let it escape, and I don't intend to let it pass us by."

John pulled her to him again, and again he kissed her. This time, Crystal began to return the kiss with a passion equal to his own. Then, from somewhere, she summoned the strength to pull away again.

"Please, no," she said. She was trembling in his arms now like a frightened bird. Tears spilled from her eyes. "John, I need your help. You must help me to fight it. I can't fight it all alone."

"Help you fight it? Do you hear what you are asking me, Crystal? You are asking me to deny everything I want, everything I care for in this world. No, I won't help you fight it. I can't help you fight it. I want you to become a part of it. I want you to share not only this moment but your whole life with me."

John tried to kiss her again, and when she turned her lips away to avoid him, he moved his kiss down to her neck. Her skin was incredibly warm, and the pulse in her neck was beating rapidly. For one instant she leaned against him, pressing her body to his, then she gasped for breath with a crying, pleading sound. "I beg of you," she said. "Don't you know what you are doing to me?"

A bewildering, frightening, overpowering sensation swept over Crystal. This was not her first time to be in this situation with John, and the sensations she was feeling were not unknown to her. At Trenton Town, she had abandoned all caution, and not only permitted, but urged him to go on,

further, beyond all limits. But she had not known
the terrible secret of her father's plan at Trenton
Town. Now she did know, and that made the
situation more difficult, more fraught with danger.

Despite all that, there was a part of her which
welcomed that danger. Indeed, it more than welcomed the danger, it embraced it with a wanton
desire. Crystal's hunger grew more intense as the
kiss deepened, and soon, she was at the same
degree of sweet agony she had been at Trenton
Town. And this time, there was no Willie to stop
them.

John's hot kisses lingered on her lips and she
bent to his pressure until she realized, with some
surprise, that they were lying down. She could
feel the soft moss beneath her. John's lips moved
hotly, relentlessly, down her throat and to the
nape of her neck. Crystal abandoned all pretense
of fighting him now, and she surrendered to his
will, eager to please and to be pleased.

John's fingers opened up her bodice and moved
underneath, across her scorching skin and to her
breast, warm and throbbing, straining to be touched.
A final, soft cry of protest formed in her throat,
only to emerge as a sigh of ecstasy. John's busy
hands finally freed her of all her clothes, until
Crystal was aware of a gentle breeze blowing, caressing her naked thighs, making her aware of
her nudity. Now she was as naked as the day she
was born, even more naked than she had been on

that sensuous night at Trenton Town, and she knew there was no stopping, and no turning back. It was a feeling so sensual and so delightful that the sensations of pleasure washed away any fear or embarrassment which she might otherwise have felt.

Crystal's legs were smooth and soft, under the hard, muscled limbs of John, and Crystal looked at their legs as if to steady herself. She tried hard to fix the image of them in her mind to catch up with events which were sweeping her along with dizzying speed.

Bubbles of fire ascended from somewhere deep inside, and Crystal hungered for the ultimate, the joining of their bodies which would fulfill the demands her own body was making. When finally John positioned his demanding body over her soft, yielding thighs, she didn't resist, but rose to meet him.

Crystal let out a low gasp of pain as he first entered, then a sharper exclamation as she felt him thrust into her. But the pain was so quickly washed away with the pleasure that she quickly forgot it. Now all pretense was put aside. No longer would she play the coy or the helpless young girl. Now, at last, she was a woman, and she was a woman with hungers and desires. She felt a need to be satisfied, and that need was being fulfilled. The stars which were so bright above her came down to her, or perhaps she went up to them. She didn't know which, because there suddenly burst over her a pleasure so exquisite that it defied all description. A hundred thousand tiny eddies of pleasure joined into one, rapturous explosion, and that was followed by another, and by yet another. Her skin tingled with exquisite ecstasy, and the stars became multi-colored lights which danced before her eyes as her body began jerking in orgasmic, convulsive shudders.

Crystal whimpered and moaned in her rapture, and her cries were buried in John's throat as he captured her mouth with his and used his tongue in a stabbing, darting motion to correspond with the powerful, sensory-laden thrusts below.

Crystal felt John grow tense, pause for a moment, and then, as if struck by lightning, he made one final, convulsive jerk as he spent his satisfaction in her. That was when suddenly, and unexpectedly, Crystal experienced new pleasures, achieving sensations so far above what she had already known, that she feared she would pass out. She hung precariously balanced on the precipice between consciousness and unconsciousness for several seconds, and during that time wave after wave of rapture burst over her, until all conscious awareness was redirected to absorb the experience.

And then, with every muscle in her body limp from fulfillment, she felt John slacken above her, and she put her arms around him and held him tightly to her, prolonging the moment that they were one.

Later, much later, John rolled off her, then he slid his arm under her so that her head rested upon his shoulder. Crystal didn't feel the least bit strange, lying naked on the top of a cliff in the arms of an equally naked man. In fact, it seemed almost as if they belonged here in this place and in this state together. Adam and Eve must have felt this way, she thought.

Finally, but only after several minutes of silence, John spoke.

"I love you," he said.

"I know," Crystal replied with a contented sigh.

"And you love me."

"Yes," she admitted.

"Then you can't do it," he said. "I won't let you. You can't marry anyone else."

Crystal tensed. Until that moment she had known contentment and satisfaction, just lying in his arms. It was a piece of eternity, shared in an instant. And now it was done, for by his comment he had reminded her that this was all still just a dream, after all. It was a wonderful fantasy, but it was just a fantasy and it could never really be attained. She was going to marry David. She had no other choice.

John felt her tense, and he sat up quickly and looked down at her.

"Crystal, no," he said. "No, you can't mean you are still going to marry him? Not after this? Not after we have been what we just were to each other?"

Crystal had not said a word, but so atuned were they to each other now that she didn't have to speak. John knew that she had made her decision.

"Oh, John," she said. "I have to, don't you understand? I owe it to my father, or at least, to the man who has been my father."

"No, you don't owe it to him," John said. "You know you don't love him, Crystal. You know you don't. It is time now for you to live your own life. He can't expect this of you."

"But he does," Crystal said. "And I have an obligation."

"What about the obligation you have to me? You do love me, don't you?"

"Yes," Crystal said. She began crying then. "I wish I didn't love you, John. It would be so much easier if I didn't."

John stood up and looked down at the girl who was crying softly. The last connection between them was broken now. A few moments before, they had shared only pleasure and passion, and the wonderous joy of life.

Now, they shared only pain.

Chapter Sixteen

When Crystal opened her eyes, she was aware of the throbbing of the engine and the motion of the boat. She lay there for a moment wondering about it, then she realized that it was late in the morning and the boat was already underway. Her father must have let her sleep late this morning.

Crystal had remained on the top of Castle Rock for several minutes after John left last night. She sat up there, all alone, until all the music and the laughter had died on the boat below, and the lamps had been extinguished one by one. When she finally did return to the boat, she was surprised to see her father standing on the deck in the darkness.

"I was beginning to get a little worried," he said. "But I saw you going up to the rock, and I figured you needed a little time to yourself."

"Thanks, Dad," Crystal replied.

"Is there anything you want to talk about?" Marsh asked.

"Talk about?" Crystal asked, nervously. What did he mean? He saw her go to the rock; did he follow her? Did he know she met John up on the rock. My God, did he know what they did up there? No, surely not! He wouldn't be this calm if he knew.

"Yes," Marsh said. "I know your life has suddenly changed, right before your eyes. I just want you to know that I'm always here if you need to talk about anything."

"No," Crystal said. "I'll be all right, Dad. You're right, it has been a drastic change, but I'll be all right."

Marsh put his arms around Crystal and pulled her to him. He hugged her tenderly.

"Darlin', believe me, if I didn't honestly think this was the best thing for both of you, I wouldn't do it," he said. "But it is—I believe it in my heart. Besides, it isn't like you have someone else, or somethin', now is it? Remember, I told you not to fall in love with anyone else."

"I remember, Dad," Crystal said.

"Good, good. Now, it's late. It's very late. Why don't you go on up to bed and get a good night's sleep. Everything will be all right tomorrow."

"I am tired," Crystal agreed.

"Goodnight, darlin'," Marsh said, kissing her

lightly on the cheek. "Remember. By tomorrow, everything will be just fine. You'll see."

"Goodnight, Dad," Crystal called back to him. She climbed the ladder well to the hurricane deck and the entrance to her cabin. Just before she went in, she looked back up at Castle Rock. There, just a short while ago, she had glimpsed the portals of heaven in the arms of the man she loved. But it was to be a glimpse only, for she was sure that never again would she know such passion.

Crystal dressed quickly, and as she did so, she felt a strange soreness in her loins which puzzled her for a moment. Then, as she realized what caused it, she felt a sudden warmth and a burst of pleasure, reliving for just an instant the rapture of the night before. But soon after that was the realization that the joy she had known last night would never—could never—be repeated. What she had done was wrong, even more so now that she was committed to marrying David.

When Crystal was dressed she stepped out of the cabin onto the hurricane deck. A long, frothy wake rolled out behind them as the boat pushed down river. Crystal could feel a fresh breeze in her face from the speed of the passage. It was good to be underway again.

"Good morning, Miss Crystal!" Willie yelled up to her. Willie was at the end of the boiler deck, working with a line. He smiled at her. "Did you enjoy sleeping in?"

"Why didn't someone wake me?" Crystal called. She looked at the sun which was almost at noon height. "I've never slept this late before."

"Well, maybe it was about time you did so, lass. After all, everyone is entitled to a rest every now and a bit, and I know of no one more entitled than you."

"Oh, but I must get to work right away," Crystal said. She started toward the wheelhouse, then stopped just before she got there, because inside, standing behind the wheel, was none other than her brother, or, at least the man she had always thought to be her brother. He smiled at Crystal as she stepped into the wheelhouse.

"Hello, Crystal," he said. "Isn't it a beautiful day, today? I'm glad you woke up before you missed all of it."

At first Crystal was prepared to make a response to counter his taunting, then she realized that he wasn't taunting her. In fact, he was being quite pleasant to her, and that surprised her.

"David," she said. "You look different."

And indeed, he did look different. Gone were the silks and suits of his cardsharp days, to be replaced by the blue serge of a riverboat officer. Gone too, was the almost constant look of belligerency he wore.

"I am different," he said. "For one thing, I'm sober." David laughed. "I haven't been completely sober in a long time," he said. "But I'm vowed to stay sober now."

"I'm glad," Crystal said.

"Are you, Crystal?" David asked. "Are you really glad?"

"Yes, of course," Crystal said. "Dad has worried about you, so. And the thing which has worried him most has been your drinking."

"No," David said. "I don't mean Pa. I mean *you*. Are you glad to see that I am staying sober?"

"Yes," Crystal said.

"Crystal, you don't know what that means to me," David said. "You don't know how glad I am to hear that. I'm doing it all for you, you know."

"For me?" Crystal said weakly. Now she knew, even before he said anything else, that Marsh Lee had told his son of his plans. Crystal felt a dizziness. She had hoped, an irrational hope she knew, that all this could be avoided. But it could not. The time had come to face up to it.

"Yes," David said. "Pa told me of the plans he has for us. Crystal, I want you to know that I think they are wonderful plans. Why, I'm so happy I could shout louder than this whistle."

Smiling broadly, and laughing, David pulled on the whistle cord, and the heavy bleat of the boat's whistle moved out across the flat water, hit the bluffs to either side of the river, then rolled back.

"I'm glad you are," Crystal said, surprised at David's reaction and the sudden turnabout in his attitude.

"What about you?" David asked. "Are you happy too?"

"I . . . I shall try to make a good wife for you, David," Crystal said, speaking quietly so she could cover up the fact that her heart was breaking.

"My wife!" He pulled the cord again, and again the whistle blew. Now, a few people moved forward on the boiler deck to see why the whistle was blowing, including the captain. Crystal saw him, then, because she was afraid she was going to cry and she didn't want him to see her tears, she turned away and walked to the rear of the hurricane deck: From here she could look down on the spinning paddlewheel from above.

"Are you all right?" a man's voice asked a moment later, and Crystal turned to see the man she had always thought of as her father, standing behind her.

"You . . . you told him," Crystal said, so quietly that her words could barely be heard above the thump of the engine and the slap of the paddlewheel. It wasn't a question, it was a simple, declarative statement.

"Yes," Marsh said.

"I thought you were going to wait and see if he had . . . matured any," she said, pausing to search for the right word.

Marsh sighed. "That had been my intention, yes," he said. "But that boy has drunk himself into a stupor every night since he returned. I was afraid that it would just keep getting worse, and I never would get a chance to test my idea, that being that you could be a calmin' effect on him. So, this mornin' I told him.

"Crystal, you should have seen him. You should have seen the way his eyes lighted up when I told him you would be his wife. Why, I've never seen anyone show such happiness. And right there, girl, that boy swore to me, in fact, he took a solemn oath on his mother's grave, that never again would he disgrace us, you nor me—either one—by drinkin' or by any other such action."

"Do you . . . do you believe him?" Crystal asked hesitantly, unsure of her own faith in him.

"Yes," Marsh said. "Yes, I do believe him. Oh, my darlin' daughter, I've always had a hope there was somethin' worth savin' in that boy, and now I think we're gonna be able to do it. And it's all because of you. You've made me a happy, happy man."

"I'm glad," Crystal said. She turned away from him and stared back over the paddlewheel, hoping that he would not see the tears which welled in her eyes.

"Cap'n, one of the passengers is asking for you," Willie said, coming aft on the hurricane deck at that moment.

"Thank you, Willie," Marsh said. "Oh, and Willie, would you spread the word among the crew? David and Crystal are to be married."

"No need to spread that word, Cap'n," Willie said. "David has already let everyone know. The only question remaining is—when?"

"When? Why, the sooner the better, I would think. We'll do it at Trenton Town. Yes, I think that would be the best place. After we make our turnaround downriver and come back, we'll plan to have the weddin' at Trenton Town. That'll be about six weeks from now, and it'll give everyone time to get used to it. You'd like to be married in Trenton Town, wouldn't you, Crystal? You've always liked that place. You've always liked Eb."

"Yes, Dad," Crystal said, without looking around. "I'd like to be married there."

Crystal continued to stand there for practically a full minute after Marsh left. Then, when she was sure he was gone, she turned around, only to gasp, because Willie was still standing behind her.

"Willie," she gasped in surprise. "What are you doing here?" She tried to wipe her eyes, but it was too late. He had already seen the tears.

"Aye, lass, it's just as I thought," Willie said.

"What is just as you thought?" Crystal asked. "What are you talking about?"

"You don't want to marry him, do you, Crystal?"

"Yes, of course I want to marry him," Crystal said. "You saw how happy Dad was. He, he. . . ." Crystal had to stop before she completely broke down.

"Your father is a wonderful man, lass," Willie said. "Indeed, I have often said, and I mean this from the bottom of my heart, there is no finer man on the river. And 'tis right you would wish to do something for a man with such qualities, for such is the nature of a daughter as loving and as gentle as yourself, even if you aren't his daughter, natural born. But Crystal," Willie went on, and Crystal noticed that this was the first time he had used her name without 'Miss' for as long as she could remember. " 'Twould be doing a great disservice to yourself, to your pa, and aye, even to the young lad, David, if you were to marry him without loving him."

"I love David," Crystal insisted.

"True, as a brother you love him," Willie said. "In fact, I love the lad myself, and regard him as a nephew of my own. But the love I feel for David comes from the love I feel for your father, blind though he may be in this case."

"Blind?" Crystal asked, not fully grasping what Willie was trying to say.

"Aye, blind, lass. I say that, for I can see that David is no good, and your pa cannot. I hate to see you exposed to David's own problems, for it'll only bring you sorrow and misery. Captain Marsh has no right to demand this of you."

"He didn't demand it," Crystal said, defending Marsh. "He just asked it of me and I'm willing to go through with it in order to make him happy."

"Go through with it?" Willie said. "Did you hear yourself then, darlin'? For surely if you were doing this with a light heart, you would choose words other than 'go *through* with it'."

"It was just an expression," Crystal defended.

"Yes, I can believe that," Willie said. "It was an expression of your true feelings."

"No," Crystal said. "Willie, you just don't understand. . . ."

"I understand," Willie said. "It's the cap'n who doesn't understand. But he'll understand after I've spoken to him, for I've no intention of standing by and watching you ruin your life just because you feel you owe something to him."

"I do owe something to him," Crystal said. "Don't you see, Willie? I owe him my very life."

"Then don't let him take what's remaining of it away from you," Willie said. "I tell you, I'm going to go see him!"

"No!" Crystal said. "Willie, you have no right to . . ."

"Let me remind you, 'twas me who pulled your little boat aboard that night so long ago," Willie said with a hurt expression on his face. "I've always figured I, too, had a proprietary right ever since then."

Crystal realized she had hurt his feelings, and she ran to put her arms around him. "Oh, Willie, I didn't mean that," she said. "Of course, you have the right. It's just that I don't want you to say anything. Please, Willie, let me do what I must do."

Willie sighed, and pulled her close to him, squeezing her affectionately.

"If you feel you must do this, then I suppose there is nothin' I can do to stop you. But I want you to know that I believe you are making a great mistake. I just wish there was some way I could talk you out of going through with it."

"I know," Crystal said. "I know you feel that way, Willie. And I want you to know that I appreciate your concern."

"It's a concern born of love, darlin', and of a genuine wish to see you happy," Willie said. "And if ever anything comes up where you think ole' Willie might be of service, you just let me know. Anything, anytime, no matter when or where it may be. Will you remember that?"

"How could I ever forget it?" Crystal said, smiling at Willie through her tears. "Oh, Willie, now that I know Dad isn't my real father, I can tell you even more truthfully how dear you are to me, for, indeed, you are really part of my family now. Thanks for being around all these years when I've needed you."

"You don't have to thank me for that," Willie said. "I want you to know that watching you grow up has been one of the happiest events of my life. You don't have to thank me for being around. Why, I wouldn't have missed it for all the tea in China."

Chapter Seventeen

John swung down from his horse and walked to the top of the mountain. From here he could see for miles, and the river snaked out way below him. It had been six weeks since his last glimpse of the *Missouri Mist*. Six weeks since that night on Castle Rock, when he learned that Crystal loved him as much as he loved her. Six weeks since he had heard the awful news that, despite the fact that she loved him, she was going to marry David. Crystal was the only woman he had ever loved, and the only woman he could ever love. But she was going to marry David, and bear children by him. David's children, instead of his.

John felt a nauseating sense of dizziness, then a moment of rage. He wished he had David Lee before him right now. He imagined David's smugly smiling face, complete with the diamond mark, as if it were floating in the air before him. John swung his fist at the imaginary face, hitting against it with everything he had.

Of course, there was no face there, and all he accomplished from his wild swing was a painful shoulder and a near wrench. He sighed and walked back to his horse, then slipped his canteen off the saddlehorn.

"Well, horse," he said. "We may as well not dwell on it. There's nothing we can do about it. She's going to marry him, and that's it."

John took a drink of water, then wiped his mouth with the back of his hand, put the top back on the canteen, and hung it from the saddle again. He had spent nearly a lifetime alone. Until he met Crystal, he was not only prepared, but perfectly willing, to spend the rest of his life alone. If that was the way it was to be, then so be it, he thought.

John swung back into his saddle, clucked at his horse, then rode off, away from the river. Perhaps if he didn't see the river, he wouldn't think of her. And if he didn't think of her, he wouldn't go out of his mind with the pain of it. He wished he could ride so far into the mountains that he never had to see, or think of the Missouri River again. But of course there was no way to do that. The river was the door to the Far West. It provided an avenue of exchange between the raw riches of the West, and the necessities of life from the East. It was wide and meandering; in some places little more than flowing mud, studded with dead tree trunks, and yet, it was the river of life to all who lived out West.

It hadn't always been the river of life. John thought of the tragedy of the *St. Peters*, a riverboat which had come up river in 1837. That was a long time ago, before he was born, and yet the *St. Peters* had left such a legacy of death that its story was still told around Indian campfires, and its history was recorded on the pictographs of a dozen winter-count chronicles.

The steamer *St. Peters* had come upriver to Fort Union, from St. Louis, carrying with it several passengers with visions of wealth from the riches of the new territories, and one passenger with small pox. . . .

When the boat stopped at Fort Clark, a Mandan Chief stole the blanket belonging to the infected passenger. Three days later the chief grew sick and died, but not before he had transmitted the disease to others, who, in turn, transmitted it to others. The Indians had no resistance to any of the white man's illnesses, and the disease swept through them like wind before a raging fire. They died by the hundreds, dying so quickly and so horribly that there was no time for ceremonial burial, or burial of any kind. The bodies were thrown off cliffs, leaving piles of bones which still existed. Within a few weeks all but thirty of the

1700 Mandans who lived near Fort Clark were dead. Many of them died by their own hands, leaping off the cliffs while still alive, preferring suicide to the slow, agonizing death they knew was waiting for them.

The *St. Peters,* not unmindful of what it had done, nevertheless continued on upriver. It carried its deadly cargo of death on, infecting the Assininboin Indians next, who in turn spread the disease on to the Crow and the Blackfeet. The deadly seed sown by the *St. Peters* took one full year to run its course, and by the time it was finished, more than 15,000 Northern Plains Indians had died. That was more Indians, John knew, than had been killed in all the wars, battles and engagements thus far fought with the white man.

For several years afterward, steamboats had to pay for the callousness of the *St. Peters,* because all the Indians were, quite naturally, suspect of them. At best the Indians refused to trade, denying game, skins, pelts, and other commodities which would have made the white man's trip upriver profitable. At worst, the Indians sometimes attacked the boats, burning them with fire arrows, or blocking their passage with mud and stick dams, then killing everyone on board.

It was only reluctantly that the Indians began to recognize the mutual benefits they derived in trading with the passengers and crews of the boats; thus safe passage was generally assured once again.

John's relationship with the Indians was one which had come about over a period of time and through a checkered course of events. He had grown up in Missouri where his father was killed during the Civil War. At the age of seventeen he left Missouri when a couple of distant cousins, Frank and Jesse James, began to achieve an unwanted degree of notoriety. He went West, where he represented himself as a plainsman and an expert guide and scout. He wasn't expert of course, at least, not when he started. But he was a courageous young man, and he did have a great deal of common sense, and those were the two prerequisites most needed for scouting service.

He became friends and worked with the great scout, William Comstock. John learned quickly, and when Comstock was killed, John became one of the most dependable of all remaining scouts.

John worked for Custer for two years before quitting in protest over the continued encroachment of white men and their support by the army into the Black Hills. The Black Hills had been guaranteed the Sioux by treaty.

"John, I don't blame you for leavin' this business," Charley Reynolds told John on the night he announced his intention to quit. Charley Reynolds was Custer's chief scout, and, like Comstock, was a close friend of John's. "All this business is goin' to come to a head real soon, you mark my words. The white man is a'lookin' for gold, and the Indian is determined to keep 'im out. They's gonna be a battle soon that'll be the greatest Indian battle ever fought on this here continent.

"There needn't be," John said. "If Custer would keep the prospectors out of the Black Hills the way he is supposed to, there wouldn't be any problem."

"Ha," Charley said. "Custer don't want to keep the prospectors out, 'cause he wants there to be a problem. Didn't you hear about the article in that *New York Magazine?* The writer quoted Custer as saying, 'Come on out to the Black Hills, fellers. You'll find gold nuggets just a'clingin' to the roots of grass. You can pull up a clump of weeds 'n make yourself a rich man.' And them was his exact words."

"But why?" John wanted to know. "Surely, Custer knows the trouble that can cause."

"Custer knows exactly the trouble that can cause," a familiar voice said behind them. John turned to see Custer standing there, leaning against the tent support pole. Custer preened his golden mustache. "But you see," Custer went on, "A Custer also knows that the trouble will be amply covered by the eastern press, and he understands the value of publicity."

John had worked for Custer for two years, and he was used to the fact that Custer often spoke of himself in third person.

"Publicity?"

"I want the name, 'Custer' to be known in every home in the United States. I don't want a man, woman or child, to hear the name without knowing who it is. You see, a man doesn't become president, unless he is known."

"President? Of the United States?" John asked. "General, are you serious?"

"Of course I am serious," Custer replied. "You should know me well enough by now to understand that I am never frivolous about such things. I am a firm believer in manifest destiny, and the manifest destiny of George Armstrong Custer is to occupy the highest office in the land."

"But, my God, President of the United States!" John said. "It is overwhelming just to think about it!"

"Presidents are but men, John, just like everyone else. They have to come from somewhere. Look at the man who currently occupies that position. A failed store clerk, a failed farmer, and, until the war came along to rescue his military career, a failed army officer."

"Yes, but the war did come along, and it did make him famous."

"Precisely my point. I, too, had the Civil War of course, and I, too, was a general. Unfortunately, I was known then as the 'Boy General,' and the public does not elect boy generals to the office of president. Therefore, I must re-establish my credibility as a leader, and that can't be done, just by playing nursemaid to a bunch of Indians on a reservation. I must go to the sound of the guns."

"Go to the sound of the guns? General, if you will pardon me, that's utter nonsense."

"I'm sorry you feel that way, John," Custer said. "I am certain you would have been a great help to me on the summer campaigns ahead."

"I wish you success in politics, General," John said. "But I hope you don't have to get to Washington over the bodies of a lot of good men, red and white."

"We all do what we must do," Custer replied. "It is my destiny to be president of these United States. It may very well be that in the overall scheme of things, a lot of men, a lot of good men, must die, in order that I can fulfill my destiny."

"Maybe so, General, but I sure don't plan to be one of them," John said, tendering his resignation on the spot.

John left the Army Scouting Service and began to make a living by trapping and hunting. The furs he sent back to St. Louis; the meat he sold to trading posts, railroad workers and riverboats. He learned to coexist with the Indians, becoming a friend to, rather than an enemy of, the red man.

That summer, which was the summer of 1876, Custer disregarded the advice of Charley Reynolds and divided his forces in the face of the largest concentration of Indians ever to assemble on the American continent. He ordered Major

Reno to take the opening sortie, an attack against a tremendously large Sioux and Cheyenne camp on the Little Bighorn River. Reno was not up to the task, and he failed in his attack, panicked, and lead a retreat which was so disorganized that many of his men didn't even know the retreat had been ordered. Those unfortunate men were trapped and they stayed back in a draw of timber to fight on alone. One of those who died in that lonely valley in Montana was Charley Reynolds. On that same day Custer and more than two hundred of his men were also killed, annihilated in a battle that quickly became legend.

To the Indians, the fight was known by its location. It had taken place in an area known as Greasy Grass, and by Greasy Grass, it was known. By that strange Indian telegraph, word of the fight, and of Custer's death, spread very quickly. John was one hundred miles away, but he learned of it on the very day it happened, and two days later, he was at the Little Big Horn. He watched as the members of the Seventh Cavalry went through the somber task of finding, and burying the men where they had fallen. John saw Charley Reynold's body, as well as the bodies of the Custers. Custer had died bravely, of that there was no doubt. But he had died foolishly, and, as a result of his foolishness, many had died with him. Included in the dead, were Custer's two brothers, one an army captain, the other merely a schoolboy on summer vacation. He also lost a brother-in-law and a nephew.

John respected the Indians, and their way of life, and, a measure of their respect for him was that they allowed him to continue to have freedom of movement through their territory, even after the Custer battle. When the army was ordered to push the Indians out of still more territory, Angry Wolf, chief of the Mandan, came to John and asked him to represent them in Washington. Though he wasn't 100 percent successful, he had, at least, turned back the army and preserved much of the Mandan land.

John continued to ride, thinking of his past and lamenting over the future that could have been, had he been fortunate enough to have Crystal's love in fact, as well as in spirit. Then, later in the day, he saw the new camp. He was surprised by it, because it was a camp where no camp was supposed to be. In the first place it was clearly beyond the boundaries imposed by the latest agreement, and in the second place, it was outside the normal hunting area used by the Mandans. Why would anyone be here, John wondered? And who was it?

John swung down from his horse, tied it off, then started walking toward the camp. To many this might have seemed like a foolish move, but John knew it was much easier to sneak up on an Indian encampment on foot, than on horseback.

A man could walk quietly, and keep below the skyline and not be seen. A horse made too much noise and was too big to hide. John also knew something else that many white men didn't know. John knew that, most likely, the encampment would be unguarded. He remembered riding into a Sioux camp with Bill Comstock, way back when he first started scouting. It was wintertime and it was cold, and the smoke from the tipi fires had alerted them for several miles that there was an Indian camp nearby.

"There are no guards," John observed in surprise as they approached.

"Would you stand guard in weather this cold?" Comstock asked.

"I'd have someone do it," John insisted.

"Who? Do you think anyone would volunteer to stand guard in this weather?"

"I don't know," John said. "It wouldn't be very pleasant."

"That's the way the Indians have it figured," Comstock said. "Standin' guard in weather like this is just about the most unpleasant thing around."

"But someone should do it," John said. "If no one volunteers, then someone should be appointed."

"Who does the appointin'," Comstock asked.

"Whoever is in command, I suppose," John answered.

Comstock laughed. "That's just it, sonny. There ain't nobody in command."

"What? What do you mean? What about the chief?"

Comstock laughed again. "Sonny, chiefs is somethin' the white man thought up. Ever' now 'n then some Indian will come along and his medicine will work for a while, and he'll get lucky in a few things, and folks'll listen to him. That is, they'll listen to him if they want to. But if they don't want to listen to him, well, that's all right too, because the Indians figure they got damn few equals and no superiors a'tall. Now, if a fella don't figure he's got 'ny superiors, he ain't likely to let someone tell him to go out 'n stand ass-deep in the snow to keep on the lookout."

True to Comstock's word, there had been no guards on the village that time, and there were no guards on the village John found himself approaching.

John stopped behind a rock just before the edge of the village, and he looked into it for a while, studying it, as he wondered who it was and why they were here. The mystery was solved a few moments later when the flap of one of the tipis opened and War Horse stepped outside, into the circle formed by the tents. War Horse was talking animatedly with another Indian who John didn't recognize. Then, as John studied the markings of the other Indian, he saw that it was not a Mandan but an Arikawa. Why would War Horse be talking to an Arikawa? He crept closer to the village, close enough to hear the conversation. He could speak a little Mandan and a little Arikawa, but not enough of either to eavesdrop on a conversation between two Indians speaking their own language. In this particular instance he was most fortunate, however, for the two Indians were talking in the one language which was universal to all Plains Indians. They were speaking in the tongue of the whites. English was their common ground of exchange.

"In three more days," the Arikawa was saying. "We will strike the boat at the Place of Much Sand."

The Epson Sandbar, John thought. It would be a good place for an attack, for the boats invariably had to grasshopper over the bar.

"Good," War Horse answered the Arikawa. "Your attack will be a sign to the others. The Missouri River on both sides is closed to the whites. Even the medicine of Angry Wolf cannot protect those whites who would try to violate our ancient and sacred river."

The medicine of Angry Wolf? John thought. Then he realized what War Horse was saying. He was planning on defying Angry Wolf's protection of the *Missouri Mist*. That was the boat he was going to attack.

Crystal was in great danger!

Chapter Eighteen

The *Missouri Mist* didn't go all the way to St. Louis on this trip. Instead, it made its turnaround at Omaha, thus taking nearly three weeks off the normal time of one of its trips.

Once in Omaha, Marsh gave Crystal enough money to go into town and buy a wedding dress. She bought one, but probably never had such a dress been bought with such a heavy heart.

The woman who altered the hem for her knew nothing of Crystal's heartbreak. As a result, she bubbled over with happiness and enthusiasm and talked in glowing terms about the beauty of marriage and how lovely Crystal would look in this dress when she walked down the aisle. All the time she was talking, Crystal was fighting hard to keep the tears from coming.

Oh, if only she could buy this gown for a wedding with John, then she would be as happy as the woman thought she was.

Crystal went into town to purchase her wedding dress, Willie, Pete and Hank visited their routine haunts, but David never left the boat. The whole time they were in Omaha, David stayed aboard. Marsh pointed that fact out to Crystal, as evidence of David's intention to keep his promise to reform. Willie confided to Crystal however, that he had heard talk in town to the effect that David's life might have been in danger had he ventured out. He still had enemies in Omaha, as in fact in most of the cities of the country.

Finally, after four days in the port of Omaha, the *Missouri Mist* pulled out into midstream and started beating its way back upriver, bound for Fort Benton.

But before it got there, it would reach Trenton Town, and there, in Trenton Town, Crystal would be married.

Even before John reached the river, he could hear the cannonading of the steam pressure relief valve. It boomed proudly, defiantly, and the thunder of its noise gathered up resonance from the sandstone bluffs and rolled across the breaks.

Once, from the top of a hill, John managed to get a view of the river, and there, coming around a distant bend, he saw the *Missouri Mist* beating its way back up river.

It would reach Epson Bar just before dark, though, early enough that they would be able to spar across it before it was too dark to see. It would be there where they were occupied with sparring and in a particularly vulnerable situation, that the Indians would attack. Begrudgingly, John had to acknowledge that the Indian plan was a good one. They had learned their lesson well over the past several years, and though they knew nothing about the mechanics of a steam engine, they did know, by now, its limitations, and they often put that knowledge to their good use.

As John continued on down the trail, he lost sight of the river again, though the sound of the boat never left his ears. It took him the better part of an hour to get to the water's edge, and in all that time he was able to mark the progress of the boat just by sound alone. Finally he came out on a large, flat, sandy section of riverbank and he stood there and waited, looking toward the bend at which he would first see the boat.

The noise grew louder as the boat approached, and finally, John could see the smoke rising above the trees and hills. At last the *Mist* itself appeared, swinging wide around the bend, picking its way carefully under the skillful piloting of either Crystal or Marsh, through the deepest part of the channel.

John took off his shirt and began waving it overhead, signaling for the boat to stop and put over a skiff for him.

"Bridge, there's a man signaling from the shore!" the lookout called.

Crystal was at the wheel, and she looked through the windows surrounding the wheelhouse, toward the man who was signaling for them to stop. She gasped when she saw that it was John.

"No, John, please!" she said under her breath. "Go away. Can't you see what this does to me?"

For an instant, but just for an instant, Crystal continued on as if she hadn't heard the lookout's shout. Marsh heard it, however, and he stepped out of his cabin to look toward the river's edge. Then he realized that Crystal had not signaled the engineer to stop engines.

"Darlin', didn't you hear the lookout?" Marsh asked. "We've a signal from the river bank."

Crystal telegraphed all engines to stop, and the paddlewheel halted as the boat drifted on under its momentum. She would have to pick him up now; she had no choice. If she refused to, she wouldn't be able to explain it to her father.

"I'm sorry," she called down. "I guess I didn't hear it."

Marsh looked at the man on the riverbank. "I wonder who it is?" he mused.

"It's John Riley," Crystal said, then she blushed

almost as quickly as she spoke the words, for if she knew who he was, then she certainly knew that he was signaling to be taken aboard.

Her father looked up at her, curiously, but she suddenly found something to study in the river, thus avoiding his gaze.

"David," Marsh called down to the boiler deck. "David, take a skiff over to the bank and pick up Mr. Riley."

"Pa, I don't think that's such a good idea," David protested.

"Oh? And why not, may I ask?"

"You know how he is with those Indians," David said. "How do we know this isn't some sort of a trick? He may be in with them. They may be planning to rob us."

"If you believe that then you have been too long in the East. You can measure the worth of a man by the man's actions, and I have total confidence in John Riley."

"I'll go get him if you say so," David said. "But I'm going to keep an eye on him, nevertheless."

Crystal listened to the exchange between Marsh and David, then she telegraphed the engineer to advance the engines just enough to hold their position against the river current. It was obvious that there was already bad blood between David and John, begun no doubt by the card game in which John had lost all his money. Crystal's father had explained the story to Crystal. The situation was certainly not improved from John's point of view, by the fact that David was soon to be Crystal's husband.

Crystal jockeyed the boat against the current and watched as the skiff rowed ashore, then returned with John. John climbed aboard, and spoke intensely to Marsh. Crystal could see them, but she had no idea what they were talking about. Whatever it was, she saw that David disagreed.

"You say the Arikawas are planning on attacking us?" Marsh asked.

"The Arikawas, and those Mandan who are following War Horse," John said.

"I don't believe it," David said. "Not for a minute do I believe any of it."

"Well, now, a few moments ago you were all set to believe there might be an Indian ambush," Marsh said. "What made you change your mind?"

"It's simple," David said. "Anything this man says, I believe just the opposite. Why would you warn us, anyway?" David asked John. "You are an Indian lover, aren't you? I would think you would be on their side."

"I'm on the side of justice," John said. "There have been times when the Indians didn't get justice and I am on their side in that. But this is something entirely different. War Horse is planning on attacking this boat when you begin to spar across Epson Bar. I just can't stand by and do nothing."

"Well, John, I thank you for your warning," Marsh said. "But the question now is, what, exactly, do we do about it? We have to go over Epson Bar, and when we do, we'll be there for them. There's no way we can avoid it."

"Perhaps there is," John suggested.

"If you have any ideas, I'm all for it," Marsh said.

"About what time do you expect to reach the bar?" John asked.

Marsh pulled out his pocket watch and looked at it. "I figure we'll make the bar at about five-thirty tonight," he said. "We'll grasshopper for about an hour or so, 'n we'll be through it by six-thirty or seven, just before it gets dark."

"Slow down the boat," John suggested.

"Slow down? What are you suggesting?"

"Slow down the boat so that you don't reach Epson Bar until later," John said. "Much later . . . say, around ten o'clock."

"Are you serious? You want us to take that bar at night? It's hard enough to take it when we have enough light to see what we are doing. It'll be even harder at night."

"Perhaps so, but at least we won't have the Indians to contend with."

"What do you mean?" David asked. "That would be the perfect time for them to hit us. We would be occupied by the bar, and it would be so dark they could sneak up on us."

"The Arikawa won't attack at night," John said. "They consider it bad medicine."

"Who are you trying to kid?" David asked.

"No," Marsh said. "That's right. I've heard the Indians won't attack at night."

"You may have heard it, but can you count on it?" David asked.

"I don't see that we have any choice," Marsh replied.

"Captain Lee, I don't want you to misunderstand," John said. "Some Indians will attack at night, and I'm sure even some Arikawa might. Indians are just like white men, some are more religious than others. The most religious ones won't attack at night because they think it will anger the Great Spirit. But you get someone who doesn't care, and it won't make any difference whether it's night or not."

"What do you think about these fellas?"

"Well, I think we are probably dealing with some pretty religious Indians," John said. "In fact, I think this whole war is a Holy War. They believe the land that was taken from them was given them by the Great Spirit in the first place. Anyone who would fight a war for that reason, has to have some religious convictions; therefore, I believe they won't attack us if we take the bar at night."

"We?" David said. "What do you mean, *we?*"

"I'll stay on the boat with you until you have cleared the bar," John said.

"Oh, no. I'm not having any Indian lover on board while we are just waiting for an Indian attack."

"David, be sensible! If we have any trouble, it will be good to have Mr. Riley along!"

"Humph," David snorted. "If we have any trouble, it will be *because* Mr. Riley is along."

"John Riley is welcome on board the *Missouri Mist* anytime he wants to come aboard," Marsh said, speaking in a tone of voice that informed David he had no intention of continuing this discussion.

David, realizing that he had lost the argument, snorted once, then spun angrily on his heel, and walked away.

"Captain, I don't want to talk out of turn here," John said. "But your son seems to have an awful lot of hate stored up inside."

"I know," Marsh said. He rubbed his chin and watched as David moved through the passengers toward the stern of the boat. "The thing is, I'm afraid it's all my fault. I think I may have made a mistake with that boy a few years ago. But I hope what I'm doing now makes up for it."

John knew that Marsh was talking about the marriage he had planned for David and Crystal, and he wanted to speak out against it now, to tell Marsh that he wasn't helping David, that he was ruining Crystal's life . . . as well as his own. But, for the time being at least, he said nothing.

"Well," Marsh said. "If we aren't going to try and make Epson Bar before dark, I may as well slow us down. Do you have any ideas what we should be doing in the meantime?"

"We might construct some walls to provide cover, just in case the Indians decide to fire on us from shore," John said. "Shift some of the cargo around to take advantage of it."

"All right," Marsh said. "And if we are going to grasshopper at night, I need to get everything ready for that as well."

"I'll see to the building of some barricades," John said. "If you don't mind, I'll get Willie to help me."

"No, of course I don't mind," Marsh said. "Take whomever you need. Draft some passengers, if need be."

The *Missouri Mist* was carrying several boxes of farm machinery, and because they were heavy, they provided excellent cover. John and Willie and several of the passengers spent the rest of the afternoon moving the cargo out to the edges of the deck, providing a large, sheltered area for the people to hide behind, just in case anyone did fire at them from the river's edge. By the time they were finished, it would have been virtually impossible for a chance shot from the shore to hit anyone.

During the afternoon, while John was busy, he

had no opportunity to speak with Crystal. For that, Crystal was thankful. In truth she didn't know how she would be able to handle it. It had been at least six weeks since that night on Castle Rock, but Crystal had only to look at him, and the intensity was just as great as it had been that night. She didn't think she could carry on a conversation with him, no matter how innocent.

Crystal stayed in the wheelhouse all afternoon because her father was busy making preparations for a night-sparring across the bar, and that meant she had to pilot the boat. Her situation had the advantage of insulating her from unwanted contact with John, but her unique position also gave her a commanding view of all that went on aboard. It seemed that John was in view all afternoon. As she was alone with her thoughts, and John was constantly in sight, he was also constantly in her mind, and she couldn't help think how things might have been.

Marsh came up to the wheelhouse just before dark, and he leaned against the doorframe and looked in at Crystal. He stroked his chin.

"You've done an excellent job all afternoon, darlin'," he said. "There's not another pilot on the river I would have trusted today."

"Thank you," Crystal said. "Do you want me to stay up here when we start to spar?"

"No," Marsh said. "I'm going to need someone with good eyes, and someone who can read the river, to be on the bow. Darlin', that means you are going to be pretty exposed if the Indians do try anything."

"Do you think they will?"

"I don't know," Marsh said. "I want to believe John Riley. He says they won't. I know David sure doesn't believe him."

"What does David know?" Crystal scoffed.

Marsh looked at Crystal with a strange expression on his face.

"Darlin', that doesn't sound like the confidence a girl should have in the man she is going to marry."

"I just meant, David hasn't been around Indians and John ... that is, Mr. Riley has," Crystal stammered.

"Yes," Marsh mused. "Yes, I suppose you are right on that score. Well, you'd better get on down there."

"All right, Dad," Crystal said. She smiled at Marsh. "And don't worry. Everything is going to be all right, I just feel it."

Crystal went down two flights of steps until she reached the main deck, then she went out onto the bow. As she looked back onto the deck she saw all the passengers huddled as instructed, behind the barricades which had been constructed around the outer edge of the boat.

Crystal also saw David, and she couldn't help but make the unkind comparison between David, who was staying carefully behind the barricades, and John, who was carelessly exposed as he helped to fit the sparring poles.

"Ready to spar, Cap'n" Willie called up. Willie and Pete would handle the poles, while Hank would handle the steam capstan. Crystal took her place out on the bow.

Under Crystal's guidance they came to the first bar, then, gently, the bow slid upon it until they were grounded.

"Spar," she called.

"All right, laddies, here we go now," Willie said. He put his pole down into the water. A few seconds later, Pete had his pole down, then they signaled Hank, who opened the throttle on the engine which operated the capstan. The capstan began winding up, pulling on the cable, and the cable put tension on the spars. The front of the boat was lifted slightly, and the paddlewheel churned mightily, whipping up a muddy froth at the rear of the boat. Gradually the boat began to slide forward, until finally enough of it was over the bar that it could move under its own power. After only a hundred or so feet, they had to spar again.

John had nothing to do with the sparring, as the crew was quite skilled at that particular operation. John did keep his eyes on the shore, however, and, though he said nothing to anyone on board lest he unduly frighten them, he saw the Indians watching them. He held his breath and said a little prayer, and his prayer was answered, for the Indians, deciding that this particular boat wasn't worth violating their religious code, let it pass through the bar unmolested.

It took a lot longer to negotiate the bar at night than it would have had they done it during the daylight hours, so it was nearly midnight by the time they were free and clear, and started up the other side. Long before that, however, John saw that the Indians had given up and left.

"Thank, Bill," he said under his breath, thanking Bill Comstock. He had learned from Comstock that most Indians didn't like to attack at night. He'd also learned that Indians didn't like to make war at all, unless the odds were strongly in their favor. Now that the odds were no longer in favor of War Horse, there was every chance that the *Missouri Mist* wouldn't be bothered at all.

John went up to the wheelhouse to tell Marsh that he felt they were out of danger. Marsh thanked him for his help, and offered to take him anywhere he wanted to go, but John just asked to be put ashore.

"I'm obliged to you, John Riley," Marsh said. "I figure you saved our skin on this. Oh, by the way, I'd like you to come to the weddin'. You will come, won't you?"

"The wedding?"

"Yes. Didn't you know? My son is marrying Crystal. Crystal isn't my real daughter, you know.

So this marriage will take care of that. It's going to take place at Trenton Town next week. If all the boats are keepin' pretty close to their schedule, there should be about four or five boats tied up there then, so we will have quite a shindig. Won't you come? There'll be lots of dancin' and drinkin' goin' on."

"Oh, I don't know, Captain Lee," John said. "I just can't believe I would be very welcome at something like that."

"Nonsense, you're welcome because I say you're welcome," Marsh said. "Oh, I know David doesn't seem to think too much of you now, but the truth is, I figure that's nothin' but embarrassment 'bout as much as anythin' else. He knows that you know he was a card cheat. But that's all behind him now, and I'm hopin' he's turned over a new leaf. But, in the meantime, you could come to the wedding, for Crystal's sake. I know she likes you, and I know she'd want you to be there."

"I'm not so sure about that, either," John said. Then he smiled. "But I'll tell you what. I'll be there, provided you don't say anything about it to either one of them in advance."

"You got yourself a deal," Marsh said. "Now, just go on down and see Willie. He'll see to it that you get ashore. Thanks again, John Riley. I'll see you at the weddin'."

John waved good-bye to Marsh, then went back down to the main deck to look for Willie. He asked Hank about him, and Hank said he thought he had seen Willie at the stern of the boat. John went back there, but he didn't see Willie. Instead, he saw Crystal standing in the same spot he had seen her so many times before, just aft of the starboard engine, listening to the rhythm of the pistons, and watching the paddlewheel slap against the water.

"Hello," he said.

Crystal was startled by his sudden appearance, and she jumped at the sound of his voice.

"I'm sorry," he said. "I didn't mean to frighten you."

"That's all right," she said.

"I'm about to go ashore," John said. "But I didn't want to go until I had a chance to talk to you. We haven't spoken since I came aboard."

"I don't think we should speak," Crystal said.

"Why not?"

"John, you *know* why not," Crystal said. "Please, don't do this. Don't make it any more difficult than it already is, for you or for me."

"I'm sorry, Crystal," John said. "But you see, that is exactly what I intend to do. I intend to make it as difficult as I possibly can. Don't you understand? I love you, and I don't want you to marry David. And if I can make it difficult, then I will. In fact, I hope this makes it impossible."

Before Crystal could react to his last statement, John grabbed her and pulled her to him, and kissed her, deeply, passionately, crushing her against him. For an instant, she forgot time and place, and some wild, insane desire inside her told her that she would let him have his way with her. If he wanted to, he could have her now, and she wouldn't resist. But, thankfully for her, John had the strength she didn't have, and he broke off the kiss, then looked at her with deep, penetrating eyes.

"Yes," he said. "I want to make it very difficult."

Chapter Nineteen

The appearance of two or more boats at Trenton Town was considered a social event. Four or more was a social event of major significance, and to add a wedding on top of that made it the main event of the year. The fact that the girl getting married was Crystal Lee made it even more important, so boats actually altered their sailing schedule in order to be present for the wedding.

The wedding was set for eleven o'clock in the morning, and by nine the crowd had already gathered. Not only the *Missouri Mist* but all the boats were decorated with bunting and garlands of wild flowers. Signs congratulating the couple were everywhere.

David was leaning against the railing of the *Missouri Mist*, looking out at all the activity with an expression of bemused interest. He was drinking quietly, but very heavily.

"Aren't you drinkin' a bit too heavily lad?" Willie asked. "I mean, this bein' your weddin' day 'n all."

"Ha!" David said, laughing without mirth. "You, the biggest drunk on the river, are going to tell me about drinking? After all the times my father has had to pull you and your drunken cronies out of jail?"

"Aye, lad, you have me there, for I've been known to imbibe a bit too freely on more than one occasion. And, I confess, I'm not the one to be preachin' the evils of demon rum. But, lad, this be your weddin' day."

David held his glass up and it caught a shaft of sunlight, split the light into a spectrum, and projected a rainbow burst of color against the deck. "Well, then let us say I am drinking to the happy event."

David finished what was in his glass, then started back for more.

Willie shook his head sadly, then walked away to look for Captain Lee. Perhaps the Captain had no idea of what he was actually doing to Crystal.

Marsh Lee was nowhere to be found on board the *Missouri Mist*, nor was he on either of the adjacent boats. Willie finally thought to walk up the path to the trading post, and look for him there.

Willie shook his head sadly as he climbed up the path. Everywhere he looked he saw people; laughing, dancing, eating, drinking, all having a wonderful time at this most wonderful of all parties . . . and yet, all at Crystal's expense. How ironic that the celebration was for a girl who had no cause to celebrate.

Inside the trading post the band was playing, and squares were already formed for dancing, though Eb, traditionally the caller, was not calling. Willie walked over to the bar.

"What'll you have? It's all free today," the bartender said, wiping the bar down with a damp cloth.

"Nothing, thank you, friend," Willie said.

"What's that? Nothing you say? The bartender gasped. "Willie, are you ill?" Mockingly, the bartender put his hand to Willie's forehead.

"Enough of that," Willie said, pushing his hand away. "I'm a man who enjoys his drink, but I'm also a man who can pay his way. I don't have to drink just because it's free. Now tell me, would you have seen Cap'n Lee, by chance?"

"Yeah, I saw him," the bartender said. He pointed to some stairs at the back of the room. "He went up those stairs with Eb. You'll find 'em both up there."

"Thanks," Willie said.

Willie pushed his way through the crowd of celebrants, a crowd which seemed to grow with each passing second, until he reached the bottom of the stairs. He looked up the stairs, then drew a deep breath before we went up. Probably he had no business butting in like this. But he thought it was time someone talked to Captain Lee and told him just what the score was.

"Oh, she may have been infatuated with him, Eb. But I wouldn't go so far as to say she was in love with him," Marsh's voice was saying as Willie reached the top of the steps. Marsh and Eb were just inside a small room, right off the landing, and Willie could hear them easily. He stayed just outside for a moment before he went in, listening to their conversation, since it obviously pertained to the subject he also wished to discuss.

"I tell you she is in love with John Riley," Eb said. "She told me as much."

"Crystal told you that?" Marsh said.

"That she did."

"But, when did she tell you such a thing? And why has she never mentioned it to me?"

"She told me some time ago, when you delivered John back from his trip to Washington. You'll remember we had a dance here?"

Marsh laughed "That long ago? Well, excuse me, Eb, but you haven't been around young girls as I have. Why, I happen to know that a time that long is almost like two or three years to Crystal. I've no doubt that she thought she was in love with John Riley. But that was before David returned, and that was before I told her what I had in mind for her. And, after all, John is a handsome fellow, and a nice enough sort. I can see how she may have been attracted to him. Believe me, though, that's all over now. Indeed, if it ever really existed, that is. Now she wants to marry David. Why, she has told me so, half a dozen times."

"And you believe her when she tells you that, Cap'n?" Willie suddenly asked, stepping into the room at that moment.

Willie's unexpected appearance startled the two men who thought they had found a private place to conduct their conversation.

"Willie, what are you doing here?" Marsh asked.

"Pardon me for buttin' in, Cap'n. I know it ain't my place. But I got the same interest in Crystal's welfare I've always had, and I figure it's time I say somethin'."

"Willie, you are the oldest and most trusted crew member I have," Marsh said. "And I like to call you friend. But you have no say-so in this at all."

"Pardon me, Cap'n, but I beg to differ with you. I figure I have as much say-so as you do, seein' as you never legally adopted her, and I was the one who brought her aboard that night."

"But I'm the one she calls 'Dad'," Marsh said. "And it's father I am to her."

"How can you call yourself 'father' to the lass and force her into a marriage like this?" Willie asked.

"Believe me," Marsh said. "I've thought this marriage through, and I'm convinced it is the best thing for her. It is the best thing for both of them."

"Tell me, Marsh," Eb said. "How can a marriage to a woman who doesn't love him, be good for David?"

"David needs a good woman to settle him down," Marsh said stubbornly. "I know Crystal can be that woman. I've discussed it with her, and she understands what her role is to be. Look, maybe she doesn't love him in the manner of the romantic fairytales. But she does love him and that is more than most marriages have. Trust me! I'm doing what I think is best for both my children."

"Uh, huh," Eb said. "Now, you be truthful with me, Marsh. If the situation was the other way around, if Crystal was your real daughter 'n David a tyke you found in a basket, would you still be all hot to get 'em wed? Would you really want your daughter marryin' someone who has raised as much hell as David, knowin' the unhappiness he has caused?"

Marsh looked at Eb with an expression of surprise on his face, as if he had not previously considered the situation from that point of view. He paused for a long moment.

"Well, would you?" Eb asked again.

Marsh sighed. "I . . . I won't lie to you, Eb. But the truth is, I just don't know." He shook his head. "I just don't know," he said again, quietly.

"Then, I'll answer for you," Willie put in. "You wouldn't do it, and you know it! Cap'n, that boy is down there right now, gettin' drunker'n a hoot owl, 'n here it is on the very mornin' of his weddin'. Are you goin' to marry Crystal up with the likes of him?"

Marsh sighed, then looked at both men with an expression which was an appeal for help.

"Please, try to understand," he said. "I've thought this out several times, and I'm convinced that I'm doing the right thing. We're going through with it. Crystal is marrying David—and that's that!

In another part of the trading post, in the room that had been Crystal's for many years now, Crystal was getting ready for the wedding. She was standing in front of a mirror, and a heavy-set woman, named Martha Brown, was helping her get dressed. Martha was the wife of the captain of the *River Queen*, one of the other boats tied up at Trenton Town.

"Oh, what a lovely dress," Martha said, as she looked at the white gown. "Where did you get it?"

"I got it in Omaha," Crystal said.

Martha ran her hand across the lace bodice and clucked her tongue. "I've never seen one more beautiful," she said. "I didn't have such a dress for my own weddin'." Martha chuckled. "Of course, I was a mail-order bride. I was just happy to have a weddin' at all."

"You were a mail-order bride? What is that?" Crystal asked.

"I read an ad in the paper that there was a shortage of wives in the Northwest," Martha said. "So, I put an ad in a newspaper saying I would come West and marry any man who would pay my way out. Captain Brown was that man."

"You didn't know him?"

"I never set eyes on him 'till our weddin' day," Martha said.

"Mrs. Brown, have you been . . . that is, are you happy?"

"Yes, of course!" Martha said. "And I'm sure you will be as well."

There was a crashing sound from outside, then loud laughter. Shortly afterward the music began again.

"Listen to the laughter," Martha said. "Everyone is so happy for you."

"They must be terribly confused," Crystal said. "First they think of me as David's sister, and now they must get used to the idea of my being his wife."

"Everyone knows now," Martha said. "There's no confusion anymore."

"You knew all along, didn't you?" Crystal asked.

"Yes," Martha said.

"I must have been a big joke to everyone," Crystal said. Everyone knew the truth about me. Everyone but me. I didn't know anything."

"Believe me, darling, no one treated it as a joke. And besides, there weren't that many who actually knew. I knew, because my husband and Captain Lee are old and fast friends. And I was a friend of your moth. . . . that is, of Mrs. Lee. Oh, how she would have loved you, if she had been alive when you were found."

"Oh, Mrs. Brown, I . . . I need a woman friend now," Crystal said, and suddenly tears spilled from her eyes.

Martha was moved by the young girl's poignant cry, and, quickly, she put her arms around her and cushioned her against her rather ample bosom.

"Dear," she said. "You have me."

"I just don't know," Crystal sobbed.

"You just don't know what, dear?"

"I just don't know if I am doing the right thing."

Martha smiled. "Oh, is that all? Why, every girl worries about that on her weddin' day. Of course you're doin' the right thing. It's only natural that you would be a little nervous right now . . . a little frightened. After all, you're going to be married soon, and that's a big step."

"I thought girls were supposed to be happy on their wedding day," Crystal said. "I thought I was supposed to be in love with the man I was going to marry."

"Why, surely you love David?" Martha asked. "After all, you've known him for all these years."

"I thought I loved him as my brother," Crystal said. "But I've never been in love with him."

"Heavens, child, consider yourself very lucky. At least you know him. Remember, I didn't even know Captain Brown when we were married. And yet, it worked out very, very well. And it will work out well for you too—you'll see. Now, wipe your eyes and put a smile on your face. Everyone has come to see a beautiful bride, and they can't see one if she's crying."

The wedding ceremony had a sense of unreality to it. Crystal would have preferred an Episcopal priest to perform the wedding, but the nearest vicar was in Omaha, many miles away. Instead, the service was performed by a perfect stranger, a passenger in one of the other boats, who was going West to start his own church. The preacher had railed long and loud to all who would listen, how he and the Lord had both been betrayed by the organized churches which were prevalent back East. Only out here, the preacher insisted, could a ray of light and a breath of fresh air be let into a new church, to be formed by him for the glory of God. His new church would be called the Church of God Through the Word of Jeremiah, because when he was looking for a name he decided to leave it in the hands of the Lord. He let the Bible drop open of its own accord. It fell open to the Book of Jeremiah.

The preacher was dressed, not in black, but in white, in order, he explained, to better show the stains of sin. Crystal wasn't too sure of the stains of sin, but she saw several food and tobacco stains on his clothes, as well as many other stains of an undetermined origin.

The music for the wedding was provided by the same group of musicians who had provided the music for the square dancing, and some of the square dancers voiced a little irritation that the wedding party would be interrupted by something as trivial as the wedding.

Crystal processed to the makeshift altar on the arms of her father, and as she looked at him, and saw how happy he appeared to be, it fortified her decision that she was doing the correct thing. After all, maybe Mrs. Brown was right. Maybe everything would work out for the better.

David was already standing at the altar as Crystal approached, and he watched her with a rather laconic smile on his face.

The music stopped and Crystal took her place beside David and faced the preacher.

The preacher looked at Crystal and David and then out over the people who were gathered for the ceremony. There was, in the preacher's eyes, a somewhat wild, somewhat frightening look, and if Crystal felt uneasy about her wedding to begin with, he certainly did nothing to ease the situation.

"It is written in the Book of Jeremiah," the preacher began, "In the seventh chapter and the thirty-fourth verse; 'Then will I cause to cease from the cities of Judah, and from the streets of Jerusalem, the voice of mirth and the voice of gladness, the voice of the bridegroom and the voice of the bride: for the land shall be desolate'."

Crystal looked up in surprise. This was clearly not the "Dearly Beloved" ceremony she had witnessed before.

"Our Lord, speaking through the prophet Jeremiah, mentions the role of the woman in marriage, in chapter three, verses eight, and nine. 'And I saw, when for all the causes, whereby backsliding Israel committed adultery, I had put her away and given her a bill of divorce; yet her treacherous sister Judah feared not, but went and played the harlot also. And it came to pass through the lightness of her whoredom, that she defiled the land, and committed adultery with stones and with sticks.' "

The preacher continued in that vein, citing chapter and verse in a convoluted marriage ceremony, until finally, he proclaimed, by the powers vested in him, Crystal and David were man and wife.

Chapter Twenty

The grandest salon on the most elegant boat of the small fleet was given over to the newlyweds for their wedding night. The *Delta Miss*, a boat once used on the Mississippi River, and thus considerably more elegant, if not more practical than the others, was one of the boats docked at Trenton Town. The captain of the *Delta Miss* was an old friend of Marsh's, and he insisted that the Royal Stateroom be used. The Royal Stateroom was extremely elegant, and it was justified in using the name, "Royal," since it was once used by a Russian prince during an American visit.

It was nearly dark when Crystal finally went to the stateroom. She was embarrassed by the fact that everyone watching her knew where she was going and what would be going on there. She tried not to look into their eyes but she couldn't avoid it. In the men's eyes, she saw unrestrained envy of David. Only in Willie and Eb's eyes did she see sympathy, but she couldn't look at them, either, for fear that, somehow, she had let them down.

Crystal learned that John Riley had been invited, but, fortunately, he was not present. For that, Crystal breathed a sigh of relief.

The Royal Suite had a bathroom, and Crystal felt a sense of gratitude when she saw it. If ever she needed a bath, she felt, it was now. There was something about this entire ceremony which seemed unclean.

Later, after the bath and the toweling had left her body pink and clean, Crystal put on a dark-green, silk, sleeping gown. The silk clung to her body like a second skin, and as she examined herself in the gilt-edged mirror, she saw every curve and dip of her body. Even the two nipples protruded through the silk to form two, sharp points.

Crystal sat at the dresser mirror and brushed her hair with long, luxurious strokes as she waited for David. Within a short time her hair was glowing like the shining brass in the bell she kept so polished. Her red hair, contrasting with the green silk of her nightgown, created a picture of loveliness.

There was a light knock on the door, and for just an instant Crystal felt a knot in her stomach.

It would be David, and he was here to claim that which was his right. Could she go through with it?"

"Crystal?" a man's voice called quietly. "Crystal, it's me."

"Dad?" Crystal said in surprise, recognizing the unexpected voice of her father. "Dad, is that you?"

"Yes, darlin'."

Crystal got up from the dresser and moved quickly to the door, then opened it. "Dad, what is it?" she asked. "What's wrong?"

Marsh was standing on the other side of the door, with a long, sad expression on his face. When he saw his daughter he gasped in surprise.

"My God, child, what a beautiful woman you have become," he said. Then he sighed. "And to think that I must come to you on this night of all nights to tell you what a fool I have been."

"Dad, what is it? I don't understand," Crystal said.

"It's your broth ... hus ... it's David," Marsh said.

"What about him?"

"As you know, he's been drinking heavily all day. I turned my eyes from it, and tried to pass it off as nervousness. I guess I just didn't want to admit that he had failed ... that I had failed. Anyway, as I said, he was drinking all day, and he was probably not aware of what he was doing," Marsh said. "I don't suppose that excuses him, but it might help explain what happened. What he did."

"Dad, what did he do?"

"There was a card game," Marsh said. "I know David's history with gambling, especially with cards. I should have been more alert. I should have stopped him. But I didn't, and David was caught cheating. There was a scene, and David wound up pulling his gun and shooting a man."

"Oh, Dad, no!" Crystal gasped. "Was the man killed?"

"No, thank God," Marsh said. "As it turns out, he wasn't even hurt all that bad. But David didn't stay around to find out. He stole one of Eb's horses and headed into the hills. He's run off, Crystal."

"I'm sorry, Dad. I'm sorry for you that it didn't work out the way you wanted," Crystal said. She sighed. "But I must confess to being relieved that this night is being postponed."

"It's not being postponed," Marsh said.

"What do you mean?"

"It's being cancelled," Marsh said resolutely. "Darlin', I'm that big a fool I wouldn't listen to anyone. Willie tried to tell me and Eb tried to tell me that I was making a mistake, but I wouldn't listen. Now I know what a mistake I made, and if there is anyway we can get out of this marriage that quack preacher performed, we're goin' to do it. Even if it means havin' you file for a bill of divorcement."

"A bill of divorcement?" Crystal gasped. "Dad, you can't be serious?"

"I know, a divorce is a drastic mistake," Marsh said. "But darlin' the mistake I made is a drastic mistake, and it may be that a divorce is the only way out. At any rate, I promise you, you will never have to be a wife to David. I only hope you can forgive me, and I only hope I haven't lost your love."

"Dad," Crystal said, smiling through her tears and putting her arms around him. "I've never loved you more than at this very moment."

"Go," David shouted to the panting horse between his legs. "Go, you dumb beast, go!"

David was frightened. What he had done, he had done in full view of everyone. There were well over one hundred witnesses to his act.

What will I do? he thought. How will I get away? Everyone there saw me shoot that man. They will come for me, and I will hang! Oh, God, I will hang!

The horse labored under David's insistent whipping, answering David's urging to go faster and ever faster, until its entire body was covered with lather. Still, David urged the horse on, until finally, just as it reached the top of a long, mountain pass, it fell dead from its labors.

David was thrown when the horse fell, but he got up without injury. Without looking back to the horse, without regard for the animal who had just burst his heart on David's behalf, David continued on his flight.

David ran until he was exhausted, and could run no more. He found a rock and sat on it, sucking in great draughts of air, until he managed to get his breath back, and, with his breath, some of his senses. The unreasonable fear of being caught and hanged in the very next moment left, as he realized that no one could have followed him this far, this quickly. He was free, and he would remain free.

David laughed. "I'm sorry to have to spoil your fun," he said aloud. "But you won't be hanging David Lee today."

Of course, he realized, he wouldn't be enjoying Crystal today, either.

David thought of Crystal, waiting patiently, dutifully, like a wife should, back in her bed. Their bed. Their nuptial bed.

David recalled the incident under the waterfall some years before. He had watched her during those changing years, spying on her as she bathed, or removed her layers of clothes, or, simply examined her own budding body in pubescent curiosity.

David realized that she wasn't his sister. He remembered when the little canoe had been brought aboard. He resented the fact that she was being raised as his sister. If she was treated as his sister, then she would be entitled to property which was rightfully his. And, because she thought she was his sister, she fought him off at the waterfall that time.

David wondered what Crystal thought when she learned that she wasn't related to him by blood. He laughed as he considered the difficulty she must have had in realizing that she was going to marry him . . . and share his bed.

Of course, what Crystal didn't realize was that his bed was all she was going to share. David intended to enjoy her sexual favors until he tired of them. He had spent a lifetime lusting after her, and he intended to satisfy that lust. But, as far as he was concerned, that was all. He had no intention of being a husband to her, nor did he intend to change his ways, despite the foolish dream of his foolish father.

David let out a disgusted sigh. Why couldn't he have just waited twenty-four more hours, though? By getting into a card game before he had the chance to enjoy Crystal, he had spoiled his own pudding.

Chapter Twenty One

Marsh thought Crystal deserved some privacy on this night, especially in light of all that had happened. He also did not want to have to subject her to any undue curiosity, and if she left the Royal Suite to return to the *Missouri Mist*, people would surely ask questions of her. Therefore, Marsh suggested that Crystal stay the night in the Royal Suite, just as she had originally planned. Reluctantly, Crystal agreed.

Perhaps it was because she was tired from the long day, or, perhaps she was numbed by the way events had turned out. Whatever the cause, she discovered that she was exceptionally tired when she finally turned down the flame on the gimbal lamp and crawled into bed. As a result, sleep came very quickly.

She was sound asleep when a light, tapping sound on the door to the cabin finally got through to her. At first she couldn't determine whether or not she was still dreaming, as the knocking seemed to be a part of her dream. Finally she realized that it was not a dream, it was actually happening, and she woke up to discover that the sound was coming from her door.

Crystal sat up, fully awake now, and heard the knocking again. She found a match on the table by her bed and she lit the gimbal lantern, then turned it up until a soft, golden bubble of light illuminated the stateroom.

"Crystal," a voice called. The voice was low and muffled, and she couldn't identify it by sound. Nevertheless, she moved toward it, forgetting to put a robe on over her green silk nightgown. She opened the door and there, standing in the soft glow of the golden lantern, she saw John Riley.

"John," she said. "It's you! What are you doing here?"

"You may have noticed," John said. "I was not at your wedding today."

Quickly, Crystal looked away from him toward the floor, and she had to blink her eyes several times to keep tears from forming.

"Please," she said. "John, please don't mock me so."

"I don't mean to mock you," John said. "I heard what happened. I'm sorry for all you have had to go through, but I tell you now, I am glad it turned out as it did. I couldn't stand to think of you in someone else's arms." John reached for her and tried to put his arms around her, but she took a cautious step back.

"No, John, you mustn't," she said quickly. "I'm a married woman, now."

"That's nonsense!" John said. "That is utter nonsense. You are no more married now, than you were last night. I don't recognize that marriage, do you understand me? It did not occur."

"But it did occur," Crystal said sadly. "At least, in the eyes of the law it occurred. And now, when it is too late, Dad admitted that he had made a mistake, that he should not have made me go through with it."

"Now?" John said in a pained voice. "He admits it now? But what can be done now?"

"Dad said I should get a divorce," Crystal said. "But I . . . I can't do that. I would be a marked woman for the rest of my life."

"Yes, you can do it," John said. "And the only mark you would bear would be the mark of my wife, for I would marry you as quickly as I possibly could."

"But a divorce," Crystal said. "I don't know, I just don't think I could. . . ."

"Better divorce than murder," John said. "And I tell you truly, the reason I wasn't here today was because I feared I would commit murder if I came. I was that mad with jealousy."

"Oh, darling, how I have made you suffer," Crystal said then, and this time she went to him.

"Darling?" John said happily. "Did you hear yourself then? You called me 'darling'." John put his hands on her shoulders and leaned away from her so he could look into her face. "Oh, sweetheart, I'm so happy now that I could shout for joy."

"No!" Crystal said. "No, you mustn't do that."

"Well, there's only one way you can keep me quiet," John said. "And that is to kiss me."

"No," Crystal said. "No, John, we mustn't. I told you, I am a married woman, and. . . ." What Crystal was going to say was that she couldn't control herself when John kissed her. She didn't get a chance to tell him that, though, because John sealed her lips shut with the very kiss she was protesting against.

Crystal struggled against it, but John was persistent, and finally Crystal felt herself giving up the struggle. His kiss burned through to the secret, innermost chamber of her very soul, and she grew dizzy. His hot, hungry lips forced hers apart, and his wet tongue moved inside and she felt its thrilling pressure in her mouth.

Crystal felt every fiber of her body grow weak under this relentless assault, and, as before, she knew that she had progressed beyond the point of return. Now she was his, to do with as he so desired. Not for a long, sweet, while, did the kiss end, and when finally it did, Crystal's knees were so weak that she had to lean against John for support. The nipples of her breasts, protruding against the silk gown, pressed into John's chest, and were so sensitized that even the movement of his breathing sent ripples of pleasure up and down her spine.

"John, please, you . . . must . . . go," Crystal said, making one final bid to resist, though she not only knew it would be futile, she wanted it to be.

"You know you don't really want me to go," John said, caressing her breasts, his warm breath whispering to her. "You know you want me as badly as I want you."

John picked Crystal up and carried her over to her bed, then lay her down on it. Her gown was down around her waist. She was weak before his animal strength, and weak before her own sensual desires. She was a married woman. If she had sinned before, this was a sin of even greater proportions, and yet, the sounds which came from her lips weren't sounds of protest, as much as they were sounds of ecstasy.

After John lay Crystal on the bed, then slowly, as if being in this room with her was his right, he lifted her gown up and pulled it over her head.

Crystal felt her gown being removed, and she felt the cool breath of air against her naked skin as she lay there and watched in the light of the lantern, while John removed his own clothes. She saw clearly, and for the first time, unobstructed either by shadow or distance, the broad expanse of his chest, the flat muscles of his abdomen, and the virility of his erect manhood. When all his clothes were removed he lay on the bed with her, and she felt his muscled body against her own.

It seemed to Crystal that her nipples had never been so tightly drawn, or as sensitive as they were now, and they ached with pleasure as John began moving his hands and fingers about her body. John's lips moved from Crystal's lips to her throat, and then to her shoulders, and then Crystal felt a delightful tingling, as if the wings of a humming-bird had brushed against her, and she saw his lips at her nipples. And felt the flame ignite at the center of her being.

John's tongue, hands and fingers played upon the soul strings of Crystal's sensitivity with such sensual manipulation, that Crystal was unable to discern the individual caresses from the overwhelming pulsating sensations that overtook her.

The blood in Crystal's veins turned to molten gold as she hungered for the ultimate: the joining of their bodies which would fulfill the demands her own body was now making.

Finally, John was over her and then inside her, as he thrust deeply into her very being. Crystal rose to meet him, and she clutched at him, digging her nails into his back, and nibbling hungrily at his neck with her teeth and tongue.

On deck outside the stateroom, someone walked by and John heard them and stopped for a second, holding himself rigidly in position over her, with his manhood still straining inside her. The thought crossed Crystal's mind that she was a married woman, spending her wedding night, not with her husband, but with the man she loved. As such, she was subject to discovery and humiliation. Yet that very real danger seemed only to heighten the pleasure she was feeling at this very moment, and even as John remained motionless over her, she felt herself dissolving into white-hot, liquid pleasure, throbbing in orgasmic spasms which pulled at that part of him which was inside of her.

Then, when they heard nothing else, John began anew, and Crystal felt a rebirth of ecstasy. Her skin heated, then tingled, with a million pinpricks of rapture and the golden light of the lantern seemed as brilliant as the sun and as soft as the moon.

Crystal whimpered and moaned in her rapture, and her cries were buried in John's throat as he approached his own release. Crystal felt John grow tense, pause for a moment, and then, as if struck by lightning, make one final, convulsive lunge as he spent himself in her. It was at that precise moment that Crystal managed to reach a new level, much higher than anything she had ever attained, or had imagined that she could attain.

There were two more after that: one nearly as strong, the other, not quite as strong, but intensely satisfying in its own right, and during those moments of shared pleasure, it seemed as if Crystal could feel what John was feeling, and experience what he was experiencing, so that they became not two individuals but a merged entity of pleasure, a conscious form of energy and love.

As Crystal coasted down from the peak, she came down by degrees, like a blossom floating in the river, meeting new eddies of pleasure, going back against the current a bit before slipping farther down. Finally, when every whirlpool and swirl had been explored and there was nothing left but the residual energy of what had been explosive rapture, they lay together, lost in the love they felt for each other, and in the pleasure of contact from one body to the other.

John made no immediate effort to disengage himself. Instead he continued to lay on her, and she delighted in the feel of his body against hers and the relaxed, gentle, though still intensely pleasurable sensations she was feeling. By their act here tonight, Crystal knew that they had sealed their love, once and for all.

It mattered not that she was married to another,

nor did it matter that her only hope of escape from that loveless affair would be through the scandal of divorce. Now she knew that she and John had joined their souls as one.

They had reached their magic moment in the continuum of eternity.

Chapter Twenty-Two

The *Missouri Mist* left Trenton Town to continue its trip upriver with Crystal in possession of a new name, but no husband. David did not make a subsequent appearance at Trenton Town after the cheating and shooting episode.

The man who was shot was not seriously injured, and the fact that he was awarded the pot, plus Marsh Lee's personal appeal to him, convinced him not to prefer charges against David. David was therefore free to return if he so desired, without fear of arrest or punishment. Despite that, David did not come back, and he had not returned by the time the boat left Trenton Town. As a result, the *Missouri Mist* left without him.

Under normal circumstances such a thing would have been embarrassing to Crystal, even to the point of humiliation. But these were not normal circumstances and the truth of the matter was that Crystal was elated that David was not with them. Because of that, she was able to face the passengers and the others with her head held high. Let them think what they will, she was happy.

There was, of course, another reason why she was happy. She had shared her love with John in a way which had transcended all legal and moral boundaries. Perhaps what she and John had done was wrong. Perhaps they had no right to the happiness which had been theirs on her wedding night, but whether they had a right to it or not, they had taken it. And that was the only thing that was important now. She knew that, somehow, she would find a way to give herself to John forever. That happy thought kept her buoyant during the difficult, and embarrassing days that followed her ill-starred wedding.

By the time the *Missouri Mist* reached Fort Benton, Montana, let off its passengers and off-loaded its cargo, the immediate embarrassment had passed. There, the riverboat would be picking up new passengers for the return trip, as well as cargo bound all the way to St. Louis, and points in-between. The new passengers knew nothing about the wedding, or, if they did, it was only from talk. They had not been actual witnesses to the event, and thus Crystal could look at them without feeling their scorn, or, perhaps worse, their pity. By now, things had nearly returned to normal. In fact, the only abnormal thing about the return trip was the cargo. Marsh Lee had agreed to carry one hundred thousand dollars in gold bullion, the gold having been transferred from a gold mine in Montana to a bank in St. Louis.

"You've agreed to carry gold bullion? But we have no safe secure enough for something like that," Crystal had protested.

"No one will know we are carrying it," Marsh insisted.

"What? How are you going to keep them from knowing? Something that big and that heavy is not easily hidden."

"We have disguised it," Marsh said. "And the way we have disguised it is absolutely brilliant. Each bar of gold has been covered with a thin layer of lead. As a bar of gold and a bar of lead are nearly equal in weight, our charade can be easily carried out. That way, no one but the mining company itself, and we, of course, know of the shipment. It will be stacked with their cargo in plain sight, but no one will ever suspect."

"I suppose that is an ingenious way of transporting it," Crystal agreed. "But still, the idea of being responsible for so much gold is frightening."

"I'm not belittling the danger, Crystal," Marsh said. "I'm just saying that we have taken every precaution to reduce that danger to the lowest possible amount. Despite all that, I have still demanded, and received, the highest possible tariff for its transport. This one trip shall make our entire season," he added with a broad grin.

"I'm certain it will," Crystal said, returning her father's smile. "And I apologize if it sounds as if I am not enthusiastic about it. I suppose it is just my nature to be worried."

"I know it is, darlin'," Marsh said. "And I almost didn't tell you for that very reason. In fact, I cautioned David against mentioning it to you because I didn't want to worry you. But with David gone now, I feel you need to know, just as a precautionary measure."

"David knows?" Crystal asked in a quiet voice.

"Yes," Marsh said. "I told him shortly after I made the contract."

"Dad, are you sure that was wise?"

"Why, what do you mean?" Marsh asked.

"Crystal, surely you aren't suggesting that it was a mistake to tell David? You don't really believe David would. . . ."

"I'm not suggesting anything in particular," Crystal interrupted. "But, as David has gone, who knows where, we don't know who he'll be seeing, or what he'll be talking about. Isn't it possible that he could let it slip that we are carrying gold?"

"No," Marsh said resolutely. "I can believe a lot of things about my son, including the fact that he is not fit to be your husband, but I could never believe that he would be so irresponsible that he would place us in some danger. I'm sure we are safe, at least on that score."

"I'm sure you are right, Dad," Crystal said. "I'm sure there will be no trouble."

It wasn't much of a horse, but when one stole a horse, one couldn't be choosy. Especially if the horse came from a farm, miles from nowhere.

The horse was probably a plowhorse, but it had been broken to saddle, and for that, David was glad. He hoped, though, that he would not be put into a position to have to make a run for it. This horse had probably never run a step in its plow-pulling life.

David swung off the horse, brushed some of the trail dust away from his clothes, checked his whiskey bottle, then started toward the campfire. He had seen the campfire from quite a distance and had gone to it anxious to see another soul.

David made certain that he was seen as he approached the campfire. That was so as not to startle the man by the fire, for, out in the wilderness, it was considered poor form to come up on someone unexpectedly. It was such poor form that it could get a person killed.

"I've got whiskey," David said, holding up the bottle. "If you're a drinking man, that is."

"Ole' Angus Pugh has been known to take a drink ever' now 'n again," the man by the fire said, reaching for the bottle David offered him. "Don't mind if I do, thankee."

"Angus Pugh?" David said. "You are Angus Pugh?"

The man took a long drink from the bottle, then wiped the back of his hand across his mouth before he answered.

"I may be, then ag'in, maybe I ain't," he said. "Who's askin' 'n why?"

"The name is Lee. David Lee," David said. "I'd like to do some business with you. If you are Angus Pugh, that is. I think I can make it worth your time."

"I'm Angus Pugh," the man said. "State your business."

"Mr. Pugh, I heard you tried to ship your black gunpowder up the Missouri River on my father's boat."

David had heard that story told half a dozen times since coming back on board. Willie had relished telling how Crystal had stood up to him, and how John had taken the gun away from him.

"Your father's boat?" Pugh said. He squinted at David. "Lee, yeah, that was the name all right. Marsh Lee, he was the Cap'n, and some upstart of a young girl was his First Officer. They threw me off the boat. I had to buy mules, and I been packin' my way up river ever since. As you can see, I still got a long way to go . . . may not make it before the first snow flies."

"I can guarantee you'll make it," David said.

"Eh? What's that? You are goin' to guarantee that I make it? And how's that to be?"

"I'm going to take over the boat," David said. "And when I do, I'll transport you and your powder to any place you want to go. Provided, of course, that you assist me in taking over the boat."

"You are goin' to take over the boat? What about your pa?"

"We'll put him over in a skiff," David said.

"Ha!" Pugh said. "You don't expect me to believe that, do you? You'd be puttin' your own pa over in a skiff?"

"Why not?" David asked coolly. "That's what the son of a bitch did to me."

"What about the snot-nosed daughter of his? You gonna put her over too?"

David smiled an evil smile at Pugh. "Well, now, Mr. Pugh. Perhaps you've been out with your mules too long," David suggested. "If you can't think of anything better to do with my sister than put her over in a skiff."

Pugh's eyes narrowed. "Mr. are you suggestin' what I think you're suggestin'?"

"My sister is a pretty girl, is she not?" David asked. "Or, maybe pretty girls don't interest you."

"They interest me plenty," Pugh said. "But, bein' as she is your sister, I thought perhaps . . ."

"Don't trouble yourself about that," David said. "In fact, you can consider that your bonus, if you help me out. I'll get you and your gunpowder up river and you can have your way with my sister. Now, how about it? Can I count on you for some help?"

Pugh rubbed his hand across the unkempt beard on his chin, and he studied David for a long time before he spoke.

"What kind of help are you wantin' from me?" he finally asked.

"About ten miles from here, the river passes through some narrow rapids. If we were to plant some explosives in the bluffs alongside the river we could close it down. If we waited until they were in the narrow chutes, we could close down each end of it, and trap the boat inside. They would have no way out, except by blasting their way out. And we would be the only source of gunpowder."

"What about the crew on board?" Pugh asked. "I seem to recall one fella, he spoke with an accent of some kind, an English fella I think he was. Anyway, he doesn't seem likely to be the kind that would just stand by'n let us take over. He was awful loyal to the girl. And there was one big, strong son of a bitch dressed in mountain clothes."

"The big man is no longer there," David said. "And it is the loyalty of the Englishman that I am counting on, for if he fears any harm would come to Crystal, he wouldn't do anything. Don't worry about him, or any of the others. I can take care of them."

"I reckon you can at that," Pugh said. "I got to hand it to you, mister, for pure ole' cussedness, I don't know as I've ever met anyone any meaner."

"Yes. Well, the question is, Mr. Pugh, can I count on your help?"

"You are doin' all this just to get control of the boat? Don't you think your pa can just lay in wait for you'n take the boat back whenever you come back up river?"

"By then, it'll be too late," David said. "I will already have removed the cargo."

"The cargo? What cargo?"

"Nothing much," David said. "It's just a shipment of lead."

"Lead? You are goin' to jerk a cinch into your own pa over a shipment of lead?"

"Let's just say I owe him something," David said. "Now, what do you say? Will you support me?"

Pugh smiled evilly. "Yeah," he said. "I'll support you."

There were thirty-six bars of gold, each bar coated with lead, and packed, six to a box, in six boxes. The printing on the outside of the boxes read: "To Missouri Lead Company, Virburnum, Missouri." Not even the most trusted crew members realized what the boxes actually contained, and they stacked them on the cargo deck with no more thought or concern than if they were lead bars. For that reason no one seemed to pay any special attention to them and when the *Missouri Mist* departed Fort Benton, it did so without the hoopla that would normally be attendant to a vessel transporting one hundred thousand dollars worth of gold.

The first couple of weeks of the trip down river passed without incident. Crystal spent her time at the wheel and any other moments she had alone, thinking of John, and of the love she felt for him. She had not yet told her father how she felt. Her father was now disposed toward helping her get a divorce, and she didn't want anything to change his mind. If her father approved of her divorce, then perhaps the resultant scandal could eventually be lived down. It was important if she and John were to have any chance at all of making their marriage go that this abominable marriage be put behind her.

John had left her stateroom after that wonderful night of shared bliss, the night that was her wedding night, only after she had confessed that her love for him was stronger than any further loyalty she might feel for Marsh. He had demanded, and Crystal had agreed, that somehow she would find a way to belong to him. Though she had willingly agreed to his demand, she nevertheless, begged that he leave before he was discovered, in order to give her time to work things out. Reluctantly, John agreed that it would be best if no one knew of his visit, so, even as the morning birds began their sweet song, he kissed her and left, vowing to return when the *Missouri Mist* returned to Trenton Town. That was the day of reckoning, and that day would be here tomorrow, for they were nearly back to Trenton Town on their passage back down river.

Crystal was at the wheel as the boat churned its way downriver, moving quickly with the current. It was not only the current pushing the boat. Crystal was sure that at least half the propulsion power of the boat was coming from her heart. Tomorrow, Trenton Town. Tomorrow, John. Tomorrow, she would see her love again!

"Your pa wanted me to remind you that we are coming into the narrow rapids just up ahead," Willie said, putting his head in through the wheelhouse door.

"I know, I know," Crystal said, happily. "I've been traveling this river ever since I was a little girl, but he always feels it is necessary to warn me."

"Your pa is a cautious man, that's all," Willie said. Willie looked at Crystal, and he saw the smile on her face. "Excuse me for buttin' in, but if you don't want other folks findin' out about John, you'd better try and hold that smile back."

"What?" Crystal gasped, shocked by the statement. "Willie, what are you talking about?"

Willie smiled. "Let's just say that up 'till now, I've been pretty good at keepin' a secret. But it's not doin' much good for me to keep the secret if you can't, and that smile is goin' to give you away."

"I'm, I'm sure I don't know what you are talking about," Crystal said, and her cheeks flamed pink as she blushed.

"Listen, girl, I'm not condemnin' you, why, I'm so happy for you that I can hardly keep from smilin' myself. But the truth is, I saw John leavin' your stateroom early on the mornin' after you and David were wed."

"You . . . you saw?" Crystal asked in a small voice.

"Aye. I was on mornin' deck watch, 'n I saw him sneakin' out of your room. I knew what had been goin' on, and 'twas glad I was for you. But, darlin', 'tis a secret ill-kept, if you go 'round with a big grin on your face all the time. For the truth is, by other folks' way of thinkin', you've had very little to smile about of late. When is he comin'?"

"What makes you think he's coming?"

"Why else would you be smilin'?" Willie asked.

Crystal was unable to keep up the charade any longer, and finally she smiled sheepishly.

"I'm glad you know, Willie," she said. "I'm glad for the opportunity to share it with someone. Oh, Willie, he's coming aboard tomorrow when we dock at Trenton Town. He's going with me when I get my divorce, and we're going to be married as soon as we can after that."

"Good for you, darlin'," Willie said.

"I know I'll be scandalized for life," Crystal went on. "I'll always be known as a shameless hussy, a divorced woman—but I don't care. I love John enough that it doesn't matter to me."

"Darlin', you're not a shameless woman who's divorcin' for some sinful reason," Willie said. "You are a loving daughter who did what you did because you thought to please the man you call 'Pa.' The Lord will look at your divorce and he'll take it kindly, that I can promise you. But I want to warn you now, there are those who won't, and all the love you feel for John, and all the love he feels for you, won't be enough to ease all the hurts that'll come to you. I just want you to know that, and to be ready for it when the time comes."

"I know," Crystal said then, and for a moment, the smile she had worn for the last couple of days left, to be replaced by an expression of determination. She had already surmised what Willie just told her. The best excuses for a divorce in the world did not change the fact. She had taken a vow of marriage and now she was going back on that vow. "But I'm still going through with it," she added.

Willie smiled. "I never had any doubt in my heart," he said. "And when you start sufferin'

from the slings and arrows, as it were, know that
here is one who loves you, and who will stand
beside you for as long as there is breath in my
body."

"I know that, too, Willie. And I want you to
know how much that means to me."

"White water ahead! White water ahead!" the
lookout on the bow called, and Crystal prepared
to shoot through the narrow rapids. She had taken
the boat through the rapids going upstream many
times. Going upstream the paddlewheel was just
barely able to overcome the current, and with the
pressure of the water against the rudders and the
paddlewheel beating against the current, it was a
relatively easy transit. Going downstream was something else entirely. Now the water against the rudders didn't improve control, it hindered control.
And even with the paddlewheel in reverse, the
current still took charge. Crystal had been at the
wheel going downstream only two or three times.
She was pleased that her father thought enough
of her ability to handle the situation that he not
only let her steer, he didn't even bother to come
up to the wheelhouse.

That is, he didn't come until the explosion

The explosion, when it came, was a complete
surprise to Crystal. She was concentrating so hard
on negotiating the rapids that she didn't see the
side of the bluffs erupting until she heard the

loud noise. And then, when she did look up, she saw tons of rocks falling into the river.

"Dad, to the wheelhouse!" she called, while at the same time signaling the engine room. "All back, full!" The paddlewheel had been turning slowly back, anyway, and now, with her signal, it began spinning at top speed. The boat shuddered under the effect and the bow began to swing around.

"Give 'er her head!" Marsh shouted, running up the stairs to the hurricane deck. "Let 'er come about!"

At her father's shout, Crystal let the boat swing around of its own volition, so that they were heading back upstream. By the time the boat was heading upstream again, Marsh was back at the wheel, and he had already signaled the engine room 'all ahead full'."

"Dad, what is it?" Crystal asked, still puzzled by the strange sight of half a mountain sliding down into the water.

"Someone is tryin' to dam us up," Marsh said. "They're tryin' to stop us."

"Indians?" Crystal asked. "But, where would Indians get dynamite?"

"It ain't Indians, darlin'," Marsh said resolutely.

Suddenly there was another explosion, this time at the opposite end of the straits, so that the effect was to bottle them up inside the rapids.

"Whoever it is, they know their business," Marsh

said. "We can't sit out here in the rapids, we are goin' to have to put in ashore. They've got us just where they want us."

"But I don't understand," Crystal said. "If it isn't Indians, *who* is it? And why would they want us ashore?"

"You forget, that ain't lead we're a'carryin'," Marsh said.

"You mean . . . you mean someone is after our gold? But . . . who knows about it?"

"There's your answer right over there!" Marsh said.

Crystal looked in the direction indicated by her father, and there, standing at the only possible place to land the boat, she saw a smiling David Lee.

Chapter Twenty-Three

"David, what is the meaning of this?" Marsh asked angrily, as the boat scraped ashore and David stepped easily, confidently, onto the deck.

"I want to apologize," David said glibly. "My partner and I were doing some mining; I guess things just got out of hand. The next thing you know, both ends of the rapids were dammed up, and here you were, trapped in the middle."

"Mining?" Marsh scoffed. "You don't actually expect me to believe that, do you?"

"Well, if you knew what we were mining for you would believe it," David said. At about that moment, Angus Pugh appeared on the scene, and he stood behind David, staring pointedly at Crystal. His constant and unwavering gaze began to make Crystal uncomfortable. It was a moment before she remembered where she had seen him before. Willie, who was standing close by, remembered it at the same moment, because he whispered to Crystal.

"That's Angus Pugh," he said. "Remember him? He's the disagreeable bloke with the black powder."

"Yes," Crystal replied, quietly. "I remember."

Crystal looked away once, then looked back, only to see that Angus Pugh was still staring at her with eyes which were very, very deep, and, or so it appeared, with something red in the very bottom. His constant gaze was disquieting to her.

"What are you mining for, David?" Marsh asked quietly. "Or do I already know?"

David chuckled. "Well, now, for an old man, you aren't as dumb as I thought. I guess you do know at that. You didn't think I was going to let this little opportunity pass by, did you?"

"I have to confess that I did believe we were safe," Marsh said. "I couldn't believe my own son would. . . ."

"Would what?" David sneered. "Turn on the father who loves him so?" David slurred the word, *loves*. "After all, old man, you have treated me *so* like a son, putting me overboard in the middle of the wilderness, sending me off without so much as one cent to my name. Spare me the family love nonsense, please. Now, you, Pugh, get the black powder off your mules and load those lead bars on."

"What?" Pugh asked. "Are you crazy?"

"Yeah," David said. "I'm crazy like a fox. Have you ever heard of the science of alchemy?"

"Alchemy? No, what's that?"

"It's turning one metal into another," David said. He chuckled. "I'm goin' to turn these bars of lead into bars of gold."

"What? Can you do that?"

"Yeah," David said. He chuckled again. "You see, these are very special bars of lead. Now, you give me your mules and I'll give you the boat. You can take your powder upriver."

"You said you would take me," Pugh blustered.

"Why should I?" David replied. "You are just going to go look for gold. I've already found it."

"Are you serious about bein' able to turn lead into gold?"

"Yeah," David said. "I'm serious."

"Then I'll just stay with you," Pugh said. "Where my mules go, I go."

"Aye, 'n there's a partnership formed in hell if ever there was one," Willie said.

"Ah, Willie, you never have approved of me, have you?" David said. "I'm really not such a bad sort, you know. In fact, I tell you what I'm going to do. I'm going to leave a couple of kegs of powder here for you. That way, you can blast your way out of here. Now, isn't that decent of me?"

"David, you don't expect me to just sit here and watch you take that gold, do you?" Marsh asked.

"Gold?" Pugh asked.

"Yes, gold," Marsh said. "Since the cat is out of the bag, I may as well tell everyone." By now, most of the passengers on the boat had gathered around, watching in anxious interest the byplay between Marsh and the two men who had just stepped aboard. Marsh looked at them, and addressed all of them. "You have been keeping company with some valuable cargo," Marsh said. "Those boxes you thought contained lead, actually contained gold bars, coated in lead. No one knew about it except me, my daughter, and, of course, my son."

"Son?" one of the passengers could be heard exclaiming. "You mean we are bein' robbed by the Cap'n's own son?"

"Well, I can see that I'm not too popular around here," David said. "Perhaps I had better tend to my business and get on my way. You two men start loading that gold onto the mules," David said, pointing to a couple of deckhands.

"No!" Marsh ordered, holding up his hand. "You don't really think I am going to just stand by and let you take it, do you?"

As quickly as a striking serpent, David had a pistol in his hand. He pointed the pistol, not at Marsh, but at Crystal, then he reached out and grabbed Crystal and pulled her to him, holding the cocked pistol pointed at her head.

"I thought you might try something foolish, old

man. So I have devised a way to keep you from being so foolish. If you make one move to stop us, I'll be forced to shoot dear little Crystal. Now you wouldn't want that, would you?"

"David, I can't believe you would do something like this," Marsh said. "My God, son, you are. . . ."

"Don't call me *son*!" David demanded coldly. "You forfeited that right the night you put me over in a skiff. Now, you two, get that gold loaded."

The two deckhands looked helplessly toward Marsh, and, reluctantly, he indicated that they should do as David ordered.

The passengers and crew of the *Missouri Mist* stood by in stunned silence, just watching as what appeared to be lead bars were moved from the cargo space to the cargo packs on the backs of the mules. Finally, when the mules were all loaded, David looked at Marsh and smiled, a slow, evil smile.

"Now, old man, I'm leaving some black powder for you, just like I said I would. So, you see, I'm not really stealing this gold, I'm just selling you this powder. If you think the price is unfair, let us just say that I'm a sharp trader."

"Give me that gun!" Marsh shouted, and, unexpectedly he jumped at David. David jerked away from him, and when he did, the gun went off. The bullet hit Marsh in the neck, and he put his hands to his throat with a surprised expression on his face.

"Pa!" David yelled, shocked by what had happened.

"Dad!" Crystal cried. She watched in horror, as the blood began to spill between her father's fingers.

"No!" David shouted, realizing what he had done. "No, old man! Why did you make me do that? Why did you make me do that?"

Marsh made a gurgling, rattling sound in his throat, then he fell, face down onto the deck. Crystal could tell by the way he fell that he was dead. She screamed and went to him.

"Oh, David, you killed him!" she screamed. "You killed him!"

"I . . . I didn't intend to," David shouted. "You saw what he did! He . . . he tried to jump me! I—the gun went off. I didn't mean to!"

"Yeah, well, it's done!" Pugh shouted. "Now, let's get the gold loaded and get out of here."

David had taken a step toward his father, but when Pugh spoke he stopped and backed up.

"You're right," David said. "We have to get out of here!"

"Get the girl," Pugh said.

"What?" David replied, still stunned over the unexpected turn of events.

"I said get the girl. As long as we have her, I don't figure anyone on this boat is going to be foolish enough to try 'n play hero. 'Cause if they do, they gonna find a dead girl."

"Yeah," David said. "Crystal, you come with us."

"Oh, David, lad, have you not a drop of decency left in you, now?" Willie asked. "You kill your own father, 'n now you'd kidnap the girl too?"

"It's not kidnapping," David said. "After all, she is my wife. I've got a right to take her with me."

"Your wife?" Pugh asked in surprise. "I thought you said she was your sister."

"She is," David said.

"You married your own sister?"

"It's too complicated to explain right now."

Pugh smiled evilly and rubbed himself openly and unashamedly. "You don't have to explain nothin' to me," he said. "As long as our bargain still goes, it's fine with me."

David looked at Crystal and she saw a strange and frightening expression on his face.

"Our bargain still goes," he said.

"Good," Pugh said. Pugh looked at Crystal. "Little girl, me 'n you is goin' to get to know one another better. Much better, iffen you get my meanin'," he added, and again he rubbed himself, and this time he laughed, a low, evil-sounding laugh.

"Get up on one of those mules," David said to Crystal.

There was no saddle on the mule, just a canvas jacket which had carrying pouches on each side. The mule's backbone was hard, and uncomfortable, but Crystal knew it would do no good to complain. She was numb from the shock of what had happened. She put her hands down to hold onto the cargo pouches, as it was the only thing she could hold on to. As they rode away, she was at first afraid she was going to fall off, then, when she realized she wouldn't fall, she looked around to see Willie and the others, still standing, almost as if in shock, on the deck of the *Missouri Mist*. Her father was lying on his stomach on deck, in a spreading pool of his own blood.

Less than an hour before, she had been deliriously happy, contemplating the meeting with John tomorrow. How rapidly and how drastically things had changed!

Life would never be the same again.

Crystal had no idea how far they had come. They had ridden for several hours, she knew that, but she had no way of measuring the speed of the animals. She knew only that she was exhausted, and her seat and legs were sore, almost to the point of agony from having ridden for so long without padding, on the back of this mule.

There was very little said among the three. Crystal gathered that Pugh was normally uncommunicative, and David was seemingly lost in his own thoughts. Perhaps he was reflecting upon what he had done. Maybe he had a conscience after all.

"We'll camp here tonight," Pugh said, when the sun was an orange disc low in the western sky.

"I think we should go on," David said.

"Fine," Pugh replied. "If you want to go on, you

do that. Me'n my mules and the girl is stayin'
here."

"All right, all right," David agreed. "It doesn't
make any difference to me. I was just commenting,
that's all."

Pugh swung down from his horse, then walked
back to the mule Crystal was riding.

"Come on, girl, ole' Pugh will help you down."

"I don't need, nor want your help," Crystal said
sharply.

"Well, you're goin' to get my help whether you
want it or not," Pugh said with a chuckle. He
reached up for her. Then, without the slightest
hesitation he stuck his hand under her bodice and
found a breast. He pinched a nipple hard between
his thumb and forefinger. The pain was excruci-
ating, and, for a moment, Crystal was afraid she
was going to pass out.

"David!" she screamed. "Get away!" pushing his
hand from her body.

"Huh, uh, girl, there ain't no sense in callin' to
him for help. He's done give you to me."

"What?" Crystal asked in a shocked voice. "What
is he saying? You . . . you've given me to another
man?"

"Oh, come now, Crystal, don't be so upset. That's
what whores do, and you're really no more than a
whore, are you?"

"What?" Crystal asked in a small voice. "Why
are you saying such a thing?"

"You were going to give yourself to me, weren't you, my dear? Should I flatter myself that you love me? A woman who allows a man to have his way with her, when there's no love, is a whore. You, my dear, are a whore."

"But I was doing it for Dad," Crystal said.

David smiled. "Well, now you can do it for me. I've enjoyed the services of many whores, and some, I've enjoyed watching. You, my dear, I will enjoy watching."

"You . . . you are going to watch it happen?"

"Oh, yes, my dear. I am going to watch every moment of it. After all, this is your fault, you know. All of it is your fault."

"My fault? How can you say that?"

"Do you remember the incident at the waterfall? If you hadn't denied me then, if you hadn't sent me away, none of this would have happened. I wouldn't have been caught with the Moore woman, and I wouldn't have been put overboard in a skiff. It's all your fault."

"But you can't blame me for that, David. After all, I thought I was really your sister then."

"I told you not to worry about it."

"Yes, but you didn't say *why*."

David laughed, a quiet, evil sounding chuckle. "Now, be honest with me. If I had told you that you weren't really my sister, would you have still sent me away?"

"Yes," Crystal said.

"That's what I thought."

"David, be reasonable. It didn't matter whether we were brother and sister or not. What you wanted to do was wrong, and it was wrong for anyone."

"How about you and John Riley?"

"What?"

"Have you ever done it with John Riley?"

Crystal was quiet for a long moment. "Why would you ask me that?" she finally asked.

"You have, haven't you?"

"That's none of your business."

"You have, haven't you?" David challenged again.

"Yes," she finally admitted. "But I love him."

"That is your misfortune," David said coldly.

"If you've finished with your talkin', I'll just provide you with that show you been a'wantin' to see," Pugh interrupted then, and he started to undo his pants.

Crystal saw that Pugh was busy with his pants, and David had moved quite a distance from her. If ever she would have a chance to escape, there would probably be no better opportunity than right now. She started running, moving so quickly and unexpectedly, that she was nearly out of the campsite before either man could react.

"Stop her, Lee!" Pugh called, pulling his pants back up and chasing after her awkwardly. "Don't you dare let her get away!"

Crystal hadn't run far when she realized that she stood no chance of outrunning them on foot.

She began to circle around, hoping to make a big swing back toward one of the horses. If she could just get up on a horse she felt as if she had a chance. She ran in a long, long circle, and then, with a feeling of elation, saw that her trick had worked. The horses were in front of her, and she could still hear the brush and sticks crashing as she was being chased from behind. She reached for the first horse when suddenly she felt a hand on her shoulder. She cried out in alarm as the hand threw her roughly to the ground. She looked up to see Pugh sitting on top of her, smiling down at her, showing her his crooked, yellowed teeth, and contaminating her with his foul breath.

"I thought you might be comin' back this way," Pugh said. "Now, let me show you how good, ole' Pugh can make you feel."

Pugh forced her legs apart, then he pulled her skirt up to her waist. With her skirt pulled up, he managed to pull and tear at her undergarments, until that which he so ardently sought was displayed before him, and Crystal felt a cool brush of air to underscore her vulnerability. After that, Pugh grabbed the bodice of her dress and he jerked it down until he could see her exposed breasts, two creamy mounds of young flesh, gleaming starkly white against the dark material of her dress.

"Now, look at that," Pugh said. "I tell you the truth, girl, I don't believe I've ever seen prettier tits. Though near 'bout the only tits I ever get to see is them that belongs to whores." Pugh giggled obscenely. " 'Course Lee says you be a whore, but I ain't never seen no whore as pretty as you be."

With all of Crystal's charms exposed to Pugh, there was nothing left for him to do but carry out his intention, and that he did. Crystal felt his full weight upon her, and she cried out, even though she knew her cry was useless.

Pugh entered her brutally and painfully, and Crystal had no choice but to lay there and suffer through the degrading experience. Finally she forced herself to quit crying out, because she surmised that her sounds and struggles were actually adding to his gratification. She closed her eyes as the cruel thrusts continued, opening them only once, and when she did she saw David's face watching. His expression was lust-crazed and in that moment she realized, with horror, that he was serious when he said he enjoyed it. David was actually getting a sexual satisfaction from seeing her abused so. Crystal was so repulsed by that realization that her stomach heaved, and she was afraid she was going to throw up. Finally, mercifully, Pugh was finished, and he pulled away from her with his semen running down her thigh.

The blast sent water, rocks and sand flying. Waterspray splashed back on the people on the

Missouri Mist, but when it was all settled, the river was running free again.

"All right, Pete, good job," Willie said. "I think we can go through now. Hank, are you ready to spar?"

"I'm ready," Hank called back from the capstan engine. The sparring poles were already in place.

"Then let's try it," Willie said. Willie climbed to the wheelhouse, while Hank, Pete, and the others attended to the sparring. After only two hops, the *Missouri Mist* was through the difficult part, and headed once again downriver toward Trenton Town. Marsh Lee's body was still on board the boat, because Willie intended to give him a decent burial at Trenton Town.

John Riley was standing on the dock as the *Missouri Mist* pulled into Trenton Town, and he was smiling broadly and waving at Willie. Willie returned his wave, but didn't return the smile, and John thought that a little strange, because Willie had been his closest friend on board the boat.

John strained to pick out Crystal, but, for some reason, she was no where to be seen. John was disappointed. He was sure she would be in a position to see him, and to wave to him, even if she had to go somewhere where her father couldn't see what she was doing. But then, that, too, was unusual. Where was Marsh Lee? And come to think of it, why was Willie at the wheel?

Now the smile left John's face as well, for he realized that something was terribly wrong. He watched anxiously until the boat scraped against the dock, then he leaped onto the deck and started up the steps toward the hurricane deck taking them three at a time. He was to the wheelhouse in a matter of seconds.

"Willie, what is it?" he asked. "What is going on? Where is Crystal? Where is Captain Lee?"

"We . . . we had a spot of trouble, lad," Willie said.

"Trouble? What kind of trouble?"

"Well, you see lad, we were carryin' gold bars, and when we reached the narrow rapids, why, we were set upon by river pirates. They . . . they got the gold, 'n that's not all. They killed the Cap'n."

"What? Captain Lee is dead?"

"Aye, that he is," Willie said. "The poor man is lyin' in his own bed now. We brought him back for a decent, Christian burial."

"My God, Willie!" John suddenly shouted. "Crystal! They didn't, she isn't. . . ." he couldn't bring himself to say the words.

"Ah, no, laddie, she isn't dead," Willie said. "But it may be, lad, that she's wishin' for it about now. She was taken by the pirates."

"Where?" John asked. "Which way did they go? I'm going after them!"

"If you want my way of thinkin' they're goin' to have to go to Denver to sell their gold. I figure they will head straight that way." Willie said.

"Where did they hit you? At the narrow rapids?"

"Yes."

"That means they are going to go across country that War Horse has staked out for his own," John said. "All right, so be it! I'll just race War Horse to them. Did you get a good look at the pirates? Could you describe them?"

"Aye, lad, I know," Willie said. "One of them is Angus Pugh. Do you remember him?"

"Yes, I do," John said.

"The other one is David Lee."

Chapter Twenty-Four

There was no warning when the Indians hit. They didn't have the slightest suspicion of trouble. They were just riding along with David in the lead and Pugh just behind Crystal, keeping his eye on her, when the attack came. The Indians swooped down on them, seemingly from nowhere, whooping and shouting as their horses galloped right through them.

"No! no!" David yelled, and, quickly, he threw his hands up, signaling to the Indians that he didn't want to fight.

"Lee, you cowardly son of a bitch!" Pugh shouted, and Pugh slapped his legs against the side of his horse and jerked the animal around, attempting to make a run for it.

Two braves, seeing Pugh run, let out a shout of

joy as if he had done it just to provide them with sport, and they started after him. They caught up with him in less than one hundred yards, and Crystal could hear the crack of the war club against Pugh's head, even from this distance. Pugh fell from his horse, then lay motionless. One of the braves jumped down from his own pony, and Crystal had to turn her head away in horror as she realized that the Indian was about to scalp Pugh. She certainly had no love for Angus Pugh, but she had no wish to watch something that gruesome, either.

"I've come to trade!" David shouted, still holding his hands up. "See, I've taken nothing from the Indians. I'm a trader."

The Indians circled around David and Crystal for a few moments, just looking at them. There were eight Indians, two of whom were armed with rifles. The remaining Indians were carrying bows and arrows, or war clubs. They just stared at the two for a long time. One of them rode up to Crystal and, curious about her fire-red hair, reached up and took several strands between his thumb and forefinger.

"Does hair burn?" he asked.

Crystal didn't answer. For the moment, fear had frozen her tongue.

"Do you like woman?" David asked. "Do you like white woman with red hair?"

The Indians looked at David in surprise. "Yes, I

can tell that you do," David went on. "You can have her. I have come to trade her."

"David!" Crystal said, speaking at last. "David, what are you saying?"

"Hush," David said. "You are a woman. They won't kill you; they'll keep you around until everyone has had their turn with you, then they'll make you a slave. But they won't kill you. Me, they'll kill, if I can't work out some sort of a deal."

"You want to trade woman?" One of the Indians asked.

"Yes," David said, smiling now, and bobbing his head excitedly. "Yes, I found a woman with hair like fire. She will be a good woman for you. She is very good in the robes. You will see."

The Indian who could speak English translated for the others, and they talked among themselves for a bit, as, one by one, they rode up to her and felt of her hair. One or two grew so bold as to feel her breasts.

"I have met white men who would trade their Indian women," the English-speaking Indian said. "But never have I met a white man who would trade a white woman."

"Well, sir, you have met one now," David said. "You can have her."

"What do you want in trade?"

"I don't want much," David said. "All I want is the right to ride on through your land, here. I'll just be goin' on my way and you can keep the woman."

"What if we kill woman?"

"Well," David said. He took a deep breath, and when Crystal looked at him with pleading eyes, he turned away from her. "Well, the way I figure it, once I give her to you, she's yours to do with as you please. If you want to kill her, why, I reckon that's your business. Seems to me like it would be a foolish waste, though. She can be a lot more fun alive, if you get my meanin'."

One of the Indians said something in a harsh, gutteral tone, speaking in his own language, and then he grabbed himself boldly. The other Indians laughed, and Crystal didn't have to understand their language to know what they were talking about. She felt a cold fear come over her.

"Well, what do you say? Is it a deal?" David asked. "I trade you the woman for the right to pass through your land?"

"What else do you have?" the English-speaking Indian asked, moving now toward the mules.

"Oh, not much else that would interest you, I'm afraid," David said. "Just enough food to get me through without having to take any of your game." David laughed. "You see, I'm being very particular about that."

"Powder," the English speaking Indian said. He had happened onto a cargo pack of powder which remained from Pugh's original load.

"Yes, gunpowder. Would you like that? You may take it all."

The Indian nodded and pointed to the sack, and one of the other Indians took it from the mule and put it on his own horse.

The English-speaking Indian raised up another flap, and saw one of the bars David was transporting.

"Ah," the English-speaking Indian said. "Metal for making bullets."

"No!" David shouted quickly. "No, you can't have that! That's mine!"

The Indian paid no attention to David. He nodded again, and this time two more Indians began taking the bars from the mules and passing them to the others. "No!" David shouted, angrily. "I told you, you can't have that!"

David jumped down from his horse and started running toward the Indians, screaming at them.

"David, no!" Crystal shouted. "Let them have it. They'll kill you!"

"You, son of a bitch, I told you you couldn't have that," David said, and he pulled one of the Indians off his horse and started pummeling him with his fists. The Indian was startled at first, but he recovered very quickly. Decisively he pulled his knife from his waist and slipped it quickly and cleanly, in between David's rib cage.

The Indian stood up then, and, still holding a bloody knife, looked down at David, who lay gasping and dying on the ground.

"David!" Crystal shouted, and she ran to him, and knelt down beside him. She reached out and touched him. "David, you fool, you shouldn't have fought him!" she said, and tears had already sprung to her eyes.

"I had to, Crystal, don't you see?" David said. "If I had let them take the gold, then everything I have done over the last couple of days would have been for nothing. I would have killed Pa, for nothing . . . sold you out, for nothing . . . I had to."

"But David, it isn't what you think," Crystal said. "I. . . ."

"Crystal?" David said, and in that one, clear word, he wasn't a murderer and a betrayer, he was the young, fourteen-year-old boy, back when Crystal loved him as her brother, and when all seemed right with the world. "Crystal?" David said again. And then he died.

"Get on horse," the English-speaking Indian said.

Crystal was certain she was going to be taken back to their village where she expected to be tortured and killed. If what David said was right, if they intended to pass her around from brave to brave, giving each one a chance to use her, and then make her a slave, then she hoped she would be killed.

For one instant she thought of breaking and running, hoping they would run her down and kill her as quickly and as cleanly as they had killed

Angus Pugh. That thought passed quickly, however, and when they ordered her to ride, she did.

Crystal had to ride hard to keep up with them, for they rode at a gallop, even though they were leading the pack mules. It was at least a little easier for her now, for she was on a saddled horse, rather than one of the unsaddled mules. She rode on, doggedly, blocking her mind to all thought, merely taking one moment after another to see what would happen next.

She saw all the women and the children of the village gathered along the banks of a stream, staring at her with eyes open wide in curiosity and wonder. Perhaps they were going to kill her. If so, they would not have the pleasure of watching her show fear.

"Look, I want to find her as badly as you do," Eb said. "But if we keep going on in the dark, we might miss some sign. You know that, John, as well as I do. You just aren't thinkin' straight, that's all!"

"I know, I know," John said. He sighed. "It's just that I can't stand to think of her with those two men, frightened, subjected to who knows what kind of treatment."

"Well, if we blunder around in the dark and miss some sign, we could throw ourselves off two or three days, maybe as much as a week. And I don't want to wait a week to find her."

"You're right," John said. Both men reined in their horses, then swung off them and stretched. "I guess we may as well spend the night here and get a start with first light."

"That's my way of thinkin'," Eb said. "Tomorrow, we'll head straight for Bullnose Peak. If they are headin' for Denver they'll have to go that way. If they've already been there, we'll head south. If they haven't got there yet, we'll head north."

"Eb, I want to thank you again for comin' along with me," John said. "It's good that I got you here to keep me straight."

"Ah, you're just upset'n not thinkin' too good, that's all. I can understand that. I'm a mite upset myself, if truth be known."

The horses were watered, then staked out in grass before the men began to attend to their own needs. John got a fire going while Eb started some beans. The beans had been soaking ever since they left Trenton Town, by the old trail trick of putting them in water in a buffalo stomach, so that when it came time to cook them in the evening, they would be ready. John went down to the stream and stood there with his hands poised, until he saw a careless trout. A quick slash with his hand and the trout was scooped out of the water. A moment later he had a second one, and soon the aroma of baking trout was added to the smell of coffee and beans.

After dinner John stood up and paced ner-

vously back and forth. Eb filled a pipe with tobacco and lit it, then sat down against a tree and
smoked it while he watched John pace.

"You're pretty powerful in love with Crystal,
aren't you?" Eb asked.

"Yes," John answered.

"What I don't understand is, if you are that
much in love with her, why didn't you just steal
the girl away in the first place? Why didn't you
just take her off into the hills with you?"

"I've asked myself that same question a dozen
times," John said. "I don't know why I didn't do it.
If it means anything, that is exactly what I was
going to do when the boat reached Trenton Town
this time. If only I had done it earlier."

"Don't go faultin' yourself on it, son," Eb said.
"I reckon we've all made mistakes we'd just as
soon forget about. I know I have. I made one
dandy of a mistake about eighteen years ago.

John knew that Eb was in a mood to talk, and as
there was nothing he could do to speed the night,
he sat down, lit his own pipe, and listened.

"I come up here on the *Lydia Kay*," Eb said. "Me
'n Mary."

"Mary was your wife," John said.

"Yep, that she was. She was the prettiest girl in
Virginia." Eb sighed. "I reckon I should have stayed
in Virginia. I guess things would have worked out,
somehow. But, what with the war'n all 'n me 'n her

family bein' on different sides, why, there was nothin' else we could do but leave.

We took a train from Richmond to St. Louis, 'n there, we boarded the *Lydia Kay* for Fort Benton. We figured the farther away from the war we got, the safer we'd both be. I planned to trap and hunt up here in the Northwest, figurin' to do pretty well. I did too."

Eb was silent for a long moment, but John didn't press him to go on. He knew the older man was thinking, remembering his Mary.

"I still remember the day Mary come to me with the news that she was with child," Eb finally said. "Why, I was that happy I could have flown without wings. I built us a cabin and chinked it in with mud against the winter wind . . . but . . . it wasn't enough," he said. "It was a bad, bad winter that year, and Mary come down with some kind of sickness. I nursed her the best I could, but that wasn't good enough. I made up my mind right then, that, soon as the baby was born, we was headin' back to Virginia. But, the truth is, I think that, even then, Mary knew she wasn't goin' to make it. She used to tell me though, that, even if she died, I'd only have to look at the baby to remember her. Ever'time I'd see the baby, I'd see her. The baby was all fired important to her, and she was determined that, no matter how sick she got, she was going to live long enough to have that baby."

"And did she?"

"Yes," Eb said. "She lived long enough. In fact, I was even beginnin' to think that she might make it through, and we would go to Virginia after all. We used to sit around and talk about goin' back to Virginia, the house we would build, the garden we would plant. But we was foolin' ourselves. The baby finally did come, only it didn't come out like it was supposed to. Mary was a long time givin' birth, and it took a lot out of her. It took so much out of her that she died, right after the baby was born."

Eb grew silent after that, and the two men sat around the fire, with only the crack and pop of the flames, the puffing on the pipes, and the gentle, night breeze to invade the silence.

Left unasked was the obvious question, "What happened to the baby?"

If Eb had wanted John to know, Eb would tell him. It was the mark of trust and friendship that John said nothing about it.

"Well, they're movin' a mite slower than I would have supposed," Eb said the next day, as he and John studied the trail through Bullnose Peak. There was absolutely no sign that they, or anyone else, had been this way in the past several days. If, as Willie had stated, they were leading a train of mules, it would have been easy to pick up their trail. They simply had not come this way yet.

"All right," John said. "That makes things easier. All we have to do is follow this trail back, and we'll run head on into them."

"We've got to take things easy, though," Eb said. "We don't want to blunder right into them. If they see us, Crystal will still be in danger."

"I know," John agreed. "Don't worry, we'll move easy."

John and Eb began backtracking along the trail, waiting and watching for the first sign which would indicate that they had nearly caught up with David Lee and Angus Pugh. By late afternoon, they still hadn't seen them, and John was beginning to grow worried that perhaps they had missed them. Then they saw an ominous sign, and John felt a quick-building nausea. Circling high overhead about a mile before them were a dozen vultures. Something—or somebody—was dead.

"They've been dead about two days, I'd say," John said. "When I was scouting for the army, I came upon several bodies this way. It got to a point that I was pretty good about judging the length of time."

"It's Indians, all right," Eb said. "The thing is, which tribe is it? Mandan? Arikawa? Sioux?"

"I'd say Mandan," John said.

"But I thought all the Mandan was friendly."

"This is the work of War Horse," John sighed. "At least we know that Crystal is still alive."

"What? How do we know that?" Eb said.

"If she had been killed in the attack, she would be here with the others. If she wasn't killed in the attack, the chances are they won't kill her at all. She's more valuable to them alive."

"My God, John, what will they do with her? Will they . . . will they *use* her?"

"Probably," John said.

"Oh, my God."

"Look," John said. "I'm not one of your white men who think that just because a woman has been used by an Indian that she had been defiled for life. I'm thankful she's alive. That's all I'm looking for."

Chapter Twenty-Five

The Indians were uncertain as to what they should do with Crystal, so they took her into a tipi and staked her out on the ground. She lay tied to the stakes for the rest of the day, waiting . . . waiting, for what? For the men to come and use her? For the women to come and torture her?

What was in store for her now?

Crystal had frequent visitors during the afternoon. Men and women would come in and just stand there and look down at her. Sometimes they would come alone, sometimes they would come in pairs or small groups. Nearly all of the men would kneel down beside her and touch her hair, and if there was more than one, they would make some comment, though she had no idea what they were talking about.

Once during the day, she was even the focal point of some children's game, and they laughed and squealed and ran around her, or jumped over her. A couple of times she tried to talk to them, but no one would answer her. In fact, it seemed to Crystal that she might not even be there, for many times they not only didn't answer her, they gave no indication that they had even heard her.

As the shadows lengthened, and it finally grew dark in the tent, an old woman came in and lit a lamp of some sort. The old woman sat in the flickering, gold light and looked at Crystal.

"Do you speak my language?" Crystal asked.

"I speak," the old woman said.

"Oh, thank God," Crystal said. "I was beginning to think I was going mad. Tell me, what is going to happen to me?"

The old woman smiled, a wide, toothless smile. "You will be sold," she said.

"Sold? Sold to who? What do you mean?"

"Soon we will have a great rendezvous," the old woman said. "There, many things will be bought and sold. Much fur, many blankets, knives, many things. But I think nothing will bring so much as you."

"What do you think I am?" Crystal asked angrily. "I'm a human being! I can't be bought and sold like some animal."

"Yes, I think you will bring much," the old woman said, paying no attention whatever to

331

Crystal's outbreak. The old woman leaned over and felt of Crystal's hair. "How do you do this?" She asked. "How do you make hair the color of dying sun?"

"That's my natural hair color," Crystal said.

"Everyone says there is much medicine in such hair. That is why no man has touched you. They fear the medicine."

"They . . . they what?" Crystal asked, feeling a sudden lift. "You mean the men aren't going to . . . they won't. . . ."

"They say your medicine will cause great illness among any man who has you and who does not own you. That is why you will be sold. If you are bought, he who buys you, buys your medicine. Now, many young men are checking their treasure to see if they can buy you at the rendezvous."

"They think they can buy my medicine when they buy me?" Crystal said, thinking fast. "Well, they are mistaken. Perhaps my body can be bought, but my medicine cannot be. It will always be strong, and it will always belong to me."

"Is this true?" the old woman asked.

"Yes," Crystal said. "This is true. So you had better tell everyone."

"I will tell War Horse of this," the old woman said. "He is the leader, and he should know about such things."

With that announcement, the old woman got up and left.

Night finally absorbed the last lingering shadows. The wavering orange glow of the campfires outside combined with the still flickering flame from the lamp the old woman had lit to bathe the inside of Crystal's tipi in an eerie, golden light.

Outside, the Indians were preparing for the giant rendezvous at which Crystal would be one of the principal attractions. They danced around the fires to the sounds of strange, discordant, yet hauntingly beautiful chants. The drums pounded incessantly, each drum beat measuring a syllable of time, marking its passage, yet, holding it up as well. Time and space lost their meaning. There never was a time before now; there would never be a time after now, and yet, *now* didn't exist.

Crystal may have gone to sleep, though she was never cognizant of the transition from wakefulness to sleep. She must have though, because once she saw a face standing over her, looking down on her. She closed her eyes, and when she opened them, the face was gone. It seemed as if it had all happened in an instant, though it may have been over a period of many minutes, or even hours. Then once, she opened her eyes and the face was there again, and this time the changing and banging of the drums had halted so that the only sound was the muted whisper of the burning lamp.

"You were here before," Crystal said to the face which was looking down at her. The face was nut-brown, with three, precise scars cut in the form of bars, on each cheek. The wounds had obviously been self-inflicted, obviously for cosmetic effect. Despite that, Crystal had to admit to a degree of handsomeness in the Indian who was gazing down upon her.

"I have come many times during the night," he said. He tapped himself on the chest, proudly. "I am War Horse, chief of the Mandan people."

"I thought Angry Wolf was chief of the Mandan people," Crystal said.

"Bah!" War Horse spat. "Angry Wolf is chief of the women and children, of the old men and the cowards. The true Mandan have come with me."

Crystal pulled at her bonds. "Tell me, War Horse, do the true Mandan fight their wars against women?"

"No," War Horse said.

"Then why am I tied here?"

"You are prize of war," War Horse said. "Soon you will be sold."

"I have strong medicine," Crystal said. "My medicine will make anyone who touches me, sick."

War Horse laughed. "That is not true," he said.

"What?" Crystal asked, weakly. She had counted on that as her last hope. Now War Horse was laughing it off.

"That is story I tell to keep others away," he said. "You worth more, if not used by many."

"Are you going to buy me?" Crystal asked.

"Maybe yes, maybe no," War Horse answered. "For now, I shall see."

War Horse knelt down beside her, and Crystal gasped as she saw a flash of silver in his hand. He had a knife! Was he planning to kill her?

War Horse put the blade of the knife at the bodice of her dress, then he cut it, all the way down to her hem. He opened the dress, then saw her undergarments. He looked surprised.

"I have never before seen woman wear two dresses," he said. He cut the cotton chemise as well. When he lay it open, Crystal could feel the cool air on her body, and she knew that he was gazing upon her nakedness.

"Yes," War Horse said. Crystal suddenly felt his hand on her most private part, and she tried to twist away from him. "Here is much hair, also the color of fire. Indian women do not have much hair here. Do all white women have much hair here?"

"I . . . I don't know," Crystal said. She was certainly in no mood for a philosophical discussion now. "Please," she begged. "Please, go away now!"

War Horse didn't go away, but, mercifully, he didn't do any more to her. He just sat beside her and stared at her, and she lay there feeling humiliated by the experience, but thankful that no worse had happened. Finally, without bothering her any further, War Horse left.

Crystal was glad when he left, but he didn't

replace the clothes he had cut from her, and she had to spend the remainder of the night, exposed to any who wished to see her.

Crystal dozed fitfully during the rest of the night, and she awoke early the next morning. She was cool, almost to the point of being cold, having slept naked, and without any cover. Her joints ached, as did her wrists and ankles, and she wished she could sit up. The tent flap opened shortly after she awoke, and the old woman who had spoken with her the night before came in, carrying a white, deerskin dress.

"Wear this," the old woman said, putting the dress on the ground beside Crystal. The old woman began cutting the bonds.

"Oh, thank you," Crystal said, sitting up gratefully to rub the circulation back into her feet and hands. As the circulation slowly returned, Crystal looked at the dress the old woman had lay beside her. It was, she noticed, an exceptionally beautiful dress.

"This dress is very beautiful," Crystal said. She reached for it, and was surprised at how soft and comfortable it felt. Though in truth, Crystal would have been so glad to cover her nakedness, she would have, willingly, worn a dress made of birch bark.

"I make dress," the old woman said proudly, smiling the same toothless smile she had smiled last night.

"You do lovely work," Crystal said, slipping the dress on over her head.

"Now," the old woman beamed, when she saw Crystal in the dress she had made for her. "You will bring much treasure when you are sold at the rendezvous."

Shortly after Crystal was dressed, the drums started pounding, and the singers started chanting, and she knew that the rendezvous was about to get underway. She was brought breakfast, a stew of some sort, and told that she would be sent for when she was to be sold.

They started to bind her, hand and feet again, but when she begged them not to, the old woman interceded for her, and they decided to tie her in a way which would prevent her from running away, but would allow her some freedom of movement. Her legs were hobbled, and her arms were tied straight down by her sides. It wasn't comfortable, but it was infinitely better than being staked out again, and for that, Crystal was grateful, and she expressed her gratitude to the old woman.

Since the old woman had vouched for her, she was selected to stay as Crystal's guard. Crystal was glad, because of all who had come into contact with her, the old woman had been the most friendly.

Crystal stood in the doorway of the tipi and watched as Indians began arriving from other places to take part in the great rendezvous.

"There," the old woman said, pointing to some riders and beaming with pride. "There are traders from the Sioux nation, from the Cheyenne, and from the Arikawa. And, see, there are even people from Angry Wolf's camp. Truly, War Horse is a great leader to have so many people come to his rendezvous."

"Why did War Horse leave Angry Wolf's camp?" Crystal asked.

"Because Angry Wolf is a coward," the old woman said. "Angry Wolf accepts the law of the white man. War Horse does not. War Horse accepts only the law of the Great Spirit."

Crystal looked at the old woman, surprised at the amount of emotion she displayed when she spoke of War Horse. So, this was the revolutionary band! It's funny, but she didn't think of revolutionaries being old, bent, and toothless, like this old woman. But then, she didn't think of Indians as having as much compassion as this old woman seemed to have, either. For certainly, this old woman had shown compassion for her.

"You must think a great deal of War Horse to come away with him like this," Crystal said.

"War Horse is my son," the old woman said, touching her breast proudly.

Crystal understood now. A parent's love could not be measured by race, nor even, Crystal had learned, by blood. For she had loved her father, even though he wasn't her father. Yes, love of parent for child, and child for parent, Crystal could understand.

Crystal watched as the proceedings grew more and more frenzied, and, even though she knew that sometime during the days' activities her own fate would be determined, she couldn't help but be fascinated by what was going on. She learned that the rendezvous was not scheduled just to sell her. In fact, it had been scheduled for a long, long time, and it was just a coincidence that she was captured in time to be sold here. Most of the Indians who arrived were bringing furs, horses, blankets and various other items of barter. It was, Crystal decided, almost like a country fair, only it was held, almost exclusively, by Indians.

Almost exclusively, she thought, because she saw white trappers, who, in their own way, looked wilder than the Indians. She felt a shudder go through her. If she had to be bought, she would prefer being bought by an Indian, over one of those men.

Finally, despite the excitement of the bazaar, the ordeal of her captivity overtook her, and Crystal went back into her tent and lay down to take a nap.

"Come now," the old woman said. "It is time."

Crystal opened her eyes and saw that the old woman was bending down over her. She felt a queazy feeling in her stomach. The moment of truth had arrived. She was about to be sold.

Crystal got up and followed the old woman outside, through the crowd which had gathered. She kept her head and eyes down the entire way, so that she wouldn't have to look into their faces. Finally she was led to a position by the old woman, then told to stand there while the bidding went on. As there were Indians from different linguistic groups present, the bidding was conducted in English, therefore affording Crystal the unique opportunity to follow her own fate. She heard herself being offered; then she heard War Horse bid a horse and two blankets for her. The bid was raised by another, and by still another, until she heard a voice which nearly stopped her heart. She gasped and looked up into the crowd for the first time, and there she saw John and Eb! John had just made a bid for her!

Crystal opened her mouth and took in a breath to say something, but a nod from Eb, an almost imperceptible nod, cautioned her against it. She said nothing then. Instead, she just watched the bidding. Eb raised John's bid, almost as soon as John had made his bid, then John responded by raising Eb's bid.

"You get ever'thin' you want, John Riley," Eb said angrily. "You think that just because you are a friend of Angry Wolf, that you've got all the Indians eatin' out of your hand. Well, I ain't gonna stand by and take it. I'm biddin' on this here girl, 'n I aim to keep on biddin' 'till I get her."

"What are you going to do with her, old man?" John teased. "Why, you are so old, the first time you crawl in the robes with her, she'll throw you off like a wild pony."

The Indians laughed uproariously at John's comment, while Crystal blushed, and wondered, angrily, why John was subjecting her to such embarrassment.

"Listen, sonny, I was beddin' down women before you was born," Eb said. "I reckon I can handle this one."

What had gotten into Eb? Was he actually bidding for her to take as his own? Surely not, and yet, he and John were actually getting angry with each other. The other Indians dropped out of the bidding shortly after that, and they hooted and howled encouragement to the two white men who were carrying on a spirited bidding war. The Indians thought it was great fun to see a white woman make enemies of two white men. And then in what they thought was the best joke of all, Crystal was awarded to the old man.

"I'll see you on the trail, old man!" John shouted angrily, springing to his horse.

"If you see me, you better be shootin'," Eb answered, and the Indians laughed out loud again. "Come on, woman, you belong to me, now," Eb said gruffly, and he walked over and took her,

341

and pushed her rather roughly over to one of his horses. The horse was empty now, because he had traded all it had been carrying for Crystal.

Crystal got on the horse and looked at Eb with an expression of hurt and confusion.

"Don't say anythin', girl," Eb warned, quietly. "Just go along with me, darlin'. I'll have to explain ever'thin' later."

Crystal and Eb rode out of the Indian camp to the background of hundreds of laughing Indians who were still enjoying the joke they had played. Crystal looked back at War Horse, and noticed that he wasn't laughing, and for a moment, she feared he may change his mind and demand that she be returned. She closed her eyes and started breathing a prayer, until finally they crossed the stream and climbed a hill on the other side, then rode away from the camp.

They rode on in silence for several moments, then Eb said, "Can you ride at a gallop?"

"Yes," Crystal answered.

"Let's put some distance between us and the Indians," Eb said, and he slapped his legs against the side of his horse. Crystal did the same thing, and they rode at a full gallop for about ten minutes. When they gave the animals a breather, they had covered over three miles, and at last, were safely away.

Suddenly John darted out in front of them, and he held his hand up to stop them. His sudden appearance startled Crystal, and, for an instant, she was anxious about what might happen. They had sounded really angry with each other back in the Indian camp.

John and Eb clasped hands and laughed, then John rode over to Crystal and embraced her.

"Oh," he said. "I wanted to do that the moment I saw you back there, but I knew better. If the Indians had realized how badly I wanted you."

"Or, if they had realized we were in cahoots," Eb put in.

"We would never have gotten you," John finished.

"You mean . . . the argument, the bidding, all this was a trick?" Crystal asked.

"Of course it was," John said. "We heard about the rendezvous from one of Angry Wolf's people last night. We knew that our best chance of rescuing you was to buy you, and our best way to buy you was to trick the Indians into selling you to us. Now, if we could only come up with a trick to recover the gold."

"The gold?" Crystal asked.

"Yes," John said. "As it turns out, your father signed a liability contract for that gold. If it isn't delivered, you will lose the *Missouri Mist*."

"Well," Crystal said, smiling. "Then why don't we deliver it?"

"We've got to get it first," Eb said.

Crystal laughed. "Now it's my time to explain a

trick of my own," she said. "The Indians don't have the gold. It is still on the *Missouri Mist*. It never left."

"What?" John asked. "What do you mean?"

Crystal sighed. "I never did trust David, even if Dad did," she explained. "So, I replaced all the lead/gold bars in the boxes, with real lead bars from the boat's ballast. The lead/gold bars are lying there in the hold with the other lead ballast bars."

"My God, you mean David did all this for nothing?" John asked.

"I'm afraid so," Crystal said. "I tried to tell Dad not to put up a fight, but he did anyway. I never had the chance to tell him about my trick. Now, I saved the gold, but I lost a father."

"No, darlin'," Eb said then. He cleared his throat. "A good man died, and you lost someone who was a Pa to you. But you didn't lose your father. You still have him."

"What do you mean?" Crystal asked, puzzled by his strange comment.

"Do you remember once, that I told you I could tell you a story of heartbreak?"

"Yes. You said a woman broke your heart," Crystal said.

"That she did, girl," Eb said. "But I also told you that it wasn't her fault. No, ma'am, that heartbreak was set up by my own action. You were the woman who broke my heart, darlin'."

"Me? But how? I don't understand."

"Mary died when you was born. I told myself I was givin' you away 'cause I had no way of takin' care of you. The truth is, I . . . I blamed you for killin' Mary. I know it was foolish, you were just a baby who didn't ask to come into this world, but I was that heartbroke that I wasn't thinkin' none too clear. So, one night when I knew a riverboat would be passin' soon, I put you in a canoe and set you loose on the river."

Crystal gasped. "You?" she said.

"I know you'll not be forgivin' me for what I done, girl," Eb said. "For I've never forgiven myself. Why, I'd no sooner set you out on the water than I wanted you back. But then I was afraid it was too late. I could never explain my actions to anyone. Instead, I just kept my eye on you, and loved you and watched you grow up. When you called me 'Uncle Eb,' I felt happy that you were returnin' some of my love. But I was sad, too, for it should have been me you was callin' 'pa.' There you have it, girl, my sad tale of heartbreak. Now, all is right with you again. You've got the man you love, and the freedom to marry him, and I'm tellin' you, no matter how you feel about me, 'n about what I done to you, I want you to know that I'm a happy man."

Tears filmed over Crystal's eyes and she looked at John. "Did you know about this?" she asked.

"No," John said. "Not until last night. Eb told me

everything last night. Crystal, I hope you can find it in your heart to understand what he did. Please, don't be angry with him."

"Angry?" Crystal said. She smiled. "John, darling, you have a lot to learn about me. These aren't tears of anger, these are tears of happiness. I lost one father, but I have just discovered that I am a very, lucky girl, for I have another to take his place." She leaned across and embraced Eb and kissed him, and her tears wet his cheeks.

"And now, I want to ask something of you, as your first official act as my father."

"Ask anythin', darlin', and you've got it," Eb said.

"I want you to give John and me your blessings."

"Blessings for what?" Eb teased. "Has he asked you something?"

"No," Crystal said. She looked at John and smiled. "I'm about to ask him. John, will you marry me?"

"Aren't you supposed to be on your knees when you ask that question?" John teased.

"Never mind," Crystal said. She laughed. "I can always go back to War Horse."

"Here's my answer," John said, and he took her in his arms and kissed her deeply, while in the trees overhead the birds began to sing. "Yes, darling," he said. "With all my heart, yes."